DAWN BEFORE THE DARK

WENDY BLANTON

First published by Bear Publications 2019

Copyright © 2020 by Wendy Blanton

Map by Anthony G. Cirilla ©2020

All rights reserved. No part of this publication may be reproduced, stored or transmitted in any form or by any means, electronic, mechanical, photocopying, recording, scanning, or otherwise without written permission from the publisher. It is illegal to copy this book, post it to a website, or distribute it by any other means without permission.

This novel is entirely a work of fiction. The names, characters and incidents portrayed in it are the work of the author's imagination. Any resemblance to actual persons, living or dead, events or localities is entirely coincidental.

Second edition

www.bearpublications.com

This story has been a long time coming. Special thanks goes to Jennifer Sarti, who started this whole thing; my long-suffering husband, Eric, whom I love with my whole heart; my long-time writing partners, Stephen B. Bagley and Jean Schara, who helped me develop the plot and told me to stop whining; James Feeman, who gave me the best advice I never thought I'd use; and Travis Perry, for giving me a shot.

Balphrahn Map

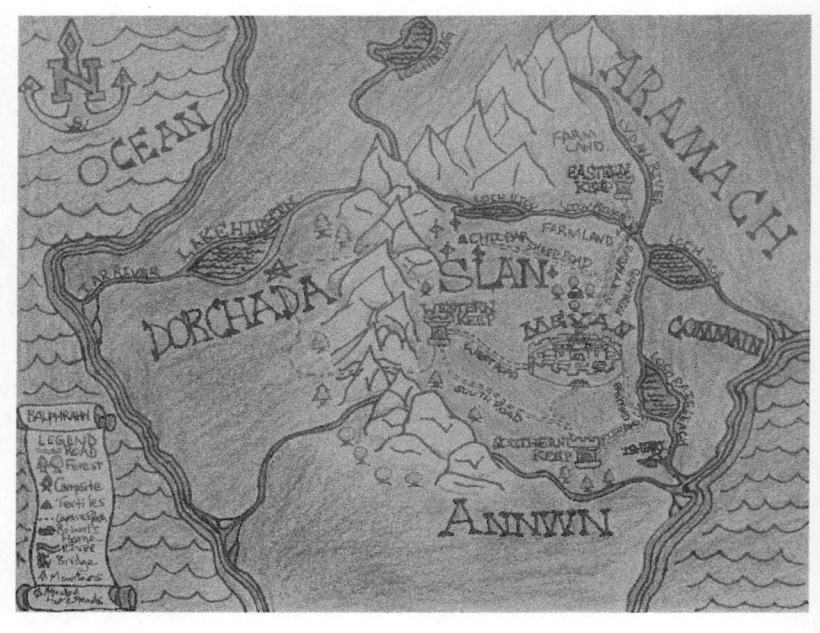

Pronunciation Guide

People

Aengus—Angus
Ailin—AY-lyn
Aithne—EYE-th-na
Arwyne—AR-win
Briant—Brian-t
Ceann—Shawn
Cruthadair—CREW-ha-dare
Dermod—DER-mod
Dougal—DOO-gal
Elan—EE-lan
Gitta—GET-ah
Hamish—HAY-mish
Lassair—LASS-air
Loach—LOE-ak
Maccha—MA-ka
Magda—MAG-da
Moira—MOY-ra
Murchad—MER-kawd
Murine—Mern
Raya—RAY-a
Ruan—RU-an
Sine—Sheen
Siril—Seeril, sort of like cereal but without the a

Dragons

Aegon—AY-gon
Saphir—Sa-FEER

Gautier—GO-tee-ay
Oriel—OH-ree-el
Peio—PAY-o
Tiemer—TEE-mer
Vieux—Veeyuh

Places

Balphrahn—BAL-fran
Mevan—MEE-van

Jobs

Raca—RAH-ka
Wreiddon—RYE-don
Wybren—WHY-bren

Curses

Galla—GAH-la
Uffern—UHF-ern

Contents

Chapter 1	1
Chapter 2	13
Chapter 3	16
Chapter 4	24
Chapter 5	34
Chapter 6	41
Chapter 7	46
Chapter 8	50
Chapter 9	54
Chapter 10	64
Chapter 11	77
Chapter 12	83
Chapter 13	91
Chapter 14	96
Chapter 15	98
Chapter 16	103
Chapter 17	108
Chapter 18	113
Chapter 19	118
Chapter 20	131
Chapter 21	139
Chapter 22	144
Chapter 23	151
Chapter 24	161

Chapter 25	174
Chapter 26	177
Chapter 27	186
Chapter 28	194
Chapter 29	196
Chapter 30	199
Chapter 31	202
Chapter 32	211
Chapter 33	217
Chapter 34	222
Chapter 35	230
Chapter 36	235
Chapter 37	240
Chapter 38	249
Chapter 39	264
Chapter 40	269
Epilogue	279
About the Author / Publisher	282

1

Three bodies lay like discarded rag dolls, all with the throats cut, but no blood. Not one drop.

Tanwen paced in the clearing. "What do you think it means?"

Her dragon, Quillon, opened one eye. His silver scales glittered in the sun. He answered telepathically. *I have not seen its like before. Speculation would be futile.*

She snorted and turned away from him to look at the carnage at the far end of the clearing. "What do you make of the tree burned into the side of the house?"

It is a fair rendering, if a bit crude.

She glanced at him over her shoulder. "Do you think it was done by magic?"

I think all of this was done by magic. He lumbered to his feet. *The others are coming. Though I wish to bask here in the sun with you, I will circle to guide them in.*

His muscles bunched as he leaped and flapped his wings to take off. He clipped the top of a spruce tree with his tail and circled the clearing.

Tanwen turned away from the wrecked homestead and focused on the flowers in the meadow. Someone had been encouraging certain wild herbs to grow in the area. She recognized feverfew, skullcap, and coneflowers. All the other plants had been pulled out, and the grass that was there was patchy. She wondered if someone who had lived in the house suffered from headaches.

From the west, she heard the clink of chain mail and the murmur of voices. "Tanwen?"

"Over here."

A few minutes later, her husband rode out of the woods, followed by two other men.

Liam slid out of his saddle and led his horse to her. His black hair was tied back, and the blue of his tunic matched his eyes. He kissed her lightly and said. "What are you doing in the woods?"

He smelled of leather and chainmail, and she wrapped her arms around his waist. "Looking for you."

He smiled, and her knees melted a little.

Behind him, Siril said, "It's the same necromancer. See the tree branded on the side of the house?"

She shivered. "Nice of him to sign his work, I guess."

The others dismounted, and they led their horses to the clearing.

Siril stopped as the sunlight reflected on his bald head. "We should tie the horses up here and let them graze. I don't like what I'm sensing over there, and they won't either, I'd wager." They led the horses to a patch of farae at the edge of the woods and tied the reins to bushes before walking toward the scene.

As they got closer, Liam nodded. "I see what you mean, Siril.

CHAPTER 1

It's odd, like necromancy, but not the same."

"I felt it at the last scene, too."

"Pity a magical signature can't tell you who it is," said Tanwen.

"Without a known signature to compare it to we can't, but when we find him, we'll know," said Siril.

"But you're sure all the homesteads have been attacked by one necromancer acting alone?"

"One bad single mage," said Colum.

Liam bent next to the nearest body, looking at the wounds. "This is what troubles me. It has to be some form of necromancy or there would be blood. We need to check the buildings."

They searched the house and outbuildings and found no people. There was evidence of cows and horses, but they were missing, too. Only the chickens and a barn cat were left.

The cat twined around Tanwen's ankles. "I wonder if the dead are the people who lived here?"

"Where are the women? There were two here, judging from the clothing I saw," said Colum.

Siril ran his hand over his bald head. "I'm not sure it's possible to say just now. We'd better get back."

Liam nodded. "It's going to be close to dark when we get home." He took Tanwen's hand. "Are you going back with Quillon?"

"Yes. I'll report to Arwyne. Should Aithne and I wait to have dinner with you?"

"No, go ahead. She'll be starving and cranky if you wait."

"I might be, too." She leaned in to kiss him. "See you at home."

* * *

Quillon flew to the Keep, and Tanwen was glad to be going over the woods instead of through them. The air carried the scents of mid-summer flowers and smoke from cook fires. She could see men coming in from the fields, their hands shielding their eyes to block their view of Quillon.

Look left, beloved, Quillon said telepathically.

She shaded her eyes as she turned toward the setting sun and saw a pair of dragons with riders coming toward them. One had red hair that matched her own.

Who is she riding?

That is Saphir. The other dragon is Peio, but I am unsure who the rider is.

She smiled. *I think it's Magda.*

That is logical. Peio enjoys her company, as Saphir enjoys Aithne's.

Do you think Saphir will Choose Aithne?

That is not for me to say, but I have encouraged it.

Saphir and Peio fell into formation with Quillon, and he led them home.

The stone walls of the Keep glowed pink in the late afternoon light as Quillon circled over the landing pad. Peio and Saphir circled higher, waiting for their turns.

When Quillon landed, Tanwen unstrapped herself from the saddle and trotted down the steps, the scent of sunbaked stone greeting her. She ducked under the ledge of the landing pad, and Quillon launched to make room for Saphir. The wind from his wings stirred the dust on the roof, and she sneezed as she headed for the stairs into the Keep.

She waited on the first landing, and a moment later she heard Aithne walking down the steps.

"Did you find anything, Mama?"

CHAPTER 1

"Yes unfortunately. Another burned homestead a few leagues from here."

"That's five now, isn't it?"

"Yes. What were you doing out?"

"Magda wanted to work on the maneuver she messed up during her leadership mission." She turned back to the stairs as Magda came down.

"Did you get it figured out?" asked Tanwen.

"We did, thanks to Peio and Saphir," said Magda.

"Excellent. I look forward to seeing it. Aithne, I have to report to Arwyne. Dinner in an hour?"

"Shouldn't we wait for Papa?"

"He came to look over the site, so he won't be back for a few more hours. He said we should eat without him."

Aithne shrugged. "Can we make it an hour and a half? We were in the air for a long time, and I'm frozen through."

"Of course." She squeezed Aithne's shoulder. "Go take a hot bath."

The girls clattered down the stairs ahead of her. Tanwen went down two flights and turned right at the hallway.

The first door on the left was different than the others in the Keep. Hewn centuries before from a single Gerdin tree, the wood was gray with age and carved with knots that flowed from one to the next. She ran her hand over the surface before knocking.

"Come in."

She found Arwyne, the Council Liaison, next to the bay windows across from the door. She wore her customary midnight blue robes, and her silver hair was braided. She had a large book in her lap and two more open on the low table beside her.

"Arwyne, we found another one."

Arwyne's brow creased. "Where?"

Tanwen walked to the map on the wall. "There." She picked up a pin and marked the spot as someone knocked at the door. One of the teachers opened it and peered inside. "Wybren Arwyne, is this a good time?"

Arwyne sighed. "Not particularly, but since I'm sure you have them all out there, you might as well bring them in. Tanwen, I'm sorry, but this should only take a few minutes."

"Of course." She leaned against the wall and crossed her arms as two teachers herded a dozen children into the study. The children looked at Arwyne, round-eyed, and she smiled at them. Tanwen grinned at how easily Arwyne covered her crankiness, but truth be told, she wanted to hear the story again, too.

"Come in, children, where you can hear me."

The teachers arranged the children on the floor at her feet before moving to stand, one against each wall, ready to remove anyone who misbehaved. Wybren Arwyne's study was the last place for foolery.

Arwyne leaned forward a little. "Children, hear the story of your past. In the beginning, our world was barren and lifeless. Cruthadair, Mother Creator, cast her eye about the stars. She saw our world and formed it into a life-giving planet, filled with food and comfort and love. In those days, everyone used magic to perform simple chores and healing.

"For generations, people lived in peace. The first ones taught their children about Cruthadair's love. Each generation talked less about Cruthadair and more about her children: Brigid, goddess of hearth and home; Maccha, her bloodthirsty sister, who eats the flesh of her slain enemies and dominates her

CHAPTER 1

lovers through cunning and guile; and their brother, Laoch, god of warriors, heroes, and champions.

"After a time, one man became envious of his neighbor. He took what he coveted by force, and his neighbor gathered others and went to take it back. No one knows what the object was, or why it was so dear that it was worth the blood spilled. One killing sparked another until all of Balphrahn was at war.

"The dragons observed all of this, and when it appeared mankind would exterminate itself, they intervened, some on one side and some on the other as they saw fit. More blood was spilled, and thousands died in dragon fire." She raised her eyebrows and paused for effect as the children shivered.

"Eventually, one side overpowered the other. Who can say if it was the right side or the wrong side? The vanquished fled east, through the woods and across the wide river. Eventually, they called their new home Aramach, and their descendants are those who harry our border to this day.

"The strongest of the dragon riders was chosen to sit on the throne and rule over all of Slan. He ordered a grand castle built in the center of the land we know as Slan, and from there, he led everyone to prosperity.

"King Fergus ruled wisely. At first. As time passed, his power overcame him and he cast his eye on his fellow dragon riders. He decreed that, as king, it was his right to have concubines and chose the female dragon riders as his own.

"Some of the women went to him willingly, smitten with his countenance and charm. Others went willingly because of his power and the knowledge that if they caught his child, they could mother the next monarch.

"One did not go willingly. Ailin protested, saying she was

in love with another and wished to stay faithful to him. King Fergus ignored her pleas. His guards brought her to his chamber, where he overpowered her and took her by force.

"When it was done, he laughed at Ailin's tears and dismissed her. Instead of leaving, she stood next to his bed and cursed all men through the power of her magic and rage—and in the name of Maccha—with a dread of dragons and cowardice. As Maccha moved to grant her wish, Laoch intervened, offended at the curse on one of his own. He was able to keep the cowardice from future generations, but not the dread of dragons. In retribution, he took magic from all women. A great cry went up in all of Balphrahn and Brigid took pity, blessing women with her healing touch.

"King Fergus rose, terrified, from his bed and ran from the castle. His dragon, seeing the cowardice upon him, repudiated him, burning his curse away with dragon fire."

The children gasped as a silver dragon flew past the window, heading for the lairs.

"If it had been only King Fergus who was repudiated, it would have been bad enough, but all the male dragon riders suffered the same fate. The bond between dragon and rider is stronger than those of a mother and her child. The dragons who were strongly bonded to their male riders also died. Those who were not bonded as strongly lived, but fled to the mountains in grief.

"A great cry went up. When Ailin realized what she had done, she fled to the woods, too ashamed to face her lover and friends. When they found her, she was great with child and insensible with grief and shame.

"The remaining members of the Dragon Council judged Ailin harshly and banished her far to the west, beyond the

CHAPTER 1

mountains. She did not go alone, for her friends were also banished. They were escorted many leagues to the mountains and through a pass, never to be seen again. It is because of the Curse of Ailin that, to this day, only women ride the dragons, and only the men are mages."

The teachers stepped in. "Thank you, Wybren Arwyne. We appreciate your time." They gathered the children and herded them through the exact center of the room where there was nothing to touch.

"It's my pleasure," said Arwyne. She held the smile until they all left.

When the door shut, Tanwen pushed away from the wall and applauded. Arwyne scowled, and Tanwen laughed. "Is that part of the liaison job?"

"Sadly, it is. I'm not sure when it became part of it, but apparently the story has more impact when it comes from an old mouth."

"I've always felt there was more to the story. I've heard it all my life, and it's always the same. No matter who tells it, there is no variation, and it's not like that with any other story I've heard. It's like a slogan of some kind that we dare not change a syllable of in case the gods are listening and punish us for getting it wrong."

Arwyne scoffed. "The gods stopped talking to me long ago." She levered herself, grunting, from her chair and joined Tanwen at the map. "It seems to be in the same general area so far. What did you find?"

"Three male bodies, the house was branded, and they took cows and horses but left the chickens, same as before."

"No blood?"

"Not on the bodies, and not much elsewhere. Enough to

account for wounded, I suppose. Siril and Liam agreed it was the work of a single necromancer."

Arwyne cursed under her breath. "That makes five sites in total, yes?"

"Yes."

"I wonder if the mages all sense the same necromancer? Or if it's a team of them going hither and yon?"

"They've read the same magic signature at all the sites. It's one mage."

"I wonder where he's from. Logic suggests he's from Aramach. Who else would have a reason to attack Slan? It does seem awfully far west for someone from Aramach. I wonder if they've had these attacks at the Eastern Keep?" She shrugged. "I'll write to Ceann. There isn't much else I can do at this point. Since you're here, take a look at this." She picked up a parchment and handed it to her.

"What is this?" asked Tanwen.

"Something that was brought to my attention recently."

Tanwen skimmed what appeared to be a poem that talked about dragons and warriors. "It seems prophetic, but it must have happened already if the warrior is male."

"Or it's about to happen." Arwyne sighed and went back to her chair. "Nothing like this has happened yet as far as I can tell, but I'm not far into the histories yet."

Tanwen frowned. "Arwyne, in the fifteen years you've been the liaison, have you ever needed to crack open the histories? We do have scribes who can look up anything you need to know."

"I know, but I don't know what to tell them to look for, or if there is anything to this. It seems odd that it's come to my attention at the same time as these mage attacks, and I don't

CHAPTER 1

know if I'm reading too much into it."

Tanwen returned the parchment to the table. "All right. You're going to do it your way no matter what I say. Let me know if there is anything else you need."

"There's nothing more that can be done now. I would be grateful if you would congratulate Quillon on his good timing. You saw him fly past the window, didn't you?"

"I did, and it couldn't have been better if I'd coached him."

"That thought crossed my mind. Go now, and get warmed up."

Tanwen grinned and let herself out. She wasn't cold from the short flight, but she wasn't about to turn down a chance for a hot soak.

* * *

As the door shut behind Tanwen, Arwyne reached out telepathically for her dragon, Vieux.

I hate telling that story. It's so misleading.

Vieux brushed her mind with sympathy. *It is the story that must be told. If they knew the whole story there would have been chaos generations ago.*

I know. But what happens if the Shunned decide to come back? We have no proof that they lived.

She shifted in her chair to ease the throbbing in her back. *But if they did, wouldn't they harbor a grudge, especially against dragons? What if this necromancer is a Shunned descendant?*

If that is the case, we will tell the truth to those who need to know, but only if and when the time comes.

It's coming, if the seers are to be believed.

Trouble is coming, but it will not be our problem. You and I will be gone by then.

I hope you're right.

Stop fretting over that. You've missed something more important. Tanwen knows it's not the whole story.

I haven't missed it, and she doesn't know it. She only thinks something isn't right with it.

Is that not the same thing?

Arwyne clenched her jaw. *Vieux, we have been partners for fifty years, and you haven't figured out the subtleties of human cognition?*

I lack experience. You are not subtle.

Arwyne scoffed. *That's true, but you didn't have to point it out. Anyway, I hope we're both wrong. If we're not, it means she is likely my successor, and I would wish better for her.*

She is the natural choice. Even Quillon suspects it is so. Do not fret. What you should do instead is ensure that whoever does succeed you learns the whole story. Whoever she is will need the knowledge, but you must safeguard it so only your successor discovers it.

I wonder, should I write it down? Only Raine knows it, besides you and I.

Vask knows it also.

Arwyne frowned. *Vask is alive? But he flew away years ago, after Lissa died.*

I would know if he had died. He has not. One never knows what might happen. Do what you think best.

2

Aithne closed her eyes and leaned her head back against the edge of the pool. Heat seeped into her bones, and she wondered if she'd get used to being cold to her core after she was Chosen. If she was Chosen.

Her heart skittered at the thought and she sighed again, trying to calm herself.

"Are you all right?" asked Magda from the other side of the pool.

"Yes. A little nervous about tomorrow."

Magda scoffed and splashed water at her. "Don't worry, you'll be fine. You've passed your other tests with flying colors. Who are you riding tomorrow?"

"Peio."

"Oh, he's good. Seriously, Aithne, don't worry."

"I'm not worried, really, just nervous...Actually, I am a little worried. I have Muirne on my team tomorrow."

"Oh."

"Exactly. The last time she rode in a leadership test, she tried to take over."

"Twice, on Alina's. I was there, too."

"Any ideas on how to manage her?"

"You can't keep her in line of sight all the time, but you'll have to watch her as best you can. You can't communicate directly with her, but you can have Peio communicate with her dragon. Do you know who she's riding?"

"I'm not positive, but I think Tiemer."

"Hmm. He's young and a little impulsive. If you get the dragons on your side, you'll have a better chance. Alina's mistake was thinking she could do it herself instead of making it a full team effort."

"That's good to know. Thanks, I'm not sure I would have thought of that." The door opened and fog swirled, but Aithne ignored it.

"I'm not sure you would have needed to. Of all the trainees, you're the favorite with the young dragons."

"I don't know about that."

"I do. Not everyone can communicate with them the way you do."

Her mother slid into the pool at the far end. "She comes by it honestly."

Aithne rolled her eyes. "Mama, can't I have something you don't get credit for?"

"Who said it was from me? Your father was exceptional at communicating with animals."

"That's magic, though. Girls don't have magic."

"His abilities can still enhance yours. Between his magic skills and my riding skills, you're a natural." She winked at Magda. "But you didn't hear that from me."

"Certainly not," said Magda with mock sincerity. "Wybren Tanwen, what advice would you give Aithne for tomorrow?"

CHAPTER 2

"Don't fall off."

Magda laughed.

"Mama!"

"Aithne, I can't give you advice. You have to rely on your training or it's not a fair test. All I'll say is you're ready for this."

"I told her to get the dragons on her side."

"So that's how the conversation started. It's the best advice I've heard in a long time. Do that."

3

Aithne sat straighter in the saddle and scanned the foothills. They were riddled with craggy outcroppings and fissures, perfect for a nest of mages to hide in.

The wind stung her face and tugged at her long red braid, trying to free it from inside her leather riding coat. She shivered despite the warm summer afternoon.

Fifty feet below, the green treetops gave way to fields. The women working in them looked up and waved. The men shielded their eyes with their hands or left altogether. Dragons had that effect.

Her safety straps dug into her thighs as she twisted to check on her team. Four other trainees and dragons followed her in a tight V. Muirne was a bit right of where she needed to be. When she saw Aithne turn, she nudged her dragon into place.

Aithne shook her head. She hadn't wanted a rule breaker like Muirne on this mission.

Behind them, in their own formation, flew the observers. Aithne knew there was a healer among them, and her mother.

CHAPTER 3

She hadn't wanted her mother on this mission, either.

Aithne, I believe I see a magic shield on the ledge below and to the east, said Peio in her mind.

Aithne squinted but didn't see anything. Then someone moved inside the shield, and she saw what he did.

Got them! Good work, Peio. Let's go take a look.

They banked right. Aithne leaned to look down. The magic shield cast a faint blue tint on the ledge. Inside the shield she saw five blurry figures. It was vaguely dome-shaped, but the edges weren't well defined. You had to be looking for it to see it. No wonder she'd missed it when she scanned the hills. Thank Brigid dragons see more colors than humans.

They flew around the hill, and the others followed. She couldn't communicate with the team verbally, but they followed suit when she took her bow off her shoulder and reached for an arrow.

They rounded the hill, heading east, and dove lower. Aithne shot two arrows at the area, trying to get a feel for the size of the target.

The other girls shot two or three arrows at various parts. They all bounced off. It was bigger than she thought.

On the second pass, they successfully planted arrows in the soil, marking the edges of the shield. Aithne squinted as she flew past and thought she saw stones marking the corners on the inside of the shield, but she couldn't be sure. It was like looking through deep water, and she was around the side of the hill before she could name the objects properly. Halfway through the third pass, Aithne waved her right arm in a circle, starting the plan they'd devised together.

She and Gitta circled around to approach from the west, while the other three continued around to attack from the east.

Aithne and Gitta threw pottery flasks at the arrows. The flasks broke and the dragons swooped to breathe fire on the spilled oil. Flames erupted and Peio dove away.

The other three arrived and sent a barrage of arrows and javelins into the shield.

Aithne looked back. Gitta's dragon ignited a spot next to the shield that hadn't lit. He was too close to the shield. *Peio! Tell him–*

As his wing swept down, they heard a loud crash, crunching bone, and the shriek of a dragon. The mage trainees ducked, covering their heads, until they realized what had happened. One of the mages inside the shield shot a bolt of magic, pushing the dragon away so he wouldn't hit the rock wall, inadvertently snapping the strap across Gitta's thighs.

Gitta held onto the saddle, leaning low with the remaining strap around her waist.

The dragon spiraled, beating frantically with his left wing while trying to steer with his right, but the spiral tightened and he shrieked again.

Peio dove after them. They couldn't do anything for the dragon, but the spiral was pulling Gitta away from the saddle.

Gitta's strap snapped, and she flew out, her scream covered by the cries of the dragon.

Aithne crouched low and clung to the back spine in front of her as Peio plunged after them. The wind stung her face, but she dared not close her eyes. Peio passed Gitta and swooped under her.

Aithne sat up and reached for her. Gitta's descent had slowed, but not enough. An unseen force shifted her toward Aithne and away from Peio's spines before Gitta slammed onto

CHAPTER 3

the dragon's back, behind the saddle. Aithne caught Gitta's arm and yelped as pain lanced through her shoulder. Gitta cried out but hoisted her leg over Peio's back. Aithne released her waist strap and handed it to Gitta. She glanced down at the wounded dragon. He had pulled out of the spiral and crashed into the ground, narrowly missing a tree.

Aithne looked up at the ledge twenty feet above. A mage instructor, her stepfather's friend, Colum, peered back at her. As Gitta fastened a spare strap around Aithne's hips, he raised his hand and shouted, "Is she all right?"

Aithne nodded, and he ducked back.

Peio circled around and up. The other riders were swooping back and forth, pelting the shield with arrows and pouches of pitch. Black splotches clearly showed the edges. The fire was out, and as they rose to rejoin the battle, Aithne saw one of the trainee mages magically cooling the hot spots.

Peio, can you get close enough to relight the oil?
Certainly.

"Gitta, hang on to me. I don't want to lose you again."

Gitta's arms locked around Aithne's waist. "That makes two of us."

Peio started toward the west side of the ridge. Aithne saw a shadow a heartbeat before Peio slammed his wings backward and banked left. Muirne's dragon flew past, almost taking Peio's head off, and flames around the shield erupted as Muirne cheered.

Aithne's heart slammed against her ribs and rage crackled inside her.

The mages rushed to the side to put the fire out again, and Aithne checked her saddlebag. *Peio, can you fly past the fire one more time? I have two more oil flasks.*

19

Yes, as long as no one else is near.

Aithne snorted and took out the flasks, handing one to Gitta. Peio flew in close, and they threw the flasks hard against the rocks as he banked away. The fire exploded behind them as he flapped hard. Aithne and Gitta turned to watch until Peio banked back around.

The shield shimmered and one of the mages, a small boy with blond hair, waved a white flag.

Aithne raised her arm in triumph and yelped a cheer. She'd won her leadership mission.

A hundred yards away, her mother shouted as Quillon blew flames in the air. She hadn't wanted her mother to observe this mission, but now she was glad. She couldn't wait to tell Papa.

She circled around toward home, and the others fell into formation. Except Muirne, who took the long way around, pumping her fist as she passed the mages.

Aithne shook her head.

Gitta leaned forward and said, "We can always count on Muirne to push the boundaries."

"I know. She's going to get someone killed."

Gitta held on little tighter, and her black curls blew in Aithne's face. "It was almost us."

Aithne patted her hand and led the way home. Peio circled to let her team land first. One by one, the dragons perched on the raised landing pad on the battlement. The riders scrambled off and ran down the stairs into the Keep, and each dragon launched again to make room for the next.

Finally, it was Peio's turn, and he landed lightly. Aithne undid the straps and helped Gitta dismount as the healer's dragon circled overhead. Gitta cradled her arm against her

CHAPTER 3

ribs. Her legs almost collapsed, and Aithne caught her, helping her down the stairs. "What's broken, do you think?"

"Ribs, probably, and I think my shoulder is dislocated. Aithne, you saved my life."

"I couldn't let you fall."

"I know, but it was dangerous. We could both have been killed if I'd landed on you."

"It would have been more dangerous if Colum hadn't magically controlled your descent. He's as much to thank as I am, probably more. Astrid is landing. She'll have you fixed up in no time."

They reached the bottom of the steps and the others rushed forward.

"Gitta, are you all right?" asked Muirne. Her short brown hair was spiky from the wind.

Gitta nodded. "I will be, thanks to Aithne."

Footsteps pounded down the stairs, and Aithne glanced over her shoulder. "You're fast, Astrid."

The healer grinned. "I've perfected the art of launching from the saddle. Gitta, let's get you to the infirmary."

"Is my dragon all right?" asked Gitta.

"He'll be fine. He broke his wing tip, but a couple of observers will see to it he makes it home." Astrid pulled Gitta's uninjured arm around her waist and helped her down the hall.

Aithne watched them go. "Muirne, I need a word."

Muirne nodded and waited until the others left. "You don't have to thank me, Aithne. I'm happy I could help."

Aithne's jaw dropped. "Help? With what? Nearly killing Gitta and me?"

Muirne frowned. "I relit the fire, which was what won the battle, and I did not almost kill you."

21

"You cut Peio off! He had to evade, and Gitta and I almost fell off!"

"Oh, Aithne, it wasn't that bad. My dragon's fire range is the longest. It made sense for him to be the one to relight the fire."

Aithne shoved her against the wall and leaned in close. "You always do this. You only play by the rules when it suits you. You're going to get someone killed."

Muirne pushed her away. "You *only* play by the rules! My improvisation made you look good!"

"It nearly killed me! If Gitta and I had fallen, you might have caught one of us, but not both!"

"Aithne!"

Her mother's voice hit her like cold water. "Mother, I need a minute."

Her mother stepped up beside them. Her leather flying coat hung open, and her red braid, nearly the same shade as Aithne's, swung over her shoulder. "I saw the whole thing." She stepped in front of Muirne. "Aithne is right. You were reckless and could have gotten someone killed. It only worked because of Peio's skill and a big bunch of luck. I would suggest you go now and come up with an explanation for the council that doesn't come across as self-aggrandizing and rationalized."

Muirne's face blazed red as she muttered, "Yes, Wybren Tanwen," and strode across the landing to the next flight of stairs.

Tanwen watched her go before turning to Aithne. "First, well done. I nearly fainted when you went after Gitta, but I'd have done exactly the same thing, and I could not possibly be more proud of you."

Aithne allowed a tiny bit of cautious relief. "Thanks."

"You're welcome. You earned every bit of celebration you'll

CHAPTER 3

get later. However, what have I told you about your temper?"

The relief was squashed by the weight of her words. "I need to learn to control it."

"Yes. Fighting with Muirne in the stairwell is not controlled."

"But – "

Tanwen held up her hand. "Muirne will take responsibility for her part, and for better or worse, her action was key to your victory. Her logic was sound, but her execution was a problem. Let the council deal with her. It's not your job. Aithne, if you can't control your temper, you won't make it through training. You can't lose your cool as a Wybren. Not ever. Giving in to emotions could get you or someone else killed. Besides, we don't have time for conflict in our ranks. There's too much to do if the seers are right."

"Mother, she's never going to learn! She's so entitled and, well, you said you saw the whole thing. Does the council need to know what happened when we got back?"

"You know I can't interfere in your training, and I wouldn't if I could."

"But if you tell the council, won't that be interfering?"

Tanwen's eyes widened. "We train like this to keep you alive. The alternative is unthinkable." She put her hands on Aithne's shoulders. "You are so gifted. You communicate with all the dragons naturally, like you're part dragon yourself. There isn't another trainee better suited to be a Wybren than you, and I'm not saying it because I'm your mother. Aithne, we need you in our ranks, but you won't join us if you don't get your temper under control." She tucked a stray lock of hair back into Aithne's braid. "Come on. Let's go tell Liam about the mission. He's going to be one proud papa."

4

The next morning, Tanwen was summoned to the Council Liaison's study. She found Arwyne behind her desk. Tanwen held out a fresh cup of arda and said, "What can I do for you?"

Arwyne took the cup and set it on the corner of the desk. "Vask is back."

Tanwen's jaw sagged. "Vask? But he flew away fifteen years ago. Dragons don't come back."

Arwyne nodded and stood, stretching her back, before reaching for the arda. "It's been eighteen years, according to Vieux. He apparently got tired of waiting to die alone and decided to come back. Along the way, he was scouting for a place to hunt and saw a boy looking at him."

Tanwen sank into a chair as her knees wobbled. "Does Vask think this boy might be an anomaly? I mean, he's old. It could be a girl with cropped hair."

"Exactly. Vask is insistent, though, so I'd appreciate it if you could take a ride and see if this boy really is a boy."

"Me?"

CHAPTER 4

Arwyne sank back into her chair. "Please don't argue. I'm too old to do it myself, and I can trust you to be discreet."

"All right. Where did he see this alleged boy?"

"I think I have the right region." She got up and went to the map on the wall. "Near as I can figure, it's somewhere around here."

"That's isolated."

"He said it was. Also, I hate to do this, but I think you're going to have to ride a horse. It's patchy woods without a lot of good places to land."

"Oh, great, Arwyne. Horseback *and* woods. You want to throw in a few stone trolls while you're at it?"

Arwyne laughed. "I'm sorry. If I could do it, I would."

"I know. When do I leave?"

"As soon as you coordinate with Vask. He's in the lair."

* * *

An hour later, she rode out, heading southwest. Quillon and Vask circled overhead, leading her to the spot and watching for trouble. It was more lightly wooded than she expected, which eased her anxiety. It was near noon when Quillon told her the boy was in the next clearing.

She rode to the edge and saw him: a lanky boy with blond hair, about Aithne's age, hunting rabbits. She watched as he reached for an arrow and shot. A rabbit jerked in the grass without a sound.

She grinned and rode out of the woods. "Nice shot!"

The boy spun, and his hand went to his dagger. "Thank you." His blond hair blew into his face and he brushed it back with one finger. Tanwen slid out of the saddle and looped the reins over the horse's head to lead him. "Have we met? You look familiar."

"I don't think so. We don't get visitors out here."

She nodded and stuck out her hand. "I'm Tanwen."

He shook it. "Briant."

"I'm sorry, did you say Briant? I haven't heard that name in a long time. Is your mother's name Agnes, by any chance?"

He shifted his weight, getting ready to run. "How did you know?"

"I think I knew her once, a long time ago. Can you take me to her?"

"She doesn't like when people drop by."

She nodded and took a step closer. "Tell you what. I'll walk with you, but I'll stay outside the yard. If she wishes to see me, or not, it's well and good, but if she's the person I'm thinking of, I believe she'll want to see me."

He squinted at her. "Are you sure?"

"The only way to find out is to try it."

"All right, then. I want to get these rabbits home anyway before the dragons come after what they want."

She followed him out of the clearing. "Dragons?"

"Yes, they've been circling for days."

"I'm surprised you noticed them."

"How could I not? They're beautiful."

Tanwen smiled. "That's not what most men say."

"Oh, I know. Curse of Ailin and all that. I don't know why, but when I see them circling, I wish they would land so I could get a closer look."

"They're bigger than you think."

"You've seen them? Up close?"

"I have. I live at the Western Keep."

They walked out of the woods and Tanwen saw a well-

CHAPTER 4

maintained homestead with several buildings and gardens. "It looks like you have quite a life here."

"I guess. If you like seeing the same people day in and day out, and never having any fun. Wait here. I'll get Mam."

He went inside while Tanwen stopped outside the fence and tied her horse's reins to a sapling. A few minutes later, Agnes stalked out of the nearest house.

"Tanwen? Is it really you?"

Tanwen grinned. "It is. I can't believe it's you."

Agnes placed her withered hand on her hip. "Why? Did you think we all died after we left the Eastern Keep?"

"No one ever knew what happened, and you made it clear you didn't want us to look for you."

"Fair enough. What brings you out here? It must have been a long ride from the Eastern Keep."

"I didn't come from there. I live at the Western Keep now. How's Colin?"

"Dead for five summers."

"I'm sorry."

"Why are you here?"

"It's about Briant, or it might be. I have it on good authority he may be a player in this." She handed the parchment to Agnes.

She scanned it and looked at her, eyes wide. "After all I've given, you have the nerve to come here and tell me my son could be the fulfillment of this dusty, vague prophecy? I nearly gave my life! That's enough! You can't have my son, too."

"But Nessie – "

"Don't!" Agnes stepped back, holding up her good hand. "No one has called me that since I left the Keep, and I'm not about to start hearing it again."

Tanwen held up her hands in surrender. "I'm sorry. The last thing I wanted to do was bring up painful memories, but what if Briant is the warrior in this? The one wholly dragon born? You were pregnant with him when you fell, and we all agreed it's a miracle he survived."

Her laugh was harsh. "Why do you even think he could be? He's a seventeen-year-old boy."

"I know. He's six months older than Aithne."

"Then you know he's not had time to do anything to bring him to your attention."

"He came to my attention through Vask."

Agnes covered her mouth with her crippled hand. "Vask? He's still alive?"

Tanwen nodded. "We were all surprised when he showed up out of nowhere. Apparently, he'd had enough of solitude and was on his way back when he saw Briant hunting. You know how the dragon instinct is."

"That's why they've been circling. It doesn't matter. You'll not have my boy, and that's final. Vask must be senile. Men don't ride dragons anymore. Now please leave and don't come back. And for goodness sake, don't tell Skye you've seen me. She'll come roaring out here with her hair on fire trying to make everything right."

"All right. I'm sorry, Agnes, we won't bother you again." She turned away, and then turned back. "You should know we've had a rash of attacks north of here. A necromancer is killing, and we think kidnapping people. He brands a building at every site with a fir tree. Please be careful." She led her horse away from the homestead, going back the way she came. As she approached the clearing, her horse shied.

"Easy, buddy, what's wrong?" *Quillon, do you see anything?*

CHAPTER 4

Yes, Vask is in the clearing.

Vask? She clenched her jaw. *It would have been good if he'd said he was going to land.*

He's talking to the boy.

He's WHAT?

She dismounted and tied the horse to a bush before walking to the edge of the woods. Sure enough, Briant and Vask were together, looking at each other as if they were deep in telepathic conversation. She sagged against the tree. Could it be true? A boy talking to a dragon? She never knew males had any telepathic ability at all.

Behind her, the horse whinnied and jerked the reins free. He turned and ran. Tanwen leaped toward him. "Wait!" She ran after him, but he bolted, cutting the corner of the clearing and heading for home.

"Uffern!" *Quillon, when Vask leaves I'm going to need you to land.*

Tanwen, such language. Quillon chuckled in her head. *I'm not wearing my saddle. Shall I return for it?*

She scanned the sky. "I guess you better. I'm going to need my riding coat, too."

She walked into the clearing. If she had to wait for Quillon, she damn sure wasn't going to lurk in the trees. Vask glanced her direction but didn't interrupt his conversation. She couldn't tell what they were saying, but could sense the faint buzz of their voices.

Beloved, said Quillon, *I have spoken to Vieux. He would like you to interview the boy and see if he is willing to meet the Dragon Council.*

What? The whole council? Is he sure?

He would not make the request otherwise. Are they still talking?

They are, and I have to say, Briant seems comfortable. His body language is relaxed, and he's maintaining eye contact. Still, there's a big difference between talking to one dragon in the open and all the dragons in the lair.

If he can handle the latter, there is a good chance he is the human we seek.

The seers seem to think things are going to get bad, but they can't- or won't- elaborate. Are you dragons picking up on anything?

Vieux has asked us to keep an eye on the western border, but not even the elder dragons can say what is coming.

She sighed and rubbed her hands on her pant legs. *I'll talk to him. It looks like Vask is getting ready to leave. Hurry back, will you?*

Certainly. I am nearly to the Keep. I should be back soon, and I will bring an extra riding coat.

Good thinking.

Briant turned. He looked confused, but happy. She smiled and walked toward him. "Good talk?"

"He said there could be trouble coming, and I might be able to help."

"Dragons have a sense about those things. He didn't tell you anything more?"

"No. He was vague now that I think about it."

"Maybe because he doesn't know for sure. He's been living alone for a long time."

"How long?"

"Eighteen years. He left the Keep after his rider died. They do that sometimes – fly off to die alone."

"Do they always come back when they don't die?"

"I've never seen it happen."

Briant frowned. "You've never seen them not die? Or you've never seen them come back even though they lived?"

CHAPTER 4

"Both."

"Oh. So, you're a Wybren?"

"I am."

He frowned. "Then why did you ride here on a horse? And where is your horse?"

"You didn't see him bolt? He ran across the corner of the meadow, just over there."

"I guess I was focused on Vask."

"It happens. As to why I rode the horse here, we weren't sure if there would be room for Quillon to land, so I rode the horse, and Quillon circled overhead, keeping watch for me while Vask looked for you. Since the horse has bolted, Quillon has flown home to get his saddle. He did tell me the leader of the Dragon Council has asked if you might be interested in coming to meet with them to see if you could be part of a prophecy."

"Why do they think it's me?"

"You're male, and I watched you have a telepathic conversation with a dragon. As far as I know, that hasn't happened in five centuries or so. That's a fairly strong indicator."

"I see. So let's say I agree to meet with this council. What happens then?"

"My guess is they would set you up with a modified Wybren training so you could be formally Chosen."

"Chosen for what?"

"To be a Wybren, of course."

Briant scoffed. "That's ridiculous. Men don't ride dragons." She tried not to smile in the face of his sincerity. "The only reason men aren't Chosen is because they're afraid of dragons. You are not, right?"

"I guess not. I talked to Vask."

"Exactly. So, do you think you might be interested? I have to say I'd love to see the combination of dragons and magic."

His face fell. "Oh. Then I'm probably not your man. I hardly have any magic."

"What?"

"It's true. My brothers used to make fun of me because they all have magical specialties. Brice enhances plants and makes them more fruitful. Aengus can train animals to do almost anything. He can even keep mice and bugs out of Mam's pantry. Hamish builds things that stand up to the elements better than anything made only by hand. Me? I can direct an arrow wherever I want it. My light wisps aren't even as bright as theirs. I want to help. Truly. But I don't see how I can."

She crossed her arms. "It might be one of our warriors could teach you what you need to know, if you don't already know it. At this point, we're not even sure what your role, if you have one, would be."

"If I meet with the Dragon Council, when would they want to see me?"

"Today, I guess. Quillon didn't say, but I don't think they'd keep you waiting."

"How would I get there?"

"You can go back with Quillon and me, or I can come back later and ride back with you."

"If I wait, there's a chance Mam will find out, and I don't think she'd be happy about it. She never talks about her dragon or her time as a Wybren."

"Her life changed a lot when Aegon died."

"I know. My point is, if they want to see me, I better go now. Maybe I can write her a letter when I get there and find out if anything will come of it."

CHAPTER 4

"Are you sure that's what you want to do?"
"I'm sure."
Tanwen sighed. "All right. Quillon should be back soon."

5

Briant trembled with cold when they landed on the tiny landing pad at the top of the Keep. Tanwen hustled him down a flight of stairs as a rush of wind followed them.

"Come on. They're waiting for you. Quillon let the council know we were coming. We'll stop in the kitchen for a hot drink, but that's all we'll have time for."

She led the way down the circular stone staircase. It emerged onto a landing with a walkway leading left and right, and more stairs ahead. She turned right. At the end was a large dining room.

"Sine? Are you here?"

A woman with a long dark braid looked around the corner. "Oh, you're back. Good. The arda is hot. Are you taking it to the bathhouse?"

"No, we're taking it to the council chamber." She took a mug and passed it to Briant.

He held the mug in both hands to try to keep it from spilling, but it was uncomfortably hot, even through his gloves. "I don't

CHAPTER 5

think I've ever been so cold."

"You'll get used to it. Usually we go soak in the hot baths after a flight, but there isn't time now. Come stand by the fire."

He followed her to the banked cook fire.

She sipped gingerly. "You'll want to drink it as quickly as you can. It will help you warm up faster. Don't burn yourself."

He sipped the rich liquid, wishing he had time to sit down and savor it. "Do you always get arda when you come in from a flight?"

"Usually, unless Sine is too busy. No one makes it like she does."

"We hardly ever get arda, but we get warm milk a lot."

Tanwen gulped her drink. "Are you a little warmer?"

He nodded.

"Good. Let's take these down with us. I'll bring the mugs back later."

She led him down several flights of stairs. He wondered if they were descending all the way to hell, and started to ask, but then they reached the bottom.

"Do you have arda left?" He nodded.

"Drink it and give me your cup."

He slammed the dregs and handed the mug to her. She stooped and placed them in the corner of the bottom step. "Are you ready?"

"Do I have a choice?"

She smiled. "There's always a choice. The question is, do you forge ahead, not knowing what lies there, or back away, go home, and wonder for the rest of your life? I can take you back home tonight if you'd rather."

"I'm ready."

She nodded. "Good. After you." She gestured to the stone

archway.

He walked through it into a room so big he couldn't see the dimensions in the torchlight. It was filled with giant statues. There was a raised platform between two of them.

"Go stand on the platform," said Tanwen, pushing him gently toward it.

Just then, one of the statues moved. It turned and looked at him. His legs turned to water and a scream bubbled in his chest. He swallowed hard and forced his legs to move, ignoring the dizziness threatening to leave him in a heap on the floor. That would make a good impression.

Welcome, Briant. I am pleased to see you again.

He stepped shakily onto the platform between Quillon and a green dragon whose scales sparkled in the light. Vask was across the circle from him. He swallowed hard.

"Hello again, Vask. Thank you for having me."

The dragon next to Vask turned its head to look at him.

"Briant, son of Agnes, I am Vieux, leader of the Dragon Council. Thank you for gracing us with your presence."

Briant's jaw dropped. "You can talk too? Vask told me you talk in your riders' heads!"

The room rumbled with a growling sound and he jumped off the back of the platform.

Tanwen caught his arm. "Easy, Briant. They're laughing."

Trembling, he climbed back onto the platform. "That's the scariest laugh I've ever heard."

"I do apologize," said Vieux. "Vask has been alone for years. He will need some time to reintegrate into our society. Is there anything you wish to say before we begin?"

He shifted his weight a little. "Uh, I'm sorry about Aegon. My mother misses him every day, so I know his loss must still

CHAPTER 5

be felt here."

Vieux glanced at Vask before turning his attention back to Briant. "Thank you. We do miss Aegon. Do you know why you have been brought here?"

"Something about a prophecy."

"Indeed. You are not familiar with its content?"

He shook his head. "I've never heard it."

"Tell us about your training."

"My father taught me to fight, starting when I was six. That was eleven years ago. I practice with my brothers twice a week, and I hunt for my family."

"What is your weapon of choice?" asked a copper dragon to his left.

"Bow. I'm good with a staff, too. I can fight with a sword and targe, but my brothers are better."

A sound, like the scrape of a boot on stone, made him turn. Tanwen turned with him, surprise etched on her face. He felt a hint of relief. She hadn't kept whatever was about to happen from him because she didn't know, either. In the archway were a half dozen young women in leather armor, weapons drawn.

The one in the front had short brown hair, and she tossed a staff toward him. "Let's see what you've got," said the one in the middle. He jumped off the platform and scooped up the staff as the first two rushed forward. He parried one blow from her practice sword and dodged another, striking one in the jerkin. She backed away and was replaced by another.

He traded blows with both of them, ducking out of the way of a shot aimed at his neck. The tip of the other girl's wooden blade caught the hem of his tunic, and he jumped out of the way. His counter strike took another opponent out of the battle, and he kicked the remaining girl in the stomach, reversing his staff and striking her shoulder.

Three more opponents quickly replaced her. Fear crept into the edge of his consciousness, and he could feel his opponents' cockiness. They tried to surround him, and he took a step back, trying to keep them all in sight. They advanced on him together from different directions. Three practice blades swung nearly simultaneously. He ducked low and used his staff to sweep two off their feet, smiling at their shrieked curses. The third planted her boot in the middle of his back and shoved him toward the fallen girls. He landed face down over a girl's torso, and she gasped as his weight pushed the air out of her lungs. The other rolled away, and before he could move, he felt the tips of two practice blades on his back.

"If you take me, you take your friend, too."

"That's acceptable," said the girl underneath him.

"It certainly is not, ye silly git," said a woman's voice. "Let the lad up. Our work is done."

The blade lifted, and Briant looked up. The woman reached toward him, and he took her hand. Her grasp was hard as she pulled him to his feet and nodded. "Well done, son, very well done."

He snorted. "I lost."

"Not as fast as these lasses thought. I hope we see more of you." She released his hand and turned to the dragons. "I don't claim to understand what's going on here, but I judge him courageous, and if you don't want him, the warriors will take him."

"Thank you for your help, Cadell," said Vieux.

"My pleasure. Right, lasses, we're done here."

Only when Cadell started up the stone steps did Briant

CHAPTER 5

turn and return to the platform. His battle lust became mild irritation.

"What else do you need from me?"

Vask lowered his head to look at him. "Are you willing to be our warrior, the first of your kind?"

"I suppose it depends on what that means."

"I wish to choose you as my rider."

All of the dragons turned to look at Vask, and Tanwen's jaw dropped.

Briant frowned. "Rider? I can't be a rider. I'm not a girl."

"There has not been a man able to qualify since the Curse, but the future may require us to think and act differently than we have in the past."

"What does that mean for me, though? I mean, you have all these girls who are training to ride. Surely one of them could do what you need."

"Vask," said Vieux, "Perhaps Briant needs to observe the other riders. Might we postpone this?"

Vask looked at Vieux for a moment. "I agree. Briant, Tanwen will find you accommodations and introduce you to the others. We will meet again to discuss this further."

Tanwen moved to the platform. "Come on. Let's go find some food." She led him out of the cavern, pausing at the first step to retrieve their cups.

As they started up the second flight, he asked. "What happened in there?"

"Something that hasn't happened in five centuries."

"It sure would have been nice to know the Dragon Council was made up of actual dragons."

"They told me not to tell you. They wanted to see how you would react. Well done, by the way."

39

"Thanks. I think."

6

The next morning, Briant joined a crowd of sleepy boys in the bathhouse. No one paid much attention to anyone at first. He washed his face and hands in the hot spring pool, and as he straightened, someone handed him a towel.

"Thanks."

The boy nodded. "I've never seen you before. You're not the one who flew in with Wybren Tanwen, are you?"

Briant nodded and wiped his face, unsure of what to say. The boy's eyebrows lifted. "How did you do it?"

"I didn't do much of anything except hold on."

"But how did you get close enough to get on? Were you blindfolded?"

"No, I wasn't afraid. I just did what Wybren Tanwen told me to do."

"You're not afraid of dragons?"

Another boy walked over. "Lucas, stop asking so many questions." He stuck out his hand. "I'm Ian, and this is Lucas. Have you had breakfast yet?"

"Not yet."

"Come on, you can eat with us." He took Briant's towel and tossed it in a basket as he led the way out the door. Fog was cool on his face as they crossed a courtyard and walked through an open door. When they got to the third landing, Briant realized where they were.

Ian chose an empty table, and pages brought platters and pitchers. "So have they told you anything about your training?" Briant shook his head. "I think it's too early, and anyway, I don't think I'm going to stay. I'm not sure this is right for me."

"Why not?" asked Lucas.

"Doesn't it seem strange to you? A man riding a dragon? That's for girls."

"Only because the rest of us are afraid of dragons. You're not, which is strange, admittedly, but also amazing. I'm a little jealous. I've always thought it would be great fun to fly."

Briant grinned. "It is great fun to fly. But all the Wybrens are women, and the only women I know are in my family. How am I going to fit in when I don't know how to act around them? And besides, won't the warriors think I'm some kind of sissy if I'm doing women's work?"

Ian shrugged. "Some of them will. But being a Wybren is the best kind of women's work as far as I'm concerned. Besides, there are women warriors among the Wreiddons and no one questions that. Anyway, does it matter what other people think?"

"I wish it didn't, but I don't know."

A page trotted over to the table and said, "Briant? Wybren Arwyne would like to see you."

Ian's and Lucas' eyes went wide.

"Who's Wybren Arwyne?"

CHAPTER 6

"The Council Liaison," said Lucas.

Ian nodded. "Better not keep her waiting."

Briant's heart thudded as he got up and followed the boy out of the dining room and down a hall. He stopped and knocked at a carved wood door, and when the person inside answered, the boy opened the door. Briant swallowed hard and went in, and the sound of the door shutting made him tremble.

The woman behind the desk stood and walked over. She was old, years older than his mother, but her handshake was firm. "Hello, Briant, please come sit down. I'm sure I must have interrupted your breakfast, but I thought you could join me in here."

"Thank you."

She nodded to two chairs in front of a window. There was a table between them, already laid with plates of eggs, sausage, and early melon, and steaming cups of arda.

He sat across from her and waited for her to start eating first.

"The first melons are always the best. Have you had any ripe yet where you live?"

He nodded. "We had the first ones two weeks ago."

"Two weeks?"

"My brother uses magic to get them to grow faster."

"I see. Is that your brother Hamish?"

"No, Brice. Wait, how do you know I have a brother named Hamish?"

"I knew your family before I was the liaison. I went to the Eastern Keep often and your mother was a friend."

"You knew her? Before the accident?"

"I did, quite well. Tell me, do you know the circumstances of your birth?"

"I know I was born eight months after the accident."

"Indeed. We were all surprised you were born at all. She didn't know she was with child or she never would have been in the air."

"That's what I've heard, too."

She leaned toward a smaller table between theirs and the window and picked up a piece of parchment, which she handed to him. "This and Vask are the reason we approached you."

"Is it the prophecy I heard about?"

"Yes." He read it and looked up at her. "You don't think I'm the one wholly dragon born, do you?"

"I do, and so does Vask. The fact that you do not fear him is telling, don't you think?"

"I suppose it could be construed that way, but how can we be sure?"

"We can't, not right now. We will only know if you pass your training, assuming you plan to stay."

"I haven't decided. Wybren, may I speak frankly?"

"Oh, I do wish you would."

"Part of me thinks it would be great, even an honor, to be the first male rider since the curse. But part of me is a little insulted that I'm being asked to do women's work."

She laughed. "I had not thought about it like that, but I suppose you're right. It must be especially so since we have so many female trainees."

"Exactly."

"The problem with the girls is they did not survive a fall from a dragon while in the womb and go on to become a grown person. You are the only person I know of who has experienced that, and I cannot think of another way a person could be the dragonborn. Briant, you are free to undertake this or not as you see fit. If you choose to go home, no one will stop you or think less of you. But denying one's call can be painful, and who knows if another person will step forward to do the work in your stead? The seers have divined a time of trouble coming, and they have predicted that it will not be easily averted. If I'm right about this, if Vask is right, isn't it worth setting aside your pride to fulfill your destiny?"

The food he had eaten curdled in his stomach. "It sounds scary when you put it like that."

"I'm sure it does. Stepping out in faith should be scary."

He nodded. "Do I need to give you an answer now?"

"Certainly not. Think it through carefully. Now, eat your breakfast and tell me how your family fares."

7

"Trainee Aithne, they're ready for you."

Aithne stood and wiped her sweaty palms on her trouser legs before following the page into the Training Council room. The report from her mission had been delayed two days for an unspecified reason, although her mother assured her it didn't mean she was under consideration for expulsion.

Part of her was terrified; the other part was relieved the wait would soon be over.

Her boot heels clicked on the stone floor. The room was bare except for a long table with chairs, and a single chair in front of it. Alone.

Four people sat behind the table. Her mother was to her far right, and the combat instructors, Siril and Cadell, sat at her far left. The man in the center, Sir Donavon, was the leader of the council.

The stone walls and the pair of stone columns made the room feel cold, and the light pouring in through the windows to her left did nothing to add warmth. She shivered a little

CHAPTER 7

and sat in the lone chair when told to do so.

"Trainee, congratulations on the success of your first mission," said Sir Donavon.

"Thank you," she said, encouraged that her voice was strong and not too loud.

"Please give us your version of the events."

She twined her fingers together and gave a detailed account, trying not to place too much emphasis on Muirne's near miss. Her mother raised an eyebrow but did not comment.

As she reached the end of her battle account, she skipped Muirne's detour when they formed up, instead ending with, "I, of course, don't know what any of the other girls have told you. I want to confess, though, I handled the situation with Muirne badly when we returned. While I feel I was justified in reprimanding her for her carelessness, I should not have gotten angry with her. I should have said my piece, walked away, and let you deal with her."

"Thank you for your frankness," said Sir Donavon. "Your account is consistent with most of the reports we have gotten. Aithne, you are a valuable member of the trainee corps. You are among the oldest trainees in the program. The younger ones look up to you. While you are exemplary in most areas, you know the one in which you are not."

"I do, sir. My temper gets the better of me."

"Just so. Therefore, we have a proposal for you. A new trainee will be joining us. This trainee is your age and has some unusual skills, but no experience with dragons. We want you to take the position of primary trainer."

Aithne tried not to frown. The offer was an honor, but something felt off. "Of course, if that is the council's wish, I will do my best."

"Will you? This is no ordinary trainee."

"It goes without saying if she's sixteen and has never ridden a dragon, but I'm up to the task."

"Excellent. We feel this will be a mutually beneficial arrangement, and success will ensure both of you places within the Wybren ranks."

Aithne nodded. "I will do my best." She glanced at her mother, who was examining her fingernails, and butterflies erupted in her stomach. "I can't wait to meet her."

"How about now?" Sir Donavon nodded to the page at the door. He opened it, and Aithne heard footsteps in the hall. She stood and faced the door.

A boy walked in. His blond hair was pulled back in a tight ponytail. She spared him an appraising glance, noting the broadness of his shoulders and his blue eyes. When the page closed the door, she turned her attention away from the handsome stranger and realized the new trainee hadn't entered.

She frowned. "I don't understand. Where's the new trainee?"

The boy walked to her and held out his hand. "I'm the new trainee. Briant. Nice to meet you."

She frowned. "Is this a joke?"

"It's not a joke," said her mother. "Vask found him. He thinks Briant has a skill set that could be helpful in defeating the mage that has been killing innocent people and threatening our security. His training was approved by the Dragon Council last night."

Aithne's heart hiccupped. "The Dragon Council? How?"

"I'm not afraid of dragons," said Briant. "I'm not affected by the curse. I don't know why."

Aithne swallowed hard. She could think of nothing to say

CHAPTER 7

that would not sound defensive. Finally, she turned to her mother. "This is the wish of the Training Council? That I get him up to speed to join the Wybrens?"

"It is the wish of the Training, Keep, and Dragon Councils, actually."

"Then I will do what has been asked of me."

"Excellent," said Sir Donavon. "If neither of you has any questions, you are dismissed."

She glanced sideways at Briant, who shook his head, before turning on her heel and walking out of the room. The door closing behind her felt like her doom had been sealed.

She took a deep breath. "I'm Aithne. We have weapons training in the morning, right after breakfast. After lunch tomorrow I'll start teaching you what you need to know."

"Thanks. I'll do my best to make it as painless as possible."

She managed a weak smile. "I think you might have an uphill battle. I hope you're up for it."

"I am. I hope you are."

She shrugged. "It's the wish of the councils. I have to be."

"Me, too."

8

The next morning, Briant joined the other rider and warrior trainees for breakfast before going to weapons practice. The others were wary of him.

Word had gotten around in what seemed to him a shockingly short amount of time.

He caught up with Aithne as he stood in line to choose a bow. Her red hair glowed in the sun, but her demeanor was chilly.

"Good morning."

He chose a bow. "Is it? I've never been treated like a spectacle before."

"Don't worry, we'll all get used to it."

"Enough flirting, lad," said Siril. "That's your target, there." He stepped up beside the quiver of arrows and waited until they were given the order to draw. He shot five arrows in the time it took the others around him to shoot ten, but his were all dead center.

"You'll have to be faster, lad."

"He's slow because he's talking to himself, Siril," said the

CHAPTER 8

blonde girl beside him.

"I'm not talking to myself! It's the accuracy spell, and it worked!"

Siril frowned. "What accuracy spell?"

"The one my father taught me."

"Ah, Colin's spell. I want you to try something. Shoot ten more arrows, as fast as you can, without the spell."

His heart slammed against his ribs. "Without the spell? I haven't done that in years. What if I don't hit the target?"

The girl beside him snorted. "Why do you even need a spell? Can't you just use magic to direct the arrow?"

Siril glared at her. "Flora, go on to the fencing dummies." She sighed and rolled her eyes before walking away, shoulders slumped.

Siril turned back to him. "She makes a good point. Why are you using a spell for every arrow?"

Briant's face blazed. "That's how I've always done it."

"That's not how Colin always did it."

"You knew my father?"

"I did, when we were boys. You're not answering my question."

"My magic is weak," Briant muttered, looking at a rock on the ground.

Siril grunted. "We'll talk about that later. For now, ten arrows, no spell, if you please. If you decide to stay, you'll find I always get what I want."

Briant swallowed hard and reached for the first arrow, shooting rapidly without paying attention to where they landed. He was rewarded with ten solid thunks.

"Not bad, lad. Not perfect, but you hit the target. You'll do thirty more without the spell, but slower."

"Thirty? I think my arm might fall off."

"Then you won't be the first male rider since King Fergus, will you? Aim carefully for each shot. I'll go get you more quivers."

He walked away, and Briant reached for another arrow. It sailed into an outer ring on the target, and he reached for the next one. He was through the first quiver when he heard shouting behind him.

He turned to see his mother riding their plow horse across the field.

"Briant! Put down the bow now!"

He walked toward her, keeping the bow in his hand. "Mam, what are you doing here?"

"What am I doing here? I could ask you the same thing! Put the bow away. You're coming home."

"No."

Her eyebrows flew up. "No? I am your mother and you will heed my words."

He swallowed hard, vaguely surprised that he'd made the decision to stay. Until that moment he would have said he wasn't sure. "Mam, I have a chance to do something important with my life. I'm not coming back to the farm with you. Not right now. You don't really need me. There's enough meat in the larder and the smokehouse to get the family through the winter, especially since I won't be there to eat."

"That is not the only reason I want you home." She slid out of the saddle. "This is dangerous."

"So is hunting. You were a rider, and Da was a Wreiddon. I thought you would understand."

Her jaw sagged. "Understand? You thought I would understand? If you truly thought so, you would have told

CHAPTER 8

me you were coming here instead of skulking away like a thief in the night!"

"What if it's true what they said, that they need a special warrior? What if I'm him and I walk away? What happens then?"

She stepped toward him. "Briant, you're a boy of seventeen summers. Why would you, or they, think it's you?"

"Because I'm not afraid of dragons." He waited for her to say something, but it seemed she'd been struck speechless. "I faced the Dragon Council. I fought in their council chamber and defeated several rider trainees by myself. That's not something Da or any of my brothers could do. I'm sorry, Mam, I love you, but I'm not coming home. Not yet. I'll come home when my job here is done."

She stared at him for a long minute before turning to Siril. "His safety is on Vask and you." She clambered onto the horse. "I might not be able to kill a dragon single-handedly, but I'm pretty sure I can take you. Briant, you will come home to me safely."

She turned the horse toward home and spurred to a gallop.

Briant stared after her. "She probably didn't mean that, Siril."

"Oh, I'm certain she did, and she might be right. She's a mother. She might be able to take me. You'd best get back to work."

9

Aithne saw him at the far end of the dining hall. He sat alone at a table, pushing his food around. She sighed. Time to get to work.

She sat across from him. "You might want to actually eat something. You're going to need it this afternoon."

He didn't look up. "I'm not hungry."

Aithne was, and she dug into her food. "Everything all right?"

He stabbed a carrot with his fork and pushed it around his plate. "I saw my mother before she left, but I wish I'd had more time with her." He glanced up and away again. "Ever feel like you've said goodbye to someone for the last time?"

She paused with her fork half-way to her mouth. "Yes. Every time my mother goes on patrol."

"What's patrol?"

"Sort of a combination of courier duty and dispute resolution. She takes messages to the other Keeps and Mevan, and stops in between at the trade centers to meet with the leaders and hear any legal cases they haven't been able to resolve on their own."

CHAPTER 9

"It sounds like it takes a long time."

"It can. Luckily, the dragons can communicate with each other across long distances. She's able to keep in touch through them so we don't worry."

"That's what we're signing up for? Working a lot and making our families worry?"

"That, and putting ourselves in harm's way to defend our home." She reached for her mug. "You have time to back out if you want to."

He laughed. "Are you kidding? I wouldn't miss this for anything."

She picked up her bread and tore it in half. "Why?"

He leaned his arms on the table. "I have a chance now to be more than I would have before. I have the chance to make a difference to more than my family. I don't know why Vask chose me, but he had a reason, and I can't walk away from it."

"He hasn't Chosen you."

He sat back and his jaw sagged a little. "Sure he did. He found me and told me I'd be needed here."

"But he hasn't formally Chosen you."

"He did, in the council chamber. He said he chose me as his rider."

Aithne's heart fell. He'd been formally Chosen, but he couldn't ride a dragon. She had been training for twelve years and hadn't even had the opportunity to be Chosen.

Her appetite evaporated and she dropped her bread on her plate. "You should eat. I'll meet you in the courtyard in half an hour." She stood, and a kitchen boy scurried over to collect her dishes.

"Wait," said Briant. "Shouldn't I come with you?"

She shook her head. "I have something to do before we get

started. Meet me in the courtyard." She turned on her heel and strode out of the dining hall. Anger coiled inside her as she stalked to her family's quarters. This time of day, Mama should be there. She walked in and managed to not slam the door.

Tanwen looked up from the tunic she was mending. "Hello, sweetling, ready to start your new mission?"

"Why didn't you tell me?"

Tanwen's hands stilled. "Tell you what?"

"Vask formally chose Briant."

Tanwen sighed and sat back in her chair, gesturing for Aithne to join her.

Aithne sat on the front edge of the nearest chair, doing her best not to appear petulant.

"Vask spoke somewhat out of turn," said Tanwen. "Yes, he chose Briant. He said the words in the council. Aithne, nothing about this situation is normal. We're all feeling our way through as best we can, including Briant and Vask."

Injustice roiled in her gut. "But if Vask said the words, it's done, right? He can't repudiate him without cause, or without possible harm to one or both of them. The rest of us have been training for years to get something that was just handed to him, and *he's a boy!*"

Tanwen shook her head. "Briant can walk away. He doesn't have a beacon, so the bonding isn't complete. The council has talked to Vask. He's agreed to stay out of the way for the time being so Briant can train. If it looks like he chose hastily, he will send Briant away."

"But that's not how it works!"

"Like I said, this is as far from a normal situation as we can get, but the dragons sense a threat growing near here, and

CHAPTER 9

they think the time has come to make some changes."

"So we're recruiting boys now?"

"No. Most boys are affected by the Curse. Briant isn't. I have every confidence in your ability to whip him into shape, but remember he's left his home and stepped into the unknown. It has to count for something."

Aithne clenched her jaw. "It would have been nice if I'd had all the facts before I agreed. I better get to work."

Tanwen leaned forward and squeezed her hand. "Good luck. I can't wait to hear about it tonight."

* * *

She trudged to the courtyard and tried to focus on her mental pep talk. *I can do this. Wybrens are competent and confident. We don't back down in the face of adversity. We are fair, patient, and calm under pressure. We obey our orders to the letter, and we never, ever give up.*

She stepped into the courtyard and saw Briant watching the rest of her class launch.

Yeah, sure you are.

She sighed. "Ready to get started?"

"I am. Are you?"

Wybrens are competent and confident. She smiled.

"Of course."

"Great. Where are we meeting Vask?"

"Vask?"

"You're going to teach me to ride, right? Don't we need Vask?"

"Oh! No, you're not going to learn on Vask. He's not a training dragon."

"There are training dragons?"

"Young dragons, yes."

"Wait. I'm going to ride a baby dragon?"

"Not a baby. And not today. There are things you have to learn before you actually ride."

His jaw clenched. "All right. What's first?"

"Come with me. We can talk while we walk." She strode out of the courtyard toward the woods. "You're going to get a crash course since you're coming into this old."

"Old? I'm seventeen."

"I know, but most of us start training when we're little kids. I was four."

"Seriously? You've been riding since you were four?"

She laughed. "No, I started training. We don't actually ride until we're twelve or thirteen."

"I hope you're not planning on making me wait eight years."

"No, the early years are mostly about physical conditioning and teamwork. I figured you have that covered already."

"Yes."

"Then we'll start with easy stuff and keep going until we hit something hard. I guess you don't know anything about dragon physiology?"

"Only that they have wings and breathe fire. Oh, and they live a long time. What I don't understand is how they can fly when they're so big."

"Part of it is magic, but they're also strong, and their large bones have air pockets in the middle, so they're not as heavy as you think. Also, they use the air currents a lot when they get aloft. I'll find my old textbooks for you. You do read, right?"

"Of course I read!"

She held up her hands in surrender. "I was just asking! I know you grew up away from other people."

CHAPTER 9

"That doesn't make us barbarians."

"Fine! I'm sorry!"

They entered the first clearing and she pointed to a series of ropes tied between trees ten feet off the ground. Each rope had a net suspended beneath.

"There's your first test."

"What's my first test?"

"The rope course. You climb the ladder and walk across the ropes. Don't worry about falling. You won't get hurt."

His face turned pink. "Walk across the ropes? That's it?"

"Yes."

He clenched his jaw and stalked to the ladder. In no time, he stepped onto the first rope and, holding his arms out for balance, ran across them all, pausing on the last to take a few steps backward, turning to bow, and scrambling down the ladder on the other side.

His eyes blazed with anger, but his voice was even as he asked, "Now what?"

She stood straighter. "Do you want to skip to the advanced one?"

He scowled. "Yes, I think so."

She led him deeper into the woods to another course. This one had no safety nets and was forty feet up. "There are obstacles on that one. Do you want to watch me do it first?" He rolled his eyes, turned on his heel, and headed for the ladder.

The second one took longer since he had to climb around trees, but he finished by jumping down a series of platforms. He walked over to Aithne. "What's next? Do you want me to jump up and down while reciting the story of the Curse of Ailin? Maybe you want me to weed the Keep's kitchen garden, or prove I can read?"

She frowned. "Why would I want you to do any of those things?"

He threw his hands in the air. "Because you seem intent on giving me insultingly easy things to do!"

She pinched the bridge of her nose. Clearly, drama was not limited to girls. "Look, I just want to do this training by the book and as quickly as possible for both our sakes. I can't do it if I don't have a clear idea of your skills, so we don't have to backtrack."

"Do you think I would have made it living in the middle of nowhere without being able to climb and balance?"

"I don't know. I've never lived anywhere but a Keep, so I don't know what skills are needed for everyday life away from civilization. I thought it best not to work on assumptions. I'm sorry if I offended you."

He scoffed. "Really? Or are you just acting like it so you can have a good laugh with your friends later?"

Her jaw sagged. "Do you think I'm doing this for fun? It's not just your future on the line. If I don't teach you to ride, I'm out of the program. Twelve years of training, down the drain, and all my dreams up in smoke. I am invested in your success because it means my success. Stop being so sensitive. Act like a boy."

His eyes widened. "Act like a boy? So I shouldn't be insulted that you asked me to do things a little girl does? When did you complete this course?"

She looked away, focusing on the ropes. "Five years ago."

"Five years ago?"

She nodded. "It was the last step before we started working with dragons."

He pressed his lips together as if he were trying to keep the

CHAPTER 9

words in. "Good. We can start there tomorrow." He stalked off toward the Keep.

"Briant, wait!"

He didn't stop; didn't even turn or wave a hand at her.

She watched him go, then walked to the nearest tree and leaned against it. This would be harder than she thought.

* * *

Aithne settled across the table from her mother and stepfather. For a few minutes, she successfully dodged the questions by passing bowls around, but as they settled into eat, her mother looked at her.

"Well?"

She wrinkled her nose. "It's going to take a little work. It's different working with a boy."

"Yes, but what happened?"

Aithne put down her fork and sighed. "Apparently, I insulted him. He's so sensitive. I thought that was only girls."

Liam frowned. "How did you insult him?"

"I took him to the ropes course. I figured he probably already had physical training and teamwork down, but I didn't know how he was with heights, and I don't want to miss anything he's going to need later."

"Seems sensible," said Tanwen.

"Obviously, he disagreed," said Liam.

She nodded and pushed her food around her plate. "He got mad because I asked him to do things we girls do before our teens."

Tanwen chuckled. "Ah, well, he's going to have to get used to having his ego bruised sometime."

"So true," said Liam.

"I don't like it," said Aithne. "I don't like any of it. It's not just that he's a boy. He's so old to start training, and none of the rules seem to apply, and if there aren't any rules, what else is there? Civil society is built on rules, and it only works if they are applied to everyone and everyone obeys them. A boy riding dragons just isn't natural. What is wrong with Vask?"

Liam put his hand on her shoulder. "What's the next step after completion of the ropes course in normal training?"

"Contact with the adolescents to learn how to communicate with them, and lessons on how to care for dragons and equipment."

Liam leaned toward her. "Is it a logical place for him to start tomorrow? Or are there other things he needs to learn first? Does he need more work on the ropes course?"

"No, he did fine on the ropes. He doesn't know anything about dragon physiology."

Tanwen shrugged. "He can pick that up anytime. I'll find him some books."

"I said I'd give him mine."

Tanwen laughed. "You mean the ones written for little girls?"

Aithne rolled her eyes. "Good point."

"Start him tomorrow with communication and equipment. He'll be fine."

"Do you need me to talk to him?" asked Liam.

"No, I have to handle this on my own, Papa, but thanks. I'm pretty sure the council wouldn't want you to interfere."

"Who says they'd find out?" He looked sideways at Tanwen and laughed.

Tanwen scowled at him. "If I don't know, I'm not obligated to share. Aithne you are supposed to handle this on your own,

CHAPTER 9

but of course if you run into trouble, we can help."
"I'll manage. There's too much at stake for me not to."

10

Briant woke the next morning dreading the day. He was able to admit, to himself, at least, he'd probably over-reacted the day before. He stung from his mother leaving so soon. Not that he expected her to hang around. He was sure the Keep brought back memories she'd rather forget. Even though she'd given him her blessing, he couldn't help feeling uneasy about the situation.

He sighed and rolled out of bed. An hour later, he met Aithne in the courtyard, having successfully avoided her at breakfast.

"Good morning!" she called.

He forced a smile. "Morning."

She met him half-way. "Look, I might have been out of line a little yesterday. I didn't mean to insult you."

He shuffled his feet. "I know. I didn't think there would be anything to learning to ride beyond saddling Vask and flying."

"There is more to it. A lot more. Besides, being a Wybren isn't just about riding dragons. You have to know how to care for them and your equipment if you get stranded away from others. I talked to my mother last night and she helped me

CHAPTER 10

think through a new game plan if you're up for it."

"I am, I guess, if you are."

"Good. Come on. Let's go to the caves."

She turned back toward the Keep, and he followed. "Caves?"

"That's where the young dragons live before they Choose. We all train together. We learn how to ride, and they learn how to carry. It works great."

Briant frowned. "They don't know how to carry?"

She detoured down the left side of the Keep. "Think about it. When you carry something heavy, you move differently, right?"

"Yes, I suppose so."

"They're carrying something that moves around, sometimes a lot. They have to train so flying with a rider becomes second-nature so they don't dump us off or hurt themselves."

"Dragons can hurt themselves?"

"Just the other day, I was on a training mission, and one dragon got too close to a magic shield. He broke the tip of one wing."

"What happened to him?"

"He crash-landed. His rider fell off, but I caught her."

"You caught her? How?"

"My dragon flew under her so she landed on him instead of the ground."

"Are they all right?"

"Sure. They're healing, and the rider is a little shaken up, but they'll be fine."

"I guess this is more dangerous than I thought. What are we doing today?"

"I'm going to start by introducing you to the dragons, and then I'll show you the equipment room."

His heart sank. "All right."

She turned to look at him. "Problem?"

"I just thought I'd get into the air."

"You will, just not as soon as you'd like. You have to learn to communicate with the dragons before you can ride them."

"They don't talk? The dragons on the council did."

"Not all dragons talk. Some have better developed vocal cords than others."

"They can't just talk in my mind, like Vask?"

She frowned and stopped walking. "Vask talks in your mind?"

"Yes, since the first time we met."

She started walking about. "That's odd. That doesn't usually happen until after the dragon and the rider are fully bonded."

"When does that happen?"

"After the beacon is made."

"What's a beacon?"

She looked at him as if he'd lost his mind. "You really don't know anything about this, do you?"

"No. My mother refused to talk about it."

"Huh. The beacon is something you and your dragon—Vask, apparently—will make together. Once you complete training, you'll go out by yourself to find the right stone. When you get back, Vask will blow fire on it, and that's how your beacon is made. It will act like a homing device so he can find you if you're separated."

"Huh. So it's sort of magic women can use?"

"I guess so, yes, since dragons are part mortal and part magic."

She rounded a corner and the mouth of a cave appeared ahead. She pointed and said, "That's where the training dragons live. Just follow my lead and you should be fine."

CHAPTER 10

"Should?"

"They haven't had to deal with male humans. I don't know for sure how they'll react."

He shook his head. "Good to know. I guess."

He followed her into a large central chamber surrounded by alcoves. Each alcove was occupied by a dragon the size of the farm horses Briant had left behind. He gulped and straightened his shoulders as they all turned to look at him.

They glittered in the dim light, all of them different colors. Some sat like a cat watching a rodent, others blinked lazily as they lay curled with their chins resting on their tails.

Aithne walked in, grinning, and said, "Friends, here is the person we told you about. This is Briant."

Briant waved. "Hello."

Aithne cocked her head to look at him, eyebrows raised.

"Hello?" She sighed. "We should work on that, too."

"Work on what?"

"Your eloquence. If you're going to be the first male dragon rider since King Fergus, you should be more, I don't know, heroic." She shook her head. "Come on, let me introduce you." He followed her to the far left, and she led him past each dragon, one by one, and said their names. Peio, Juvela, Ludo, Saphir, Venka. After a while, they started to blur together and became a long string of exotic syllables.

After he greeted them all, she said, "Let me show you the equipment room."

He nodded and followed her out of the cave. Around the hill he saw a barn-like building. Beyond was a large field, surrounded by split rail fencing, in which several smaller dragons lounged and played. He could see more caves around the base of the hill, and more further up.

He pointed. "Are those baby dragons?"

She nodded. "Hatchlings from the second to last hatch. They're ten now."

"All of them?"

"Yes, there's a hatch every ten years. We just had one a couple months ago. It's a big deal. People travel for days and camp in the field, waiting for the new hatchlings to emerge."

"It must be amazing."

She looked away. "I don't know. I missed it."

"Missed it? Why?"

"My father died during the hatch ten years ago, when those out there hatched. I couldn't bring myself to join in this year." She lengthened her stride, moving ahead of him, to open the door. "This is where all the riding gear for training is kept. The Wybren gear is on the other side of the hill."

He looked around at the large open space. Saddle stands lined the two long walls, each holding a large saddle similar to the style he'd used on the farm horses, but with more straps. The saddles were wider than a horse saddle, and the stirrups looked like metal cups hung sideways from chains.

The wall ahead had large windows overlooking the field flanking a large door, and long tables with stools dominated the center of the space.

"So it's just saddles? No bridles?"

"Nope. That's why you have to learn to communicate with them. Normally, you'd spend a few months here, learning how to care for and communicate with the dragons, cleaning equipment and making repairs, stuff like that. But as my parents reminded me last night, this is far from a normal situation."

He frowned. "Parents?"

CHAPTER 10

She squinted at him. "Yes, parents. I have them."

"But you just said your father died ten years ago."

She rolled her eyes. "I have a step-father."

He felt his face heat. "Oh. Sorry. You were saying?"

She shook her head. "Since this is a special case, we'll skip the whole months-of-cleaning-and-sewing process, and I'll show you how to saddle a dragon."

"Great!"

She went to the back door and stepped outside before coming back in. "Peio and Saphir are on their way."

He looked outside. "How do you know? I can't see them."

"I have a stronger bond with Saphir than any of the other dragons. We can't really talk telepathically from a distance, but we can communicate with images."

"Saphir is the blue one, right?"

"Yes, and Peio is copper." She hoisted a saddle off a stand. "Here's Peio's. I'll grab Saphir's and meet you outside."

He took the saddle from her and went out as the two dragons ambled into the yard. Three straps fell off the seat and dragged in the dust. He frowned, wondering why there were three. It needed a girth strap, of course, but what were the other two for?

Peio waited for him in a patch of grass. Briant made sure his body language was relaxed and non-threatening, taking care to approach from an angle, just like he'd learned to do when they got their plow horses. "Hey, Peio, I'm glad to meet you. Aithne asked me to saddle you. I hope that's all right."

Peio regarded him with one green eye and stopped in front of him.

Briant hoisted the saddle onto Peio's back and reached under him for the girth strap dangling on the other side. He caught it and buckled it, taking care to cinch it gently but firmly. Peio grunted and looked around at him as Aithne walked out.

She looked at Peio and dropped Saphir's saddle in the dirt. Dust poofed around her knees as she brought her hands to her cheeks.

"What did you do?"

"I saddled him."

She rushed over and touched Peio's shoulder. "I know, I know, I'm sorry. Let me fix it." She unbuckled the strap and dragged the saddle off.

Briant's heart pounded. He clenched his hands. "What are you doing?"

"Keeping you out of trouble."

"I put the saddle on him. How is that causing trouble? I've saddled our farm horses hundreds of times."

Peio's head snapped around.

Aithne's eyes went wide and she stepped in front of Briant, facing Peio, and put her hand on Peio's shoulder. They looked at each other for a few seconds before Peio snorted and walked away.

"Thank you, Peio," she called.

"Wait! Where's he going?"

Aithne turned to him. "Briant, they are not horses."

"I know they're not horses! That's obvious! But saddling is saddling, and I'm tired of you treating me like a toddler!"

Aithne crossed her arms. "First, you insulted Peio, and I saved you from being incinerated, so settle down. Second, saddling is saddling if you're dealing with horses. You're not. You don't know about dragons, and every time I try to teach you something, you get offended. It needs to stop. Now, shut up and watch."

He started to comment but clenched his jaw and crossed

his arms over his chest. "Fine."

She walked around him, picked up the saddle, and walked to Saphir. "Sorry about the dust, Saphir. I'll clean it off you when we're done." She heaved the saddle onto Saphir's back.

He rolled his eyes. "I did that."

"Great! You did part of it right." She pulled three wide straps off the top of the saddle and let them fall. "We use a combination of straps instead of one girth strap since obviously the danger is greater if the saddle slips." She walked around in front of Saphir, and Briant followed. Reaching underneath, Aithne buckled the back strap in front, the front strap in back. Then she grabbed the center strap and said, "Come look underneath." She knelt on the ground and Briant bent to watch. She threaded the strap under the other two, wound it around the point where the other two crossed and then buckled it. "The wind in the middle gives you a redundancy and makes the whole thing stronger. Also, note I can't get a finger between her and the girth straps, but they're not cutting into her, like Peio's were." She glanced at Saphir's face. "Put your hand on her shoulder."

He did as he was told and got a mental image of a dragon swooping from the sky to pluck a horse off the ground and fly away.

"That's her way of saying she's not a horse, either."

Briant's face grew hot. "I know, Saphir. I'm sorry."

He heard footsteps crunch and looked past Aithne to see Tanwen.

"Did I hear an apology?"

Aithne stood and brushed her hands on her trews. "Hi, Mama. He just had a tiny faux pas, but it's all right now."

Tanwen's eyebrows raised. "Is it? I saw Peio going into the

lair. He didn't look happy, but he didn't want to talk about it."

Briant shifted his weight. "I accidentally insulted him."

"Ah. I see. It's more complicated than you thought?"

"Yes."

"It's good to figure that out early. Briant, Vask did some reconnaissance this morning. Your mother made it home safely."

"That's good news, thank you."

"You're welcome. Look, Briant, the next few weeks might be rough. There's a lot for you to learn, and it might seem like Aithne is treating you like a kid, but it's necessary you learn all of the basics. Did your mother talk about her time as a Wybren at all?"

He shook his head. "She wouldn't talk about it, not even when we asked her to tell her stories."

"Then you're learning everything at once. It's a lot to take in. Please be patient, and try not to take offense."

He couldn't look at her. "I'll try."

"Good." Tanwen stepped forward and lowered her voice. "And the correct response for a trainee is, 'Yes, Wybren Tanwen.'" She grinned, touched his shoulder, and walked away. "Carry on, trainees."

"Yes, Wybren Tanwen," they called in unison.

His tension eased a little as Aithne laughed. "So, any questions about saddling?"

"No."

"Good." She unbuckled the straps and dragged the saddle off. "This is a good time to teach you about dragon care, then. Saphir, we're going to use horse analogies since that's what he knows. I hope you don't mind." She touched Saphir's neck and smiled. "Oh, that would help a lot. You're the best." She turned

CHAPTER 10

and nodded to Peio's saddle. "Bring that in, would you? Saphir is going to tell the other trainers about the horse analogies so no one else gets offended."

"I guess we've had enough of that for one day," said Briant, bending to pick up the saddle. He followed Aithne inside and heaved the saddle back onto the stand while she went further down to put away Saphir's saddle. She opened a drawer in one of the tables and took out two soft brushes, a jar and two rags.

"We'll clean the saddles later, but let me show you how we help the dragons care for their scales. They're low maintenance compared to horses, but when they get dirty because of us, they like it when we help them clean up."

"So because the saddle was dusty, it's up to us to clean it off?"

"That's overstating a little, but yes." She led him out the door and handed him a brush and a rag. Saphir sprawled on the ground like a kitten. "We need to concentrate on the saddle area. Brush off the dust, and then we'll rub her scales down with this." She held up the jar. "If we each take a side, it won't take long."

He nodded and watched Aithne start, and then imitated her. She brushed briskly and kept her free hand on Saphir's back. Aithne glanced at him. "Contact with the dragons will help you learn to hear them, too."

Faintly in his head, he heard a female voice say, *Tell him why you do this.*

Aithne brushed the dust out of the crevice of two scales. "Did you hear her?"

"Did she tell you to tell me why we do this?"

Aithne nodded. "That's a good sign. We do this because the saddles cause wear on these scales. We brush off whatever dirt is on there and rub the salve in. I think it's like giving them a massage. Wild dragons don't need this care because they never wear a saddle."

Briant frowned. "Are there still wild dragons?"

"Oh, sure, in the mountains. Not too many, I don't think, but some." She set the jar of salve on Saphir's back so they could both use it. "They're pretty reclusive, so it's hard to know how many there are. They don't live as long as our dragons do. I've heard there are maybe a hundred left scattered through the mountains. They need a lot of territory for hunting."

Briant scooped out some wax with his rag and rubbed it into a large blue scale. "Makes sense. Do they only lay eggs once a decade, too?"

"That's the standard breeding cycle for all fire dragons. I don't know about water dragons."

Nor I, said Saphir, so faintly he could barely hear her.

Briant stopped rubbing. "What? Water dragons? Real ones? I thought they were a myth."

Aithne nodded. "We don't have them here anymore. Mama was part of the group that chased the last one into Annwn, where they supposedly live. That particular one wandered over our border and was causing trouble for some villages by withholding water from the river."

"How?"

"I don't know. Maybe you can get her to tell the story sometime. Honestly, if Mama hadn't seen one, I wouldn't believe they exist."

They worked in silence for a while. As Briant finished the last scale, Aithne walked around to stand beside him.

"Did you hear anything from Saphir?"

"A little, and it was really quiet."

CHAPTER 10

"Huh. I know you really want to get in the air, but I think we should focus on communication for a while first. You'll need to be able to talk to them in the air, and the wind is loud enough when you fly that verbal communication is almost impossible."

"I know. I flew in on Quillon with your mother."

She nodded with her lips pressed together. "I wondered how you got here. So that's why you're in such a hurry to get back into the sky. You've had a taste of it."

"I have. It was amazing. Your mother didn't tell you she brought me here?"

Aithne shook her head and screwed the lid back on the jar. "No one has said anything. For all we trainees know, you magically appeared out of thin air."

"I didn't, but does it help my reputation if people think I did?"

She laughed. "I think it's going to take more to win the girls over, and probably some of the dragons, too."

His heart sank. "That's what I was afraid of." He followed her back inside and sank onto a stool. "What about you, though? What does it take to win you over?"

She put the tools away. "Why? Is it important to you?"

He got up and walked to the window. Clouds had blown in, and the young dragons were ambling toward the caves. "I don't know. I haven't had a friend outside my family since I was six, so I'm not even sure where to start here."

Her footsteps were quiet as she joined him at the window.

"Sounds lonely. What happened when you were six?"

"My father accidentally killed a man. I wasn't there, and my family doesn't talk about it much so I don't know the details. I didn't even know about it until Mam woke me up a couple of nights later. It was so dark, but we left and went to the woods, and never went back. My brother told me Da was in danger because of the accident, and we had to leave before we got hurt."

He glanced at Aithne. Her face was white and her eyes were wide.

"I know that story."

"You do?"

She nodded. "I remember when your family disappeared."

His heart thudded. "You were there? But you couldn't have been. It was at the Eastern Keep."

"I know. I was born there."

"How did you end up here?"

"Mama moved us here after Da died. She couldn't stay there without him."

"So you were torn away from your friends, too."

"I guess I was." She wiped her hands on the front of her thighs. "There, now we have common ground. Come on. You need to listen to some more dragons, and you owe Peio an apology."

11

Aithne trudged into her family's quarters and dropped into a chair. She was taking her boots off when her mother came in.

"Hello, sweetling, you look exhausted. How did it go with Briant today?"

She swallowed hard, determined to stay calm. "All right. I guess. Mama, did his father kill Da?"

Tanwen's face went blank and she sat slowly across from Aithne. "Yes. Should I have told you? I didn't think it would matter."

Aithne shook her head. "We both know it wasn't really Colin's fault."

"Aithne, you're not still blaming yourself for that, are you? It was an accident."

"It was an accident that wouldn't have happened if I hadn't distracted him."

"You were a little girl."

"He'd told me before not to distract him when he was sparring." She shook her head. "You should have told me. And you should have told me you fetched him here on Quillon."

"Does that matter?"

She stood and started to pace, unable to contain her frustration."Yes, it matters! Now he's hungry to get back in the air, and he's nowhere near ready. What else haven't you told me? If I'm going to be a Wybren, you have to stop keeping important information from me."

"Get used to that. Once you join our ranks, you'll only be told what you need to know."

"Mother, I'm training him! Why would I not need to know what you know about him?"

"Good point, but you know everything I do now. Take him on a tandem ride."

She rolled her eyes. "Mother, none of the trainer dragons is strong enough to carry us both, and Vask is staying out of it."

Tanwen's brow furrowed. "That's a pickle, but it might help for him to ride with you to get a feel for how you're supposed to sit and move. Let me work on that one. For now, it will just have to be an incentive for him to learn to communicate with the dragons."

"That's what we're working on next."

"Good. Let's go find Papa and get some dinner."

"Let me get my slippers." She went to her room and dug them out from under her bed. When she went back out, her Papa was there.

They walked into the dining room and Aithne saw Briant by himself at a table in the corner. She pointed him out, and Tanwen turned that way.

He looked up as Aithne and Liam sat across from him, and startled when Tanwen took the seat beside him.

"Hi," said Tanwen. "How are ya?"

CHAPTER 11

He smiled a little. "Fine, thanks. You?"

Tanwen shook her head and poured cider in the cup at her place. "Hungry. Did you make up with Peio?"

Liam shook his head and reached across the table. "My wife is incapable of introducing people. I'm Tanwen's husband, Liam."

"Sorry," Tanwen mumbled. "I assume you know everyone I do."

Briant shook his hand. "Nice to meet you. I'm Briant." Liam took some food and passed the platters to Aithne.

"How's the training going?"

Aithne said, "Fine."

At the same time, Briant said, "Slow."

Aithne rolled her eyes. "He thought he'd be able to saddle a dragon like a plow horse and hop on."

Tanwen's eyes widened. "Like a plow horse? Is that what Peio didn't want to talk about?"

Briant blushed. "Thanks for that, Aithne."

Liam laughed. "Better get used to it. There are no secrets with women around."

"Of course there are," said Tanwen. "We keep secrets from men all the time."

"Do you?"

Tanwen nodded. "It's all stuff you don't want to know about anyway."

"Oh, well, That's fine, then. Tanwen, they finally figured out when to do the hunt."

"Oh? When?"

"Next fortnight."

"Hunt?" asked Briant. "I know how to hunt."

"You should come with us," said Liam.

"I thought you were taking me," said Aithne.

"Does that mean he can't come, too? Come on, Aithne, surely by then you'll both be ready for a break, and he knows how to hunt."

"You're only saying that because he says he can."

"Why would he say it if he can't?"

Tanwen reached across the table and put her hand on Aithne's arm. "Don't argue. There's nothing that says a warrior can only take one child, or take only his own children. If he wants to invite Briant along, it's up to him."

"I don't want to cause trouble," said Briant. "But I do like to hunt. Is it to provide food for the Keep?"

"Yes," said Liam, "And to teach hunting and survival skills to our younglings, especially the warrior and rider trainees. Why don't you come down to the training yard in the morning and meet some of the warrior trainees? I'm sure you're ready to make some friends here."

"I'd like that. Thank you."

Aithne scoffed and stabbed a bite of chicken with her fork.

"Guess I'm chopped liver."

Liam leaned toward her and kissed her temple. "I happen to love chopped liver. Seriously, Aithne, stop being such a baby. A guy needs guy friends."

"Of course they do. Don't let him stay in the training yard too long. We have work to do."

"You could come," said Briant. "We could start the day there, maybe get some training in."

"Train before we train?"

"Too much for you?"

She looked at him for several seconds, trying to figure out his ulterior motive. "Of course not. If you want to play with

CHAPTER 11

the boys first, I'm in."

Liam turned to Aithne. "For what it's worth, you should let Briant work out with the guys on his own."

"Why? I can keep up."

He chuckled. "Of course you can. But he needs time with guys without you looking over his shoulder. Aithne, think about it. If you were suddenly thrust in with warrior trainees your age and expected to catch up to them immediately, wouldn't you want to make some girl friends for support?"

"Yes, I guess so." She glanced at Briant, who was focused on his food.

Liam pointed his fork at her. "Besides, if you work with them, you'll be a distraction at best. At worst you'll make him look foolish."

"What? I wouldn't do that!"

"No? Not intentionally, but if you're there always looking over his shoulder, the other guys might think you're his girlfriend, and you're in charge, which won't help his reputation."

"Oh." Her appetite vanished, and she put her fork down.

"I guess we can move our training to the afternoon."

Briant didn't look up. His cheeks were pink. "Sounds good. I can work with the guys and have a couple hours in the cave to practice listening to the dragons." He stood. "Speaking of which, Tiemer said he has some stories to tell me. I'll see you after lunch tomorrow?"

"Sure."

Briant nodded. "Nice to meet you, Liam."

"You too, Briant." He watched as Briant walked away.

"There, see? That wasn't so hard."

"Papa, was that really all true? Could I make him look like a fool?"

"You could, if you really tried, and I hope you won't, not to any man."

"What if he's not the man you are?"

Liam grinned and leaned closer. "You'll never find a man who measures up to me."

12

Tanwen pushed the heavy door open and stepped into Arwyne's study. "You sent for me?"

Arwyne sat on a chair near the window. She had a small table in easy reach. A cup of arda steamed next to a pile of books that looked like it would topple over at the slightest breeze. Her white braid hungover her shoulder, stark against her dark blue robe, and her feet rested on a cushioned stool because she was too small for her feet to touch the floor.

She reached for the arda and nodded. "I would have come to you, but the stairs were more than I could manage today." Tanwen grinned and pulled another chair over to sit beside her. "You're getting old, my friend."

Arwyne barked a laugh. "Oh, no, *you're* getting old, my dear. I've been old for quite some time."

"Really? I hadn't noticed. After all, you're going to live forever."

"Don't you wish that on me, girl. Eternity as the Council Liaison sounds worse than death. I would like to ride off with Vieux and not come back some days."

"Don't we all?"

Arwyne smiled. "You wouldn't if you could. Leave Liam and Aithne? Not in this lifetime."

"It's true enough. I could no more leave them than I could Quillon. What can I do for you?"

"I have personal messages for Ceann at the Eastern Keep, and for the king."

Tanwen frowned. "A message you want me to hand-deliver to the next circuit rider?"

"I have made an adjustment to the schedule. You are the next circuit rider."

Tanwen swallowed hard. "Arwyne, I took my turn last month."

"Indeed you did, but this is a sensitive matter."

"So why am I the only one who can handle it?"

"Because you are the one I trust the most." Arwyne grinned as she rose slowly from her chair and shuffled across the room to the desk. Like the side table, it was piled with books and papers in precarious towers. She walked to the right side and plucked two scrolls out of the clutter. Handing them to Tanwen, she sank back into her chair with a groan.

"Are you all right, Arwyne?"

"Oh, I will be. It's going to rain tonight; I can feel it in my bones. Tanwen, I know this is inconvenient, but it really is crucial you be the one to handle this. Go on, then, and spend as much time with your family as you can before you fly off tomorrow."

Tanwen shook her head. "I'll see you in a few days."

"May you have a tailwind the whole journey."

* * *

CHAPTER 12

She pulled the wool and leather on over her clothing. Although it felt bulky, she knew she would want the extra layers. Temperatures on the ground were mild for late summer, but flying would be cold. She pulled on her first knee-high riding boot when someone knocked at the door.

"Come in."

She reached for the second boot when a boy came in with a leather saddlebag. "I've brought your courier pack, Wybren Tanwen."

"Thank you, Cameron. Is that really everything? It looks like there is some slack in the buckle strap."

His cheeks dimpled. "Not too much for you to do this trip. I'm not even sure it's worth your time."

She laughed and pulled on her boot. "Just leave it there by the door."

"Safe journey, Wybren." He dropped the pack and scooted out the door.

Shaking her head, she walked over to the pack and took it to her desk. The pack was stuffed with scrolls and letters, divided by location. She hoped nothing out of the ordinary was happening and she could get back in a couple of days. She shut the bag, tugging at the buckle to make sure it was secure. She strapped on her sword belt, stowed her boot knives, picked up her personal pack. One last look around showed she hadn't forgotten anything important, and she walked out the door.

Quillon waited for her on the launch pad.

Good morning, handsome.
Good morning.

She grinned and stowed the packs in the larger saddlebags

attached to the saddle. These had more overlap on the top and buckled to the bottom, ensuring that should one of the packs open, nothing would be lost in flight.

She climbed into the saddle and strapped in. *Ready when you are.*

She felt Quillon's muscles bunch and he launched, circling the Keep twice to gain altitude before turning east. She settled in for the flight across Slan as Quillon caught an air current. From the sky, Tanwen could see the white tops of the arctic mountains to the north. Even in the summer the tallest ones were snowcapped and inaccessible.

The land over which they flew was green and hilly, dotted with rocky outcroppings. The first summer crops were being harvested, the second crops quickly planted. Winters were brutal, and they needed enough food to last until the first spring crops ripened. When they passed over villages she kept an eye out for little girls watching Quillon and trying to note where they were. It wasn't unusual for a farmer's daughter to arrive unannounced at the Keep seeking to be a Wybren. Sometimes the desire was genuine, but usually it was to avoid a marriage contract.

Three hours later, they circled the Eastern Keep and Quillon landed on the pad raised above the battlement. She dismounted and retrieved her packs. Quillon waited until she'd reached the bottom of the steps.

She braced against the upwind side of the landing pad as Quillon took off and turned south toward the lairs, where the women who cared for the dragons would take off his saddle and bring him a meal.

Tanwen watched him go before heading for the staircase into the Keep. The liaison stood at the top, waiting for her.

CHAPTER 12

"You made good time," she said, stepping forward.

Tanwen grinned. "Not bad. How are you, Ceann?"

"Well, thanks, and you? How's the family?"

"Everyone is fine. Aithne passed her leadership mission."

Her eyes widened. "That's a big step."

"I know. Liam has started living in fear of her being Chosen."

Ceann laughed and started down the stairs. "I don't know how you do it all. I never found a man who wasn't jealous of my dragon."

"Oh, Liam is, but he's stubborn. He knew Aithne, Quillon, and I were a single unit, and he'd have to live with it if he wanted me. He's reconciled himself enough he tolerates Quillon."

"It can't be easy, though."

"Is anything worth having ever easy?"

"Good point." She led Tanwen down the hall to her study. "The guards saw you coming, so I had fresh arda sent up."

"Sounds lovely."

Ceann pushed the door open and held it for her. "Nothing like it after a long flight."

Tanwen dropped her personal pack beside the door and took the courier pack to Ceann's desk. She perched it on the corner and opened it as Ceann poured two mugs of arda. She took out the message from Arwyne first and handed it to Ceann, taking a mug in exchange. "Arwyne said I was to put that in your hand."

Ceann frowned. "Did she say why?"

Tanwen shook her head. "Only to give it to you personally, and she didn't put it in the pack because she wanted to see my smiling face."

Ceann grinned and broke the seal. "And who wouldn't want

that?"

Tanwen chuckled and sorted through the Eastern Keep contents, putting aside the letters addressed to other Wybrens. She sipped her arda, shivering a little as it warmed her insides. The subtle difference in the herbs used to make it felt like coming home. "Do you have me in the usual quarters?"

Ceann looked up, eyes wide, as if she'd forgotten Tanwen was there. "Yes. They're all ready for you."

"Thanks. I'll leave you to this."

"Is Arwyne's health failing?" Someone knocked at the door, and she called, "Come."

Tanwen shrugged. "She hasn't said anything, but she's not getting around like she used to. She looked paler than usual yesterday, too, now that I think of it. She's been more cranky than usual, but Arwyne is always cranky."

Ceann frowned and dropped the scroll on her desk. "She wrote to tell me she appreciated my hard work and friendship."

"That's it?"

"Yes." She looked up. "What can I do for you, Greer?" Tanwen nodded to Greer and noted she'd cut her hair again. It lay dark and close cropped. With her slim figure, she could have been mistaken for a teenage boy from a distance.

"Sorry to interrupt. I saw Quillon fly in. Is Arwyne sick?"

Tanwen glanced at Ceann. "She's old and likely feeling her mortality."

Ceann frowned. "Do you think that's all it is?"

"I don't think we should read too much into it," said Tanwen, willing Ceann to stop talking about it. "Unless you need me for something else, I'm going to get settled. Do we need to meet this afternoon?"

Ceann nodded. "I have some reports to go over with you

CHAPTER 12

later, but let's meet after lunch."

"Sounds good. Greer, I brought letters from your daughters." She picked them up and passed them to Greer.

"My thanks. I'll have letters for you to take back if you don't mind."

"Of course I don't."

* * *

It took longer than she'd thought to go over Ceann's reports, but she needed to know the information in case the reeve had questions.

The next morning she rose early and saw Ceann at breakfast.

"Greer gave me a letter to pass on to you. Can you stop by my study before you go?"

"Of course."

Ceann took her mug and left, and Tanwen took her food to a solitary table. She was sorry to miss the friends she had at the Eastern Keep, but there were three full days ahead and no time to slow down.

After breakfast, she stopped by Ceann's study.

Ceann handed her Greer's letter and said. "By the way, there was another note from Arwyne in the official pouch, something about necromancer attacks near the Western Keep?"

Tanwen nodded. "Yes, she said she'd write to you about that. Have you had any homestead attacks here where bodies are left with no blood, and the shape of a fir tree is branded on a building?"

Ceann's eyebrows shot up. "No, nothing like that. How many have you had?"

"Five so far that we've found. They take cattle and horses, too, which isn't really surprising. We've assumed it's a necromancer from Aramach, but it's odd that you haven't had any since they're just over your border. Anyway, I'll make sure Arwyne knows."

"Thanks. Fair skies."

"Bountiful harvest."

Tanwen left the study and went back to her room to collect her gear. She tucked Greer's letter into her pouch as she sent a mental nudge to Quillon.

She climbed the stairs to the parapet as Quillon swooped onto the landing pad. One of the guards taken by surprise swore under his breath, and she grinned as she climbed into the saddle and strapped in.

Were you suitably pampered last night, Quillon?

It was adequate. I look forward to tonight.

Tanwen snorted. *Of course you do. The women at Mevan love dragons. You'll get well fed, while I get to ride six leagues round trip on a horse.*

It is no fault of mine there are so many men located in the cities. The warriors at the Keeps don't seem to mind when we fly in and out. They live peaceably enough with us.

They're warriors, Quillon, not merchants and nobles. It could be worse, I suppose. I could be on horseback through the southern loop, while you wile your time away in leisure.

If that were the way things operated, warriors could do the circuit. Surely they could be trained to mediate disputes.

But it would take three times longer.

13

Tanwen landed at the Wybren compound outside Mevan. Three women met her and Quillon outside the lair and removed Quillon's saddle.

Tanwen ran her hand over the scales on Quillon's shoulder. "All right, my love, I'll see you tomorrow, I hope. Try not to get too spoiled."

I shall try.

Tanwen chuckled as one of the women approached. "Will you be wanting arda and a bath, Wybren?"

"Just arda, please, and a horse. I need to get to Mevan and back quickly if I can."

"Nothing is amiss, I hope."

Tanwen shook her head. "No, I just need to take care of my duties here as quickly as I can so I can get home. My daughter is in the last stages of Wybren training."

"Oh, my, what an honor to have two Wybrens in the family."

Tanwen laughed. "My husband might disagree."

"Certainly he would. Men don't understand such things."

She walked away shaking her head. Tanwen headed for

the kitchen. "They understand better than you think," she muttered to herself.

The cook gave her a cup of arda, a plate of pastries and early melon, and a seat in the corner near the fire, where she could watch the activity and talk without being in the way. The arda soothed the chill out of her, and she began to feel pleasantly comfortable when a groom stuck his head in the door and announced her horse was saddled.

She thanked the cook and left through the same door. The horse was a bay mare. She stood beside a fence, swishing her tail at flies. Tanwen's gear was already tucked into saddle bags. She swung into the saddle, and the groom handed her the reins.

"You know the way, Wybren?"

Tanwen smiled at his earnest face. "Turn right at the road and keep riding until I get there."

The groom nodded and stepped back, and Tanwen nudged her horse to a walk. The road was smooth and wide. The forest on either side was cut back several feet, for which Tanwen was grateful. She let the horse choose her speed, and entered the city an hour later. It was another fifteen minutes to wind through the streets to the castle at the center, and she rode through the open portcullis and dismounted.

A groom came to take her horse, and a guard stepped up to Tanwen.

"Wybren, what brings you here? It's not time for a circuit yet, is it?"

"No, and it wouldn't be my turn if it was. I have a message from Arwyne for the king."

He nodded. "I hope naught is amiss."

"Not as far as I know."

CHAPTER 13

"Isn't that always the way? Right, then, Matron Patson should be in her pantry. She'll see you settled and tell the chamberlain you need an audience."

She nodded and went inside. Ten minutes later she was shown to a room in the wing for messengers and visiting courtiers' staff. The room was tiny, furnished only with a bed and washstand, but private, and Tanwen was grateful she didn't have to share a room.

Settling in took minutes. She washed and changed into clean trousers and tunic. She brushed the dust off her leather vest and put it on before leaving the room with her courier pack. She found the chamberlain and gave him the messages he needed, and then took her place outside the audience chamber. An hour later, the chamberlain called her name and opened the tall doors. The king lounged on his throne. Small groups of people loitered nearby, talking amongst themselves. Their conversations made a low buzz. The king yawned as she approached, bowed, and handed him the scroll Arwyne had given her to personally deliver.

The king nodded his thanks and shifted his weight to the other side. Tanwen wondered how long he'd been sitting there as he broke the seal and read the message.

Someone near the window to her left coughed, and she glanced that direction. When she looked back, the king's jaw hung slack. His eyes widened, and he looked up at her.

"Do you know what this says?"

"I do not, your majesty. I was told only to put it in your hand."

He lumbered to his feet and held it out to her. As she took it, he raised his hands and called, "Out! Everybody out! Clear the hall!"

The people looked at each other and milled around as if unsure of what he really meant.

He scowled. "Go! Away! I will have a private audience with this Wybren."

Tanwen read the note asking the king to begin the process of finding Arwyne's replacement as Council Liaison due to health reasons, and Tanwen's heart sank. People passed her, looking for some clue about the news she bore, but she kept the note hidden from prying eyes and did not allow her shock to show on her face.

The king sank back to his throne as the doors shut behind Tanwen. "Wybren, speak frankly. Do you think Arwyne is ill?"

"She is old, your majesty, and has more difficulty getting around now. Her dragon is also old, the oldest at the Western Keep, and maybe in all of Slan. I don't believe she'll die soon, but she must feel it's time to step down if she took the time to write."

He sighed and scrubbed his hands over his face. "Of course, that is logical. Did she say anything when she gave you the message?"

"Nothing of consequence. I have been seeing less and less of her around the Keep, though, and I don't remember the last time I saw her fly."

"She is old. She must know we won't find her replacement overnight so I'm sure it's not as alarming as it seems."

"She surely didn't mean to cause any distress. Shall I pass your words to Arwyne myself, or will you have something official written?"

The side of his mouth raised a bit. "I will write her a note myself and get it to you by morning. She will accept nothing less, and she deserves at least that much."

CHAPTER 13

"As your majesty wishes."

14

The next day, Tanwen trudged down the stairs at the Western Keep, thankful to be home. She and Quillon were tired. She looked forward to a long bath and a hot cup of arda.

She shouldered the door to her quarters open. Liam was buckling on his sword belt, but took it off when she walked in.

"There you are. I saw Quillon fly away. I was coming to find you."

She resisted the urge to groan. "What's going on?"

He took her hand and led her to her favorite overstuffed chair. It only took a nudge to get her to drop into it. He knelt in front of her and started untying her boots.

"Liam."

He didn't look up. "Arwyne is ill."

"What?"

He eased off her first boot and started on the second. "She fell ill last night. She didn't want to distract you, so she told Vieux not to tell Quillon."

CHAPTER 14

She sat back and stared at the ceiling. "How bad is it?"

"Pretty bad. She's old and hasn't been in the best of health for a while anyway. It's never a good sign when someone like that goes to bed."

Tanwen snorted. "That's the truth."

He leaned forward and kissed her. "Welcome home. Get your stuff together so you can go downstairs and get your bath. I'll go see if Sine has any arda hot."

She sighed. "I love you."

15

Two hours later, she curled into Liam's side, and he stroked her back. She sighed and closed her eyes. "This is the best part of coming home."

"I have to agree, but it would be better if you didn't have to leave first."

"What if I didn't have to patrol anymore?"

"That would be amazing, but I don't see it happening anytime soon."

"It might. I saw Finley downstairs. She said I'm on the short list to replace Arwyne."

His shoulders stiffened. "Let's hope it won't come to that." Someone knocked at the outer door and called, "Wybren?" She groaned and reached for her robe. "This better be good."

Liam sat up and reached for his trews. "I have a feeling it's not."

She belted the robe and shut the bedroom door. A page waited outside the outer door. "Sorry to bother you, Wybren, but Wybren Arwyne is asking for you."

Tanwen frowned. "Now?"

CHAPTER 15

"Yes, Wybren, it seemed important."

She stopped herself from sighing. "I'll be there shortly." She shut the door and went back to the bedroom. "I've been summoned to Arwyne."

He pulled his tunic over his head. "At least she waited until we were done."

Tanwen chuckled and wrapped her arms around his waist.

"You'll still love me if things go pear-shaped, won't you?"

He pulled her close. "I'll love you, no matter what, even if the world ends." He kissed the top of her head. "You'd better get dressed. I'm going to talk to Sine about having dinner in here."

"I love the sound of that." She dropped the robe on the bed and turned to the wardrobe. "Oh, not to dump all the bad news on you at one time, but you should know Greer is back."

"What?"

She glanced at him. "She said she misses the girls, and I'm sure that's true, but I have a feeling it also has to do with Arwyne."

He scrubbed his hands over his face. "Anything else I need to know about?"

She shook her head as she took out her oldest, softest tunic. "I didn't want you to be surprised if you run into her."

"That's good, I guess. Now I know to avoid her again." He walked over and kissed her. "I might have to tell Sine we're taking all of our meals in here for the foreseeable future. I'll see you later."

She turned away and pulled the tunic over her head as he walked out. A few minutes later she was dressed, with her hair braided more neatly. She headed for Arwyne's quarters and was met by another page.

"Wybren Tanwen, I'm glad I've found you."

"Have you been sent to personally deliver me to Arwyne?"

"I have."

Tanwen chuckled and shook her head as she fell into step beside him. "She does know I just got back, right?"

"I don't know, but it seemed important that she see you right away."

"It always is with Arwyne." She picked up her pace, and the page scrambled to keep up. When they arrived at Arwyne's door, he ran ahead to open it for her.

She nodded at him as she passed, and another page opened the door to the inner chamber.

Arwyne was in bed. Not propped up against pillows and surrounded by papers as Tanwen imagined she would be. She lay on her back, hands by her side, pale against the bedclothes.

"Arwyne?"

Her blue eyes fluttered open and she whispered, "Thank you, Brigid."

Tanwen knelt beside the bed. "They said you were ill, but I didn't expect this."

Arwyne scoffed. "I'm not ill. I'm old and dying. It's a good thing you got back when you did. I need you to do something, and it's a job only you can do."

"Of course. You know I will do whatever is in my power."

"It may not be easy."

"When have you known me to take the easy way?"

Arwyne grunted. "That's true enough. Tanwen, I believe you are the only person among all the Wybrens, here and at the other Keeps, who is strong enough to succeed me."

"Oh. Arwyne, surely not."

"It's true. There is a reason the liaison has to know all the

CHAPTER 15

Wybrens well. The Royal Council will put forth names. I have told Reeve Dinsmore your name must be at the top. He has assured me it will be, but I need you to fight for it. They won't just give it to you."

"Do you know who the others are?"

"Not for sure. I believe Raya and Eve from the Eastern Keep are on the list, but I do not know of anyone here."

"Greer is back."

Arwyne closed her eyes. "She must not be the one. You know her as well as I. She will be terrible. Too much pride. Too much entitlement."

Tanwen nodded. "I agree, but I'm not sure I'm the right person. And Liam—"

"Tanwen, stop. It is your duty to act for the good of Slan. If you do not do your duty, everyone, including Liam and Aithne, will suffer. Especially if Greer is chosen. I need not tell you how Liam will feel, or how Greer will use her position to punish both of you for his choice."

"No, you need not." She sighed. "Are you sure about this?"

"I have never been so sure in my life."

"I will do my best, then."

Arwyne relaxed against the pillows, and only then did Tanwen notice how tense she'd gotten. "Thank you."

"Arwyne, please rest. We need you."

"Be that as it may, I have no control over when my time is done. I know you all think I'm alive by sheer force of will, but such is not the case."

"You'll forgive me if I don't believe that. Do you need anything?"

"Only to sleep."

Tanwen squeezed her hand gently. "Then sleep. I'll check in

on you later."

Arwyne murmured as her eyes drifted shut.

Tanwen stood and quietly left the room. The pages were at their posts by the door. "Will you come and get me if anything changes?"

"Of course, Wybren," said the one by the outer door. "Are you going to succeed her?"

"Only Brigid knows right now."

16

Someone shook her shoulder. Tanwen groaned and opened her eyes. Moonlight spilled into the room. It was later than she thought.

"What's wrong?"

Liam sat on the side of the bed. "Sorry to wake you, but they've sent for you. It's Arwyne."

Tanwen sat up. "What?"

"There's a page waiting for you."

She stumbled out of bed and reached for the clothes she'd dropped on the floor. She dragged them on and ran, barefoot, into the outer room. "What happened?"

The page held out a cup of arda. "The end is close. She wants you."

"There's no time. Leave it on the table." She ran out the door and down the corridor. She could hear the page's footsteps pounding after her, but his youth was no match for her fear. She jerked the door to Arwyne's quarters open as the second page opened the door to the bed chamber.

Dinsmore and a couple of councilors were already there. A

priestess of Brigid knelt, muttering, at the foot of the bed. She nodded to the reeve on her way to the bedside.

She took Arwyne's hand. It was cool, but not yet cold. Arwyne's chest rose and fell fractionally. "Arwyne? I'm here."

Arwyne's blue eyes opened. "Dinsmore."

The reeve walked to the other side of the bed and took Arwyne's other hand.

Arwyne lifted her arms, bringing their hands together. She pressed Tanwen's hand to Dinsmore's and said, "Serve." Her arms fell limply as she exhaled. Her chest did not rise again. The healer stepped up beside the bed to take Arwyne's wrist, and Tanwen stepped aside.

"She's gone," said the healer, and one of the councilors opened the windows. The hot summer breeze blew in. Somewhere nearby, an owl hooted.

Tanwen stepped back further, toward the door, not fully comprehending Arwyne was dead. She heard footsteps but didn't look to see who approached.

"You do realize her final wish is not the final decision."

Tanwen glanced at Dinsmore. "I am aware."

"Do you truly want the job, or did she pressure you into agreeing?"

"A little of both, truth be told."

"Truth must be told, always, if you are to serve in her capacity. She was not stupid, and of course her wish will carry weight, at least with me."

The sound of dragon wings and fire came in the window, and Tanwen looked out. Vieux blew flame in the air. Without thinking about it, she noted he flew south. They'd need to know which way he went so they could find his body. "I guess Raine is the new leader of the Dragon Council."

CHAPTER 16

Dinsmore nodded. "At least that part is easy. Dragons can be trusted to not be corrupted by power. Good luck, Tanwen."

"Thank you." She waited until the reeve walked away, then turned and walked back to her own quarters. She closed the door quietly and sank into her favorite chair.

Liam came out of the bedroom. "She's gone?"

Tanwen nodded, giving in to the first wave of grief. "She was like a mother to me."

"I'm sorry."

"Me, too."

* * *

They waited until mid-morning to start the search for Vieux. Each rider was assigned an area to fly over to look for him while the warriors conducted a ground search.

He was in Moira's grid, not far from the castle and an easy walk for the warriors.

Quillon passed her the news. *He was considerate of others and did not go too far or over rocky terrain. It will be easy to get her body to his.*

What's the surrounding area like?

It is a large field. The fire will not spread. Vieux used the last of his life to clear an area for their pyre.

He was ready to go, too.

So it appears.

* * *

The morning of the third day, before dawn, the Wybrens gathered in the ballroom of the palace, where Arwyne lay in state. They wrapped her body in a velvet shroud, each of them taking a section to stitch closed. Then they picked up her bier and carried it out to the courtyard, where a white horse and a small, flower-strewn cart waited. They placed her bier on the cart and took their positions in front of the horse. The priestesses of Brigid followed it, singing prayers to the goddess. The nobles came next, and the warriors formed up behind them.

They took Arwyne's body to the meadow Vieux had prepared, where he had waited for her to come so they could take their final journey together.

When they drew near, the Wybrens took the bier off the cart, and the women among the nobles took the flowers. They took Arwyne to Vieux and laid her bier on the ground in the curve of his body. The women arranged the flowers around them while the men stood guard in the trees.

When it was done, the Wybrens took out their beacons, and the other women joined the men. Only when they heard the dragons coming did the Wybrens withdraw.

The dragons flew in single file. As they passed, they blew fire on the bodies. When they had all taken their turn, they circled on the thermals.

It didn't take long for the bodies to be consumed, and the dragons circled lower, creating wind with their wings to scatter the ashes.

Tanwen heard rustling and knew some of the group was leaving. She stood, rooted to the spot.

"That's the perfect Wybren funeral."

Tanwen glanced to the side. The reeve stood beside her. "It's what we all hope for."

"I once saw a Wybren shudder at the thought of being

CHAPTER 16

interred in a tomb."

Tanwen smiled. "I've seen nobles shudder at the thought of dragon fire. Each to his own."

"True enough. I can't believe she's gone."

"We're going to be in for a fight."

Dinsmore nodded. "I'm losing sleep over it. The nominees from Eastern Keep have arrived."

"May I ask who they are?"

"Eve and Raya."

"Both solid choices."

Dinsmore hummed noncommittally. "I guess we'll see." He squeezed her shoulder and stepped away, heading for the Keep.

Tanwen turned back to the meadow. There was nothing left but scorched earth. She walked toward the blackened area. Heat radiated through the soles of her boots. She started to turn away and something glinted in the sun. Stepping closer, she saw a mass of melted silver with a rock in it - Arwyne's beacon.

She held her hand over it, and didn't feel heat. She tapped it gingerly. It was too warm to pick up with her bare hand, but not too hot to pick up with the hem of her wool tunic. She scooped it up and dropped it in her belt pouch. She'd figure out what to do with it later.

17

Aithne woke early. The night before she'd been sure she'd be too excited to sleep at all, even though she knew she needed to. The first day of her first hunt would be exhausting, or so she was told.

She'd challenged Papa a few times about taking Briant. Papa finally pointed out Briant didn't need a parent, and he could go if he wanted to. And he did want to.

When she saw a sliver of light on the horizon, she got up and dressed in the dark. Carrying her boots and pack, she went out to their sitting area and lit a candle with the coals from the banked fire.

She checked her pack again, making sure she hadn't forgotten anything she might need. The last thing she wanted to do was ask for something she should have.

Two hours later, they gathered in the courtyard. Tanwen hugged her cloak around herself.

"Did you pack extra stockings?"

Aithne rolled her eyes. "I packed all my stockings, Mama."

"Did you wrap them in waxed canvas?"

CHAPTER 17

"Yes, Papa told me to so they'd stay dry if it rains."

Tanwen looked at the sky. "Let's hope it won't."

"Mama, I'll be fine. Papa will be there."

Tanwen managed a shaky smile. "I know. I just miss you when we're apart."

"Me, too." She opened Tanwen's cloak and snuggled in as she had when she was little.

Her mother's breath tickled her ear as she tucked her face against Aithne's head. "Just be safe. That's all I ask."

Aithne nodded. "You, too."

Tanwen snorted and stepped back. "Be safe in my interview? I'll try not to die of boredom."

Aithne grinned. "Do what you have to do."

Tanwen glanced to the side. "Hey, Briant, are you ready to go?"

"Yes, Wybren Tanwen."

"Good. Since your mother isn't here, I'll ask if you've packed extra stockings."

He laughed. "I did, and I wrapped them in waxed canvas."

"Good lad."

Liam stepped into the group from behind Aithne. "Ready to go, younglings?"

"Ready," they both said together.

Aithne hugged Tanwen again. "See you in a few days, Mama." She turned away as Papa kissed Mama, and Briant grinned.

"Can't watch?"

She snorted and started toward the larger group of teens. "I think they do it more to annoy me than anything. Have you met any of the others going with us?"

He nodded. "I know Ian, Lucas, Aidan, and Tristan. Do you know them?"

"Sort of. We all had weapons training together until a couple years ago."

"I see. Did they have to do the ropes courses?"

"The lower ones, yes. The higher ones were only required for rider trainees to weed out the girls who are afraid of heights."

His eyes went wide. "That's why you made me do it?"

"Yes, of course. I didn't know at the time you'd ridden Quillon with Mama."

He chuckled. "Now it makes sense. I'm sorry I gave you a hard time."

She playfully punched his shoulder. "We got past it. Anyway, this week should be fun, and you get a break from trying to figure out what the dragons are saying."

"Part of me is relieved, and part of me wishes they were coming with us so I could keep trying."

"Maybe this will be good for you."

The group started out, and they joined the crowd.

Aithne's friend, Lassair, fell into step near her but didn't say anything. Her hunting clothes looked new, and she'd twisted her thick brown tresses into a bun perched on top of her head. Aithne frowned. "Lassair?"

"Not yet," said Lassair, and kept walking.

"That's odd," said Briant.

Aithne looked around and saw the riders waving to them. She waved at her mother. "Not really. Her mother is watching."

"Her mother doesn't like you?"

Aithne laughed. "Her mother doesn't like you."

"Me? Why? I don't even know who she is."

"Greer doesn't agree with Vask choosing you because it implies we need a man to save us, and women have been doing just fine for centuries, thank you very much."

CHAPTER 17

They passed through the gates and Lassair stepped closer. "Ugh, yes, that about sums it up. Mother has the same opinion of men some men have of women—they're perfectly fine in bed, but otherwise should be seen and not heard."

"So I don't stand a chance of getting her approval," said Briant.

"Not even a little one," said Lassair, laughing. She stuck out her hand. "Hi, Briant, I'm Lassair."

"You shouldn't be talking to him," said Muirne. She'd cropped her brown hair even shorter.

Lassair turned to her sister. "So? Are you going to run back and tell Mother I'm socializing with Aithne? Go ahead. Go back and miss the hunt."

"Not a chance. Uncle Neale invited me before you."

"Muirne, he saw you first." She turned to Briant. "Pay no attention to my little sister. She's a complete pain."

* * *

Two days later, they arrived at the campsite. It was lightly wooded with a large fire pit ringed with stones in an area where the pine trees and brush had been cleared away. The area was on a short plateau in the shadow of the northern mountains.

As they prepared to set up, Briant leaned toward Ian and said, "Is it odd that we didn't see any large game when we hiked in?"

Ian's brow furrowed. "I don't know. I guess, but I've never done this before. Do you think it's odd?"

"If I'm going someplace to hunt, I would expect to see animals."

"Makes sense. If it's really bothering you, ask Liam."

"I might, but I guess we better get set up first. Maybe we're hunting further north."

Ian nodded. "Can I ask you something? You don't have to answer if you don't want to."

"It doesn't hurt to ask."

"Briant!" He looked up and saw Liam. "Start gathering firewood."

Briant nodded. "Come on, you can help."

They walked into the woods and started picking up fallen branches. "What do you want to ask me?"

"It's just, when you first came, I thought I heard you tell Siril your magic is weak, but I'm sure I must have heard wrong."

"You heard that?"

"My mother says I have the hearing of a hawk."

Briant swallowed hard. "Please don't tell anyone."

"It's not my secret to tell."

"Thanks. It's embarrassing."

"I guess it would be, but is that the price you have to pay to be a Wybren?"

"I don't know. I never thought about a connection. I'll have to ask Vask when we get back."

18

Tanwen pushed the heavy needle through the leather strap and into her thumb. She hissed and cursed under her breath before sticking her thumb in her mouth.

"Tanwen?"

She took her thumb out and pressed her finger against it to stop the bleeding while she looked for a reasonably clean rag. "In the tack room."

Skye stuck her head in. "Come on, you're needed in the great hall."

Tanwen cut the clean edge of a rag with her knife and pulled an inch-wide strip off. Wrapping her thumb, she said, "That was fast."

"I guess they figured out who they don't want first."

Tanwen sighed but didn't say she hoped she didn't make the cut. Instead she left her work where it was and followed Skye out of the tack room. "I'll be back in a while to finish this," she called to the trainees who were cleaning saddles. "Do I have time to change?"

"I don't think I would," said Skye. "They might be waiting for you. It took me a while to figure out where you were."

"That was the idea."

She stopped in the bathhouse to wash her face and hands, sending Skye ahead to let them know she was coming. She grabbed a towel from the pile and knelt beside the pool. She reached for the water but stopped when she saw her reflection. She could see the fear in her eyes. She blinked. Still there. She closed her eyes and plunged her hands into the water, scrubbing her face hard. She sat back on her heels and dried her face and hands. She took a deep breath and clenched her jaw and she stood and dropped the towel in the basket beside the door.

She strode to the great hall, shoulders back, head up, projecting confidence she did not feel. The doors were closed and guarded when she arrived, but a guard opened the door for her.

The assembled crowd was smaller than she'd thought it would be and consisted of Wybrens and councilors. Dinsmore saw her enter and nodded. A few minutes later, Greer walked in, and Dinsmore stepped onto the dais.

"Thank you all for coming on short notice. I won't keep you too long. We've decided between two candidates for the liaison position. We plan to interview them this week and have a decision soon after we finish."

Tanwen swallowed hard. Greer had moved toward the front on the right side. Her smile was confident and her posture relaxed. She looked the opposite of the way Tanwen felt.

"The two candidates are Raya and Tanwen," said Dinsmore.

Greer's jaw fell open, and then people circled around Tanwen, congratulating her, blocking her view. She faked

CHAPTER 18

a smile as her stomach roiled.

Dinsmore held up his hand to call order. "I need a moment to speak with Tanwen and Raya. Thank you for coming."

Tanwen waded through the crowd to the dais and stepped up.

"Congratulations," said Dinsmore.

"Thanks." Tanwen swallowed hard and scanned the crowd for Greer.

"She's already gone," said Dinsmore. Tanwen turned to look at him.

He nodded. "When I made the announcement, her jaw hit the floor, and then she spun on her heel and walked out."

Raya joined them on the dais. "Congratulations, Tanwen."

"Thanks, you too."

She grinned. "Whichever of us gets the job, we can both sleep better knowing it's not going to be Greer."

She shuddered. "I had nightmares all night."

"She was never taken into serious consideration, but you didn't hear it from me," said Dinsmore. "I need the two of you to clear your schedules for a day, one tomorrow and the other the next day. You'll be interviewed by a panel, and they will make the decision. Who wants to go first?"

Raya shrugged. "You have home advantage, Tanwen. Do you want first or second?"

"I'll take second."

Raya nodded. "Then I'll know not to celebrate too much tonight."

Tanwen snorted. "Celebrate what? The past or the future?"

"Celebrate the wisdom of those who chose us and not Greer."

"You're up tomorrow after breakfast in the council chamber, Raya," said Dinsmore. "Tanwen, I'll let you know tomorrow when we'll be ready for you. Plan for it to take the whole day. What we talk about is not to be discussed with anyone, not even your families, starting now. No one needs to know anything beyond what I said in my announcement."

Tanwen nodded. "So nothing to anyone about other candidates."

"Exactly."

"Understood. If you'll excuse me, I have some work to finish."

Dinsmore nodded. "Don't stab yourself with the leather needle again." He nodded at Tanwen's wrapped thumb. "My father was a shoemaker. I've sewn my share of leather."

Tanwen chuckled. "I'll do my best not to cripple myself before the interview." She stepped off the dais and walked through the mostly empty great hall. She nodded at well-wishers on her way out of the Keep.

As she walked into the courtyard, someone behind her hissed, "Galla." She spat on the ground.

She was not surprised when she turned and saw Greer leaning against the wall.

"You're never happy unless you take everything you can away from me."

Tanwen stopped herself before she rolled her eyes. "That's not true, Greer, and you know it."

"Really? How did you make the cut? You, who took Liam from me? Who would have corrupted my daughters if I hadn't come back?"

"What are you talking about? I barely saw your daughters."

"Lassair says differently. She said she spent a lot of time in your quarters. I'll see to it you are not the council's choice."

Tanwen pressed her lips together and nodded once. "Do what you have to do, Greer. I can't stop you." She turned

CHAPTER 18

and left the courtyard, breathing deeply against her roiling stomach. *Quillon, do you feel like stretching your wings?*
  Of course, beloved. Whenever you wish.

19

On the fourth night after they left the Keep, Briant jerked awake. The moon had set, plunging the landscape into near total darkness. His heart pounded and he lay still in his bedroll, listening and trying to see something, anything.

One of the boys near him snored. Another muttered in his sleep. He wondered if anyone on the girls' side of the camp made that much noise.

The breeze blew the tops of the trees, and somewhere nearby a rodent rustled in the bushes. A second later there was the rush of wind as something flew over him. The rodent had given away its position, and a bird saw it. There was a muffled squeak, and then the sound of stone scraping against stone.

Beside him, Tristan stirred and sat up.

Everything went quiet. Tristan looked around and lay back down.

Briant scooted closer to him, put his hand on Tristan's arm. He could barely see the whites of Tristan's eyes.

The noise started again, along with the sound of people

CHAPTER 19

getting up and moving around. It started on the girls' side, followed by the men who were scattered around the camp. He could see silhouettes against the inky darkness. The banked coals of the cook fires glowed red, but most of the coals had already died.

He and Tristan watched as the people around the fire got up and started shuffling north. Large figures loomed around them, herding them. It looked like everyone in camp was affected, and Briant wondered if his decision to sleep away from the group had saved him, or if it was something else.

Briant leaned close to Tristan, hoping the sounds would hide his words from everyone else. "Wake Aiden. I'll get Ian and Lucas. Play along like we're doing what they're doing."

Tristan nodded, and they rolled over as if they were waking up. Briant put his hand over Ian's mouth and shook him awake. Ian jerked under his hand, reaching for the sword he wasn't wearing.

"Shh," said Briant. "Something is wrong." He pointed to the people mindlessly shuffling past them and took his hand off Ian's mouth.

"What in the name of Laoch?" whispered Ian.

"I don't know." He woke Lucas and turned to Tristan. He grabbed his sword as another group shuffled past. "Let's follow, but stay close to each other."

They nodded and fell into line with the group. They walked about a league to the edge of the tree line, and Briant ducked out of the group, grabbing Aiden's and Lucas' arms and dragging them aside. Lucas grabbed Tristan and Ian. They met nearby in a grove of trees, close enough to hear the others walking past.

"What is going on?" asked Ian.

"They're under some kind of spell," said Aiden.

Briant nodded. "That's how it looks to me, but it's not anything I ever imagined. Even the older warriors who have been using magic for years are affected. We should split up. I'm going to follow them, but someone needs to go back to the Keep and tell them what's happened."

"Why are you following?"

"Because I'm a rider, and I have a training beacon. I can summon a dragon for help if I need to."

"I'll come with you," said Aiden.

Briant nodded. "Tristan, can you come, too? You have the best magic, and we might need a diversion."

"Of course."

"Ian, Lucas, can you get back to the Keep?"

Lucas nodded. "We can get there, but we won't get back until mid-day."

Briant swallowed hard. "Just get there as quick as you can. We'll follow and see where they stop. I don't know, but maybe I can talk long-distance to Vask. Anything is worth a shot. When we find out where they're taking them, we'll come back." They joined arms, grasping each others' wrists.

"Be brave," said Lucas. He and Ian turned back, melting into the night, and Briant, Aiden, and Tristan bolted north to catch up with the group.

When they saw the back of the group climbing over the rocks at the base of the mountains, Tristan grabbed their arms. "We should stay back and try to stay under cover until we know where the mage is."

"Should we shield?" asked Aiden.

Briant's face went hot. "I can't shield."

The other two looked at him. "What do you mean?" asked

CHAPTER 19

Aiden.

"I can't shield. My magic is weak. I can barely make a light wisp."

Aiden's jaw went slack, but Tristan nodded. "Maybe That's why you're not afraid of dragons. Anyway, we don't know how long we're going to be following, so I think it's too early to shield. We don't want to have to rest if they keep walking, and we might need our magic for defense. Let's just try to stay out of sight for now."

Aiden and Briant nodded, and they veered a bit west before they started climbing, relying on catching glimpses and listening to the group.

As the sun came up, they were able to see the crowd better, and Briant's stomach jumped into his throat. "Guys. Stone trolls."

They looked over. A dozen stone trolls circled the group, climbing faster than creatures their size should be able to. The smallest was easily ten feet tall and four feet across, and although they looked like they'd been carved from rock, Briant knew they were flesh and blood.

Tristan nodded. "Good."

Briant's jaw dropped. "How are stone trolls good?"

Tristan started climbing again. "It's likely the mage spelled them. Stone trolls are far from intelligent, so he could have cast an area of effect spell on them and sent them down to collect our group, saving himself the trouble of coming with them."

"But how could he know where we were?"

"We rotate three hunting grounds. This is the one furthest north," said Aiden.

"But how would a mage know? And why didn't we hear

them coming?"

Tristan glanced over his shoulder. "A sound-proofing component in the spell maybe? I don't know. Maybe we can find out, but you should stop asking so many questions. Save your breath for climbing."

Briant nodded and reached for the next hand hold. Tristan was right, but Briant burned with questions. The answers might be what they needed to save Aithne. And Liam. And all the others.

* * *

Briant wished they'd had a chance to at least grab water skins. He trembled from climbing all day and wondered what kind of spell the mage had used to keep several dozen people climbing with no food or water. Was there an energy component to it, or did the others simply not realize how hard they were pushing?

As darkness fell, the group stopped on a wide ledge where a man in black and red robes waited. He gestured with one hand, and the entire group, including the stone trolls, sat where they were.

The boys hid in the brush, watching for a few minutes, before finding a place nearby, out of earshot and downwind where they could keep watch.

They huddled close together, and Tristan said, "We need to rest. I'll take first watch. Who wants second?"

Briant said, "I'll take it. Do you think there's a water source near here?"

Aiden looked around. "I think I sense one. Give me a few minutes." He darted into the gathering night before they could

CHAPTER 19

stop him.

Briant and Tristan sank to the ground, stifling groans.

"Tristan, what do you make of the stone trolls?"

"What do you mean?"

"They climbed all day. Stone trolls hate daylight."

Tristan grunted. "Good point. It must be one powerful spell."

Briant shuddered. "If he can do that, what else can he do? Do you think he can see us?"

"I think if he could, he'd have done something about it, but we should be extra careful."

Several minutes later Aiden came back, gesturing in the gloaming. They followed him to a small spring where they could see the ledge.

They took turns drinking, and then Briant and Aiden settled in to rest. Briant barely noticed the hard rock he settled against. He watched the edge of the moon peek over the horizon and closed his eyes.

It seemed he'd just fallen asleep when Tristan shook him. The moon was a quarter of the way up, a bare crescent that gave almost no light.

He got up and drank more water as Tristan settled into the spot Briant had occupied.

Briant washed his hands and face at the spring and found a place to stand where he could see those close to the edge of the ledge. The mage had put a shield around them, and Briant wasn't sure if it was to keep those close to the edge from falling off, or to prevent escape if someone overcame the spell. He supposed it could be both.

He shivered as the night wind blew against his neck, and he was grateful he'd chosen to sleep in his cloak the night before. He pulled up the hood, shocked that it had been less than a week since they'd left the Keep.

He looked at the moon. Almost three days. He wondered if he should activate the beacon, but decided to wait. If the dragons came, it might provoke the stone trolls into killing everyone. He couldn't live with that.

He watched until the moon was high in the sky before waking Aiden and taking his place. He closed his eyes, and when he opened them, fingers of light broke the horizon.

He heard rustling above him from the ledge and rolled to his feet to drink. Silently he cursed himself for not keeping a water skin close at hand when he'd gone to sleep. He wouldn't make that mistake again.

They hid under the ledge and waited for the group to start on their way. When it sounded like the last of them had gone, they peered over the edge.

The last of the group went over another outcropping and onto a narrow pathway. They followed it, three abreast, to the east.

Briant watched, and a flash of movement caught his eye. Liam looked at him and tossed something down before turning back to watch where he was going. When the last of the stone trolls was out of sight, Briant scrambled up.

Liam had tossed an empty water skin down the hill. It had bounced half-way down and stopped. He retrieved it and tossed it to Tristan, who grinned and went down to fill it.

Aiden came up to join Briant. "They're not all spelled. Someone scratched, 'Kill them or us' in the dirt."

"How are we supposed to do that? We have one sword between us."

"I don't know."

Tristan climbed up to join them, the full waterskin dripping

CHAPTER 19

from his belt, and they started after the group.

* * *

They climbed all day again. The terrain was rocky and unforgiving, and the wind gusted frigid air through the opening in his cloak. By late afternoon, the path leveled out and they saw three lean-to shelters, their openings facing a central area.

The stone trolls herded the captives into them, and the mage stepped out of a cave. The stone trolls went into the cave as the mage cast a shield over the lean-tos before returning to a small tent on a nearby ledge.

Briant and the others hid behind some rocks and watched as the captives lay on the ground. All except one.

Liam walked around the edge, despair on his face.

Briant watched him for a few minutes before turning to the others. "I'm going to talk to him."

Tristan grabbed his arm. "What are you doing? It could be a trap."

"If it's a trap, it's up to you two to get away and bring back help." He slipped around the rock and ran to the shield, taking care to be as quiet as possible. Liam met him.

His voice was muffled as he asked, "Do you have a training beacon?"

Briant nodded and drew it out of his tunic.

Liam's shoulders slumped. "Summon them here. If nothing else, they can communicate with the other dragons and figure out how to drop this shield." He glanced over his shoulder at the tent. "Go now, before they notice you're here. Ask them to tell Tanwen I love her, and I'm looking after Aithne."

Briant nodded and ran back to the hiding place. "He said to summon the dragons." He held the beacon in his hand, palm up, for several minutes.

"Is it working?"

Briant shrugged. "I'm not sure. You guys get some rest. I'll keep the beacon on. It's going to take some time for them to get here."

Aiden bit his lower lip. "Can you let us know before they arrive? So we can take cover?"

Briant nodded. "Of course."

* * *

He woke Tristan a few hours later and settled in with the beacon in his palm. It was there when Aiden shook him awake. "Briant, wake up! We have to find a better hiding place."

He peered around the rock. The stone trolls were coming out of the cave in the pre-dawn light. It appeared they had food and water for the captives.

He looped the beacon's thong back over his head, and followed the other two toward a scooped out area in the rocks facing away from the shield. They hunkered down and hid in silence until everything went quiet.

Aiden leaned close to Briant. "Are the dragons coming?"

"I don't know," Briant whispered back. "It seems like they should have been here by now, but maybe they've alerted the Dragon Council, and they're all going to come for us."

Aiden gulped. "Great."

Tristan nodded. "Keep telling yourself they're coming to help us, not eat us."

Briant grinned. "I'll protect you both." He couldn't bear to tell them he didn't think they were coming, that maybe the

CHAPTER 19

beacon didn't work at such a long distance, or maybe it didn't work at all. Or maybe they'd ignored him.

Muffled yelling made the boys peer around the edge of their shelter. Briant's heart pounded.

Everyone was awake. Some of the girls were crying. The men and boys were using magic to try to dispel the shield.

The mage came out of his tent and shouted taunts at them. Briant crept closer, trying to hear the mage's words.

Aiden touched his boot. "What's he saying?"

He crept back. "Something about how they will become part of a great army, and how they were lucky to have been chosen. He has a strange accent. I've never heard one like it."

"What does that mean? They were chosen for a great army for who?"

"I don't know, but we were idiots not to grab a bow and some arrows. One arrow would end all of it, and we could go home."

"We have to do something to help," said Tristan. "What can we do? Can we try to help them dispel the shield?"

"From here?" asked Briant. "If you could drop the shield from this distance, wouldn't you have done it already?"

"I don't know! But they're all trying, so maybe a little extra help would get it done."

Aiden shook his head. "I think the best way we can help is to go back and tell the council where they are. No offense, Briant, but I don't think the dragons are coming."

Tristan nodded. "It might be easier to at least take the path at night. If we stay near the wall, we'll be fine."

"All right," said Briant. "Let's wait until dusk and head back." As the sun started to sink into the horizon, the captives settled down, their hunger and thirst finally overpowering their panic.

The mage was nowhere in sight, but Briant knew the stone trolls would be out after dark. He leaned toward the others." Do you think we should head out?"

"Yes," said Aiden. "The sooner we get back to our campsite, the sooner we can get food and extra water. Then we can make better time."

"I think I should tell them we're going, and tell them all to use their beacons tonight."

Tristan frowned. "You don't think they have been?"

"How would I know? They're girls. I don't know how they think."

"Go," said Aiden, "And hurry up. The stone trolls will be back any minute."

Briant scrambled up the hill to the shield. Aithne looked at him and stumbled over. As she neared the edge, she appeared to distort, as if she was standing inside an inverted fishbowl. Briant wondered if his lack of magic kept something about how the shield looked hidden from him. Did he see it like a girl, or maybe like a boy before the curse? Could girls see it at all?

"What are you doing here?" She sounded like she was talking through water.

He reached into his tunic and pulled out his beacon. "Do you have yours?"

She pulled it out of her tunic.

"I don't think mine works. You should all try to use yours. We're going to get help."

Aithne waved him off. "Go!"

"Stay strong." He turned and scrambled down the hill as the

CHAPTER 19

first of the stone trolls came out.

He ducked behind a rock and ran hunched over to the others. "Let's get out of here, but be quiet! The stone trolls are coming out."

* * *

Aithne watched him leave before turning to the others. "Briant said he doesn't think his beacon is working, so we should try ours."

Muirne scoffed. "What do you think I've been doing?"

"Me, too," said Lassair. "I figured the shield was stopping it."

Aithne held her beacon up beside the shield. "It might be, but we have to do something."

"It never hurts to try," said Liam. He walked over and squeezed her shoulders. "Don't worry, he'll go get help."

She tried to smile, but her body froze. Liam's hand stopped mid-clench, pinching hard, but she couldn't cry out.

The shield shimmered and she heard shuffling and the sound of the mage's voice.

She whimpered as the shield reappeared. Liam's hand released. She looked around. The stone trolls had brought food and water.

Before she could start toward it, someone said, "Where's Ruan?"

"There!" yelled someone else.

Aithne looked in time to see Ruan disappear into the caves with a pair of stone trolls. "Papa, what's happening? Where are they taking him?"

He stepped in front of her, blocking her view, and wrapped his arms around her shoulders, drawing her face to his chest.

His heart was pounding, but his voice was calm as he said, "I don't know, sweetling. Don't worry, I won't let them have you."

20

The boys stumbled into their former camp at mid-day. It looked like it had been pillaged. The small game they'd taken was gone, as were most of the water skins and trail rations. The carnage was surrounded by the tracks of stone trolls.

Briant scrubbed his hands over his face. "There must have been some we didn't see taking provisions for our people."

Tristan stood still, his eyes roaming the camp. "We'll just have to gather what we can and press on." He walked to the nearest pile. The packages had been ripped open by rodents. He picked up a pack and started stuffing food into it. "Come on. We can make another league or two and find a place to camp. Gather what we'll need—food, water skins, weapons, blankets."

Briant picked up a bow and quiver. He filled the quiver with extra arrows as Aiden gathered water skins.

"These are mostly empty," he groused.

"Take them anyway," said Briant. "We can refill them." Tristan set aside his pack and said. "We might as well eat these before we go. Is there enough water for a meal?"

"I think so," said Aiden, "And the stream is close."

They sat next to the cold fire pit eating travel rations and passing the water skins around. The water was tepid and tasted like leather, but Briant didn't care. After two days with no food and not enough water, it felt like a feast.

Food revived them, and they went to the stream. Briant splashed water on his face knowing he wasn't making a dent in the grit, but they didn't have time to stop and bathe.

They filled the water skins and divided them up, and then started for home at a brisk walk.

Tristan said, "Briant, keep your beacon going. Maybe we were out of range before."

"I hope so," said Briant. He swallowed a lump in his throat and tried to ignore the voice in his head that said the dragons had left him to the wolves.

* * *

Briant left the beacon out, but he didn't bother to hold it up anymore. It had become clear either no one could hear him, or they didn't want to hear him.

He trudged on, trying to keep the pace up, but they were all exhausted.

What am I doing here? Why did I even leave home? I'll never fit in.

Briant? The voice was faint and feminine, and he stopped, unsure if he'd even heard it.

Yes. Can you hear me?
I can. What is wrong?

He shook his head.

Tristan walked back to him. "What's wrong?"

CHAPTER 20

"Either I've contacted one of the dragons, or I'm going crazy with desperation. I can barely hear her, and I'm not sure if it's real."

Aiden joined him. "Can't you amplify it with magic or something?"

Briant shook his head. "It doesn't work that way. Just give me a minute."

He closed his eyes, concentrating. *If you can really hear me, we need help.*

Briant, what is it?

Briant's eyes flew open. The light filtering through the trees seemed to pierce his skull, and his head started to throb.

Vask? You can hear me?

I can. Why are you stretching your telepathy instead of using the beacon?

I've been using the beacon for two days. Vask, we need help. Almost everyone has been kidnapped. I wasn't affected by the magic, and I have two others with me. There were stone trolls and a mage.

We are in the process of trying to decide how to proceed. The boys you sent back told us what happened. Where are you?

I don't know. In the woods somewhere.

Describe your surroundings. Is there a place anywhere near where I can land?

Briant would have wept with relief if the others hadn't been with him. *Not here. All I see here are trees.*

What kind of trees?

Hardwood.

What direction are you heading?

Due south. We left the hunting ground yesterday about mid-day, so at this rate we should be back late tomorrow afternoon.

Not if you find a clearing. Spread out and tell me when you find a place to land. I will find you and relay the location to Quillon to have warriors to rendezvous with your companions. Do not contact me before you find the clearing. Stretching your telepathy will cause you pain.

Thank you, Vask. He swallowed hard. "We need to find a clearing, someplace where Vask can land."

Tristan's eyes flew open. "Vask? But he's male, and you said you could barely hear her."

"I know. I don't know who the other one was. Vask said if we find a place he can land, he'll find us and send warriors to rendezvous with you."

Aiden grinned. "Dragons would be faster. Now you're going to beat us home and take all the glory for yourself."

Briant laughed. "I'll beat you home and have wine and women waiting for you. Who's the best tree climber?"

* * *

A few hours later they found a large clearing.

Aiden looked from one end to the other. "Looks like a good place to camp, right?"

Briant laughed. "For you? Sure!" He walked into the field, taking note of the details. *Vask, we found a place. As far as I can tell, it's longer than you by a tail length.*

That will be tight but sufficient. What do you see around you?

It's all hardwood trees. The clearing seems to be unnaturally rectangular.

Walk toward the center and tell me if you see what could be the remains of a stone foundation.

Briant frowned and walked toward the center. *It's not so*

CHAPTER 20

much a foundation as something that could have been stone walls. Stay there. Prepare camp. I will arrive soon.

Briant walked back and relayed the information. He and Aiden began collecting firewood while Tristan cleared a spot for the fire. When he brought back a pile of branches, Tristan looked up with a grin.

"Any chance you could talk Vask into lighting the fire for us?"

Briant laughed. "If it's ready to light, I'll ask him."

They worked together to get things set up for Tristan and Aiden, and by the time Vask circled overhead, they had a fire laid and water skins refilled from a creek nearby.

"Time for you to take cover," said Briant. He clasped wrists with them, and they ran for the woods as Vask circled lower.

Do I see a fire laid?

Yes. They'd like you to light it if you wouldn't mind.

Certainly. He circled again before seeming to drop out of the sky. He landed with a puff of leaves, and Briant walked toward him.

I guess this might be the time to tell you I haven't actually ridden a dragon on my own.

I am aware. Did Aithne instruct you on usage of the safety straps?

Yes.

That is all you need to know right now. I will light the fire when you are mounted. I do not wish to cause your friends more fear than necessary.

Briant climbed into the saddle and fastened the safety straps. Vask leaned close to the fire pit and breathed a tiny flame onto it.

Hold on to the front of the saddle or the spine in front of you while I launch. It will be less smooth than launching from the pad at the Keep.

Briant gripped the front of the saddle, and butterflies quivered in his stomach. *I'm ready.*

He felt Vask's muscles bunch seconds before he leaped into the air. Briant's stomach lurched and he bit back a yelp as Vask angled sharply. The wind from his wings pushed Briant forward and he leaned toward Vask's neck to try to reduce wind resistance.

Did Aithne tell you to do that? Vask's voice was laced with amusement.

Do what?

Lean forward in the saddle during take off?

No, it just seemed like the right thing to do.

Interesting.

Was I wrong?

Not at all. I'm curious about how you knew to do it, though.

Briant bit his lip. *The last time I had a conversation like this, I insulted dragons without meaning to.*

Riding horses?

Well, yes.

Let me guess. You offended Peio.

And a few others, I think.

They are young and easily offended.

He leveled off, and Briant sat up. *Is that why they don't talk to me? Because they're still angry? I didn't know it would offend them, Vask.*

They are not angry with you. Dragons do not hold on to anger. They do talk to you, but you cannot hear them.

But why? And why can I hear you perfectly well, even from a distance?

Because you are my Chosen.

CHAPTER 20

So I won't ever be able to hear them?

I do not know. I must consult with the others about the future of your training.

They won't make me stop, will they?

No, you will not need to stop training, but it may be different from the standard course.

It already is.

Briant let go of the saddle and drew his cloak tighter. The sun was almost below the horizon when he saw the Keep.

Vask, do you know if the warriors have been sent to Tristan and Aiden?

They left when I did, but it will take them several hours to arrive. I will land on the pad at the top of the Keep and you will dismount. I believe Tanwen is waiting for you near the stairs.

Thank you for coming to get me, Vask.

We are partners, Briant, although we are not fully bonded yet. When we are, we will be formidable together.

I never thought about being formidable before.

Do not dwell on it now. There is time enough to come.

He circled the Keep a couple of times, dipping lower and lower until he came to rest on a large stone pad.

Briant unfastened the straps and scrambled out of the saddle. He went down a set of steps and across the battlement to another set of steps.

Tanwen waited halfway down, and she held up her hand as Vask launched.

When he was gone she led him back up the stairs. "Do you see how the pad overhangs the pedestal?"

Briant nodded.

"When we have a lot of dragons landing, you'll come down the first steps and wait under that overhang until your dragon launches to make room for the next one. We usually take cover under there and tell our dragons when we're clear. After they launch, you'll have time to cross the battlement while the next dragon circles."

"Thanks."

She turned back toward the stairs leading into the Keep. "Normally you'd learn that during your training, but it seems you're getting an unorthodox education. Do you need to warm up before you report?"

Briant's brow furrowed. "No. I mean yes, I'm frozen through, but don't you need the information?"

Tanwen blinked back tears. "Honestly, I'm about to come out of my skin with the not knowing. But I've also been in your shoes."

"They're alive, Tanwen. Everyone was alive when I left, at least I think so. I didn't really take time to look for everyone, but Aithne and Liam were well as of last night."

She drew a shaky breath. "Thank you. You're good to report then? The Keep Council and the riders for the Dragon Council can be ready in ten minutes."

"As long as I can get some arda and maybe a chair by a fire, I'll be fine."

21

Two hours later, after holding herself together to get Briant's report in the council chamber, Tanwen sank into her favorite chair. Briant's voice rang in her head: *They're alive.*

She breathed deeply to calm her fear, but she knew it wouldn't go away until they were home.

Someone knocked at the door, and she nearly jumped out of the chair. She took a deep breath and pressed her hands to her chest as she called for them to enter.

Dinsmore came in. "I tried to catch you after the meeting, but you got out of there too fast. Are you all right?"

"Not really, but thanks for asking. No offense, but you look very grim. I hope you don't have more bad news."

He sat in the chair across from her. "Tanwen, I know the timing to fill Arwyne's role couldn't be worse, but Raya isn't going to work out."

Tanwen stared at him for a long moment before leaning back and rubbing her face with both hands. "You're right. The timing is awful."

"I would rather do this publicly, but between the missing people and Greer stirring the pot, I think we need to make a decision quickly. Are you willing to fill the position?"

"If I say no, what happens?"

"Honestly, I don't know. I'd have to talk to the council. There's a chance Greer might win after all, or they might decide to summon Ceann back for more candidates."

Tanwen shook her head. "Ceann is stretched thin as it is. We might have to shift some of our Wybrens out there, at least temporarily, as it is." She got up and went to the window.

"I hate to point this out, but you're already thinking like a liaison."

She sighed. "I know." She leaned her head against the glazing and closed her eyes. "Damn you, Arwyne." She turned and went back to her chair. "She was adamant I succeed her. Do you know why?"

"Of course. You're the best person for the job. I'd have appointed you at her death bed if it had been in my power."

"I hate being backed into a corner."

"I know, Tanwen, but that's where you do your best work."

She swallowed hard against the panic rising in her chest. "I'll do it. I don't want it. Liam really doesn't want it. But if I'm the only one, I don't have a choice. I just have one request."

"What?"

She blinked back tears. "I really need a drink."

He reached into the inside pocket of his jacket. "I thought you might." He placed a small bottle on the table in front of her. "I hope this will take the edge off. Is noon tomorrow too soon to make the announcement?"

She shook her head. "As you said, we have to do it quickly before Greer gains a foothold."

CHAPTER 21

"I'm sorry, Tanwen."
"Don't be. We can't outrun our fate."

* * *

Tanwen, the dragons are preparing to fly north to look for the captives. Would you prefer I stay behind for your installation?
No, I'd rather you go with them and bring my family home. I will do my best.

She'd spent the night dozing in her chair, and she felt awful. She took off her clothes and put on a robe, stopping in the kitchen for bread and arda on her way to the bathhouse. A long soak relaxed her tense muscles, and she was grateful no one else came in. She escaped to her quarters and dressed in her best clothing.

She reported to the council chamber an hour before the announcement. Dinsmore and two of the councilors sat at the far end of the table.

Dinsmore looked up as she entered. "Tanwen, thank you for coming."

"We've got quite a crowd gathering in the great hall."

"Good. We want all the witnesses we can get."

"The dragons are flying north. I hope Briant's description of the place was good enough to get them there."

"As do we. Did Quillon go with them?"

She nodded. "He asked if I wanted him to stay, and I told him to get his butt out there and find my family."

Dinsmore grinned. "Any woman who can boss around a dragon is welcome in my council chamber."

"Don't say that. Greer is bossier than I am." Councilor Seamus paled. "Perish the thought."

The door opened and Councilor Briaca came in. She smiled when she saw Tanwen. "You're here early! Congratulations, I'm happy to have this resolved so quickly." She sank into her seat. "I've talked to Sine. She's got the food under control."

"Food?" asked Tanwen.

"Of course! You didn't think we'd install you and not have a feast, did you?"

"I never thought about it. Food isn't high on my list of priorities right now."

"Of course, with everything going on. Don't worry, we have people seeing to everything. You just show up, eat something, and you can start moving into your new study straight away."

Tanwen faked a smile. "Going through Arwyne's books and papers will give me something to do to take my mind off my missing family."

* * *

At exactly noon, they all filed onto the dais. Tanwen's heart pounded, and she concentrated on at least looking calm and self-assured. The five councilors lined up along the back, and Tanwen and Dinsmore took their places in front of them.

Dinsmore caught the attention of the people in the front, who shushed those behind them, and soon the crowd quieted. "Thank you all for coming," said Dinsmore. "After careful consideration, the council has decided to choose Wybren Tanwen as the next liaison. Wybren Tanwen has agreed, and her willingness under difficult circumstances shows her mettle and determination. She will be a fine asset to the council." He turned to Tanwen. "Wybren Tanwen, do you swear to serve the Dragon, Keep, and Royal Councils fairly and unreservedly, putting aside your

CHAPTER 21

personal ambitions, and putting the welfare of Slan before your own?"

"On my life, I so swear," answered Tanwen.

"Do you swear to uphold and defend the decisions made by the councils and report accurately between them?"

"On my life, I so swear."

"Wybren Tanwen, I pronounce you are found worthy of the position of liaison, and I welcome you to the councils."

She faked a smile and clasped his wrist. "Thank you."

Over his shoulder, Greer glared at her, and Tanwen shivered.

No turning back now.

22

Ruan didn't return. Everyone kept an eye on the cave, even though they were sure he was probably already dead.

Aithne and several other girls took turns trying to dig under the shield. They'd been disarmed, so they had no tools. Instead, they kicked the frozen earth loose and scooped it away with their hands. It snowed intermittently, and it collected on top of the shield. They all grew up seeing snow on the high peaks all year, but none of them, not even the oldest of the warriors, had gone that high.

Early in the morning of the third day, Aithne woke shivering. She rolled over, pulling her blanket around herself, and tried to snuggle against Liam for warmth. She squirmed, unable to find him, and reached her arm out. No Papa.

She sat up, squinting into the darkness.

Her heart slammed against her ribs as she saw him outside the shield, flanked by stone trolls.

She stumbled to her feet. "No! Noooo! Stop! Papa!" She ran to the edge of the shield, both hands out as if she could run

CHAPTER 22

through it. "Papa!"

Someone caught her, trying to turn her away, and she fought to watch as he walked into the cave without looking back.

"Papa, no!" She buried her face in the chest of the man who held her. She couldn't breathe, and she gasped for air around the shock clogging her throat.

"Ssh, Aithne," whispered the man into her hair.

"Why did they take him?"

"I don't know, but we'll look after you."

She stepped back. She didn't know who it was, couldn't see through the tears blinding her. "That's what he said, and now he's gone."

She turned back to the shield and dropped to her knees, sobbing into her hands.

Papa. Please. Please don't die.

* * *

She stayed there all day, watching the mouth of the cave. Lassair joined her, tried to coax her to eat or drink some water, but she couldn't. Her stomach was a tight ball, her heart a gaping wound.

Night fell, and she kept vigil. The next morning she woke, curled in a fetal position, with no memory of falling asleep. Someone had covered her with a blanket, and a warm body curled around her.

Papa?

She gasped and sat up, startling Lassair.

"Aithne, **uffern**, you scared me!"

Aithne turned away as tears streamed down her face, unable to choke out an apology. Lassair put her hands on Aithne's shoulders. "Are you all right? Did you have a nightmare?"

She shook her head. Curling again on the cold ground, she covered her head with the blanket and wept.

* * *

Briant was sure his directions and descriptions would lead them right to the captives, but it turned out there were several areas that fit his description.

The dragons left at first light to look for them. Vask touched his mind as he flew away, and Briant rolled over in bed, having been ordered by the healers to sleep late. He didn't need to be told twice.

He woke at mid-day, parched and hungry.

He pulled on the first clothes he put his hands on and headed to the dining room.

The trainees had not yet arrived so it was easy to find a solitary table in the corner. He finished a pitcher of water by himself and held it up when a page looked his way. When the boy fetched it, he looked at Briant wide-eyed and looked away. Briant frowned and reached for another slice of bread.

He looked up at a commotion in the doorway. Tristan and Aiden walked in. Briant grinned and waved to them, and they walked over.

"Glad to see you made it back in one piece. I thought you'd be later."

They joined him at the table as the page brought two more pitchers.

"Our escort brought horses," said Tristan. "Not as fast as dragons, but faster than walking."

"Less tiring, too," said Aiden. He poured water for all of them.

CHAPTER 22

"I think I'm going to sleep for a week."

"Not before the Keep Council debriefs us. We saw the dragons flying north an hour or so after dawn. Any news yet?"

Briant shook his head. "I haven't heard anything from Vask."

"Briant."

He looked up to see Tanwen weaving between tables.

"Uh oh, looks like I spoke too soon."

She stopped at their table and put a hand on Tristan's and Aiden's shoulders. "Welcome back, gentlemen."

"Thank you, Wybren," said Tristan.

"Is there news?" asked Aiden.

"I don't know, but I've come to collect Briant. The dragons are back."

Briant frowned and pushed his plate away. "Already? Why didn't Vask tell me?"

"None of them have spoken to their riders. It's usually not a good sign."

Briant gulped the last of his water. "I'll catch up with you later, guys."

"Goodluck!" called Aiden as Briant trailed behind Tanwen.

He caught up with her in the hallway. "What weren't you saying in there?"

"Nothing. You know what I know. More, maybe, since you have the memories of the captives in your head. Who knows what you saw that your mind dismissed as unimportant. Come on, the dragons are waiting."

* * *

They entered the Dragon Council chamber. The dragons

individual lairs lay down tunnels off the main cavern and not all of the dragons had gathered.

Tanwen walked to Quillon and sat on his right front paw. "I suppose you're going to make me wait."

"Oriel, Vask, and Raine are on their way. It shan't be much longer."

She crossed her arms and ignored it when he leaned his snout against her side in what passed for an affectionate gesture.

Quillon rumbled deep in his chest—the dragon version of a chuckle. "I forget, sometimes, human impatience. After one has lived a few hundred years, a fortnight seems a breath."

"It wouldn't if stone trolls captured your family."

"Even hatchlings make stone trolls flee. We have faced worse, you and I."

"Not worse than my family being missing."

The remaining dragons lumbered into the cavern and took their places. Briant walked to Vask and sat on the ground beside him.

Raine, the matriarch of the dragons, looked around the circle before speaking. "We flew far and wide today and have news to report. Gautier found the captives and alerted us. As I was the nearest, I joined her for reconnaissance. Their numbers were fewer than they should have been, which we expected. There are, perhaps, a dozen left, but we dared not fly close enough to identify individuals. There may be a few more in the feeding rooms we may rescue. We have a preliminary plan to save them, but we need to do more reconnaissance first. We could not tell where the tunnel entrances were. Razo and Gautier will fly back this afternoon and observe their movements. If any of our captives are outside, it will, perhaps, give them hope that help is on the way."

"When should we be ready to attack?" asked Moira.

Gautier said, "It depends upon what we find. If we are able to detect the proper entrances, we can fly in first thing tomorrow morning. We will have to be sure they are not false entrances. It is a defense tactic stone trolls employ."

Tanwen's hands flexed. "How will you be able to tell? Shouldn't you be there when they move inside so you can see where they go?"

Gautier lowered her head. "We will observe when they come out, and if necessary, stay until morning. We will need to find sufficient cover, or maintain high altitude for the safety of the captives. If the stone trolls see us, they may kill all the captives to stop a rescue."

Raine nodded. "We will meet back here tomorrow to finalize our plan."

Quillon nudged Tanwen's shoulder. "It is too soon to give up hope."

She faked a smile and drew her shawl closer. "I know." She followed the other women back up the staircase, and Briant jogged to catch up. "I'm sorry they couldn't tell us more. This must be really hard on you."

She nodded. "Not knowing is the worst. If you know, even if it's terrible, you can face it a little at a time." She smiled weakly. "Right now I wish we had a way to communicate with your mother so she'd know you're safe. Mothers always worry."

"I thought all mothers had an intuition when their child is in trouble."

Tanwen snorted. "It's more wishful thinking than anything." She shook her head. "They have to be all right. Aithne has the potential to be a great Wybren. Her empathic abilities are almost as good as mine already. And we both need Liam. I don't know which of us would take it worse if something happened to him."

"She's really close to him, isn't she? Even though he's her stepfather?"

Tanwen stopped, her eyes wide. "She told you that?"

"She said she'd never seen the dragons hatch because it reminded her of her father, who died when she was young."

Her face went neutral and she started walking again. "He did die when she was young. That's how I know it's worse not knowing if you'll have to grieve again."

Skye looked over her shoulder and stopped. Her pale blonde hair almost glowed in the dim light.

"It's not good, only a dozen are left."

Tanwen nodded. "There might be more. Hopefully we can rescue the ones we know about, and they can tell us if anyone was moved to another location."

Skye shivered. "Do stone trolls do that?"

"We're livestock to them. We buy and sell cattle all the time."

"My people just stole cattle," said Skye.

Tanwen chuckled. "Truth be told, so did mine."

23

Tanwen woke from her uneasy doze in a chair when Quillon touched her mind. A bird chirped outside her window, and the sky was turning pink, chasing away the dark.

Tanwen, Gautier and Razo are returning. They saw Aithne.

She sat up straight. *Oh, thanks be to Brigid. What about Liam?*

They did not see him.

What does that mean?

They could not tell me more. I apologize.

Thanks for telling me.

She closed her eyes and pinched the bridge of her nose. Falling asleep in the chair had been a stupid thing to do. Her head was beginning to throb. Levering herself out of the chair, she gathered her clothes and headed for the bathhouse.

She slid into the empty pool and closed her eyes, trying to focus on the positive news that Aithne was alive. Fear and uncertainty gnawed in her gut.

Steam swirled as the door opened. Finley came to the edge and knelt beside her. "Have you gotten the news?"

Tanwen nodded. "Quillon told me Aithne is alive, and Liam is unaccounted for."

"Don't read too much into that. They couldn't see everyone. He might have been in one of the shelters."

"Not if Aithne was outside."

"You don't know that. Maybe some of the men were trying to figure out how to drop the shield holding them in. They wouldn't stand out in the open to do that."

"You're right. Of course you are."

"You have time for a long soak and breakfast. Quillon will let you know when Gautier and Razo are back so we can make a plan."

Tanwen nodded and managed a small smile, and Finley left.

* * *

Briant entered the cavern and saw Vask on the far side. Only Quillon and Tanwen had beaten him. Tanwen sat on Quillon's paw, her shawl pulled tight, looking like a statue in the dim light. He paused beside her. "Have you heard anything?"

"They saw Aithne, but not Liam."

His heart sank. "I'm sure he's fine."

She nodded. "That's what Finley said, too."

Unsure of what to do, he walked to Vask. *I know you can't tell me anything yet.*

I cannot.

Briant sighed and stuffed his hands in his pockets. *Any idea how high the ceiling is in here?*

About one hundred feet. Why do you ask?
I just needed one question answered.

The others arrived and took their places. Raine's voice

CHAPTER 23

echoed through the chamber. "We are assembled. Razo, please tell us what you observed."

Razo nodded, and his bronze scales glittered. "There are more alive than we initially thought. I counted eighteen of the twenty-five we seek, and Gautier confirmed this. It appears to be a new place for this group. There is only one entrance."

"That's good news," said Moira.

"Maybe not," said Greer. "They've probably got it heavily guarded if it's the only one. If this is the work of Aramach, we can't rule out mercenary guards."

"We can't be sure it's Aramach," said Skye.

"Who else could it be? The Commains don't attack anyone."

"And the Aramachs don't usually come this far west! Sure seems like they'd have started at the Eastern Keep if they wanted to do this."

Moira stood before Greer could retort. "Ladies! We have no way of knowing who did this or why! If we can rescue our loved ones, we might be able to find out something, but right now all we know is someone is holding them captive. Gautier, can you tell us anything about who is holding them?"

"Nothing specific, I'm afraid. I saw them inside a magic shield. They have three crude shelters that face each other with some space between. There was a tent on a ledge nearby. I would surmise this is for the mage. I did not see him, but I did see seven stone trolls." Her green head cocked to one side like a kitten observing a mouse. "It is unusual for stone trolls to use a single entrance. Whether this is the work of the mage, or whether it is because they have lately taken over the mountain is impossible to say at this point, but it does seem odd that they are not working diligently to mold the area to their own liking. They seem to feel themselves safe because none of the usual defenses with which I am familiar were visible. I do beg your pardon, Razo, please continue."

"As Gautier said, the captives are in barn-like shelters within a shield. We will not be able to break them out quietly, but instead will have to find and kill the mage to nullify the spell. For that reason, I cannot suggest one battle plan. I think we must make contingencies."

Briant tried to step unobtrusively behind Vask's shoulder so no one would realize he was there. Greer looked up and said, "The boy shouldn't be here. He's not fully bonded with Vask yet."

"It is a mere formality," said Vask. "It is because of him we found the captives as quickly as we did. His actions may save their lives if we do not waste time arguing about his right to be here."

"I'm sorry, Vask, but I don't think he belongs here at all. Doesn't anyone else think it's interesting that Arwyne died so suddenly after Tanwen brought him here, and that she succeeded Arwyne? I can't be the only one who thinks something might not have been quite natural there."

Briant tensed, not sure he could have heard right. "Are you really accusing me of murdering a woman I met once? I wasn't even in the room when she died!"

Tanwen stepped forward and shot a warning look at Greer. "Of course she's not. Even Greer wouldn't stoop that low. Vask, for efficiency we need to begin coordination of other parts of the operation. With the permission of the council, I would like to step outside with Briant for a moment."

"Of course you may," said Raine.

She looked across the room at him, and her expression reminded him of his mother. He sighed and followed her out

CHAPTER 23

of the council chamber and up the stairs to the first landing. Before he could speak, she turned to him. "Briant, I know you want to be in there. I agree you should be allowed to stay. But this is time sensitive, and Greer is right in saying you're not an official member of the council yet."

"Tanwen, she accused me of murder! Both of us, really."

"I know. Let me deal with that. Briant, you don't know how we operate, and you could slow us down by trying to help." She held up her hand when he tried to protest. "I have another way you can help. First, I need you to find Cadell and tell her to join us. We might need a warrior representative to coordinate. Clear so far?"

"Yes, Wybren Tanwen."

"Good lad. Next, I need you to go to the cave and let the trainer dragons know we will be attempting a rescue mission, and we will likely need their help. Last, do you still have your training beacon?"

"Yes."

"Good. Find Siril and show it to him. Tell him about how you tried to summon the dragons and no one heard you."

"But how will Siril—"

"Briant, I don't have time to answer questions right now. Just do as I've said, and then get yourself ready. You and Vask will ride with us, and if the council disagrees, I'll tell them what they can do with it. Do you understand?"

"Yes, Wybren Tanwen."

"Good. Hurry. We need Cadell now." He nodded and ran up the stairs.

* * *

He found Cadell on the archery field and waved with both

arms.

She frowned and walked toward him. "What is it, lad?"

"The Dragon Council needs you. They've found the captives and are figuring out how to rescue them."

Cadell grinned. "I'll be right along. Are you returning to the council?"

He shook his head. "I have more things to do."

"Go, then. Thank you."

"You're welcome." He turned and sprinted for the caves, slowing to catch his breath when he got close.

Briant? Is that you?

He stopped, unsure if he actually heard it. *Yes. Who is this?*
Saphir.

It was you! The voice I wasn't sure I heard. That was you?

I heard you, but you could not clearly hear me, and then I heard Vask.

Now I understand why you don't hear us. Come inside and tell us the news.

He walked into the cave. "Forgive my interruption. I have news about the captives. They've found most of them, and Wybren Tanwen asked me to tell you we will need your help with the rescue mission."

Saphir walked to him, and he put his hand on her shoulder.

What do you mean when you say they've found most of them?

Some of the other dragons nodded and he realized they'd heard her question. "Razo and Gautier counted eighteen of the twenty-five captives. We don't know what has happened to the seven who were not accounted for."

The buzzing of dragon voices echoed in his head. He closed his eyes and put his free hand on his forehead. "Please. I can't.

CHAPTER 23

What is that?"

The noise stopped, and when he opened his eyes, they were all looking at him.

"Interesting," Saphir said out loud.

Briant jumped, and the dragons rumbled in laughter. He rubbed his palms on his pant legs. "Sorry. I didn't know you could actually talk. You have talked to me before now."

"It is a skill we must develop. It does not come naturally to us. The sound you heard was all of us talking to each other, and it is interesting you perceived it after having such trouble communicating with us. It is possible your communication with Vask is opening your telepathic channels."

"Indeed," said Peio. "We will have to take care what we say to one another now."

Saphir looked at him. "Peio, now is not the time to experiment with human humor. Briant, do you know who is missing?"

"No. I'm sorry. They didn't get close enough to identify all who were left, but they did see Aithne, Muirne, and Lassair in the group."

Small waves of relief rolled over him. One of them came from Saphir, but he couldn't tell where the others originated. "I don't know what else I can tell you. The council is meeting now to develop a strategy, so as soon as they figure it out, I'm sure they'll let you know."

"Thank you for the information Briant," said Saphir. "We will be ready to mobilize when they call."

He nodded and backed out of the cave. Once outside in the sunshine, he took a deep breath and went back to the archery field. He'd seen Siril there when he'd fetched Cadell.

He waited a few minutes for the training to end, watching

the technique and accuracy of the shooters. His hands itched to get in there and join them. He'd outshoot all but a few.

When the class dismissed, he waved at Siril and walked over to meet him.

"Hello, Briant, welcome back."

"Thanks. Wybren Tanwen asked me to bring you my training beacon."

Siril grinned. "It's Wybren Tanwen now, is it?" He chuckled. "You'll do, lad, very well, I think. Let's see the beacon."

Briant slipped the thong over his head and handed it to Siril.

Siril looked at the pendant, turned it over, and turned it back. "This is your training beacon?"

"Yes, they gave it to me right before we left."

"Who gave it to you?"

"Greer passed them out to all of us. Is something wrong with it?"

"Yes, but I'm not sure what. Come with me. You can pass what we learn to Wybren Tanwen." He grinned and walked away.

Briant trotted after him. "She told me that's the right title."

"Oh, to be sure. It's exactly right. It's just been a few short weeks ago she was just Tanwen to you. You've come a long way, lad."

"Oh. Thanks."

They walked into what appeared to be a small dark workshop. Siril strode in and called, "Elan, are you here?"

"Out back."

Briant followed Siril through the space. Another door stood open, and they went through it to find a small thin man wearing a workman's cap and a leather apron removing a wood paddle from a stone oven. He closed the door and

CHAPTER 23

glanced up.

"I don't have it ready yet, Siril."

"That's not why I'm here. Did you make this?" He handed over the beacon.

Elan frowned. "Where did you get this? It disappeared a couple of weeks ago before I had a chance to spell it."

Siril's eyebrows flew up. "Interesting. It was given to young Briant here as a training beacon."

"Oh, so you're Briant. Welcome. I don't envy you. It can't be easy working with a bunch of women."

"It's been an adjustment, sir."

"Very diplomatic. I'll have a new batch of training beacons ready next week. Do you want me to hang on to this and spell it with the others?"

Siril shook his head. "Let me have it back for a few days. I'm sure this was accidental, or a bad joke, but right now it's evidence."

Elan handed it back. "I'm sure you're right. If you get it back to me, I can make it more than ornamental."

"I'll bring it back to you in a few days. Thanks, Elan."

"Ofcourse."

Siril walked around the corner of the shop and handed the beacon back to Briant. "Take this back to Tanwen and tell her what Elan said. Make sure she knows Greer gave it to you, and I'll catch up with her when she has a minute. I hope we'll be able to get to the bottom of this soon. What's the word on the captives?"

"A couple of the dragons found them, and the Dragon Council is making a rescue plan. They've got me running everywhere so I'm not in there getting in the way."

"Ah, well, you're new."

"And male."

Siril laughed. "Women can be controlling, and there's no doubt you face an uphill battle gaining the trust of all of them, but you're doing well. Give it time."

"I have all the time in the world, but I don't think that's enough time to win the trust of some of them. Thanks, Siril." He stuffed the beacon in his belt pouch and headed back to the Keep. By midday there was still no word from the council, so he wandered to the dining hall, catching up with Tristan and Aiden on the way.

"Hey, Briant, how'd it go with the council?" asked Aiden.

Tristan shoved his arm. "You can't ask. You know he can't tell us council business."

Aiden shoved him back. "I wasn't asking for specifics."

Briant stepped between them and put an arm around each of their shoulders. "It was all right but not what I expected. Let's grab the corner table and I'll tell you what I can."

They settled at the table and filled their plates before Aiden leaned forward. "Well?"

"I don't know if I'm supposed to tell anyone this part, but they found them."

Tristan grinned. "See? I said you'd get all the glory."

"Not all of it. We don't have them back yet, and I got kicked out of the planning session. But I did get some news you two will find interesting. My training beacon is a fake."

"What?" gasped Aiden. "How do you know?"

"I showed it to Siril and Elan. It disappeared from Elan's shop a few weeks ago and ended up around my neck."

"That's a sick joke," said Tristan.

Briant nodded. "I hope that's all it is. I hope it doesn't end up costing lives we could have saved by getting there sooner."

24

They flew in an hour past sunrise the next morning and landed on the other side of the mountain. All of the training dragons joined them to help evacuate the captives. Those who were not needed would stay behind and incinerate the stone trolls when they came out of the cave.

I would feel better about this if we'd been able to make your beacon first, Briant, said Vask as Briant dismounted into ankle deep snow.

I know, but Tanwen gave me this one, and she made sure it works. Indeed. Let us focus on the task at hand.

Briant patted Vask's shoulder and joined the riders. They hiked around the mountain, swords drawn, Greer and Skye in the lead, and Tanwen beside him. Even though it was late summer, their elevation meant snow half the year. This high, winter had started, and he hoped the captives had a way to stay, if not warm, at least alive in the cold.

They approached the shelters from the back, weapons drawn. There was little chance of encountering stone trolls; at this time of day they would be sleeping, or in deep caves, away from the sunlight they hated. But if they were working with a mage, they couldn't rule out mercenary guards. After all, Aramachs did such things, and who else could it be?

Greer picked up a rock and threw it toward the back of the nearest shed. It ricocheted off the shield surrounding it and Skye ducked, colliding with Briant's right shoulder, as it flew over her.

"Not so hard," she hissed.

"Sorry, Skye," Greer murmured. "I didn't think it through."

"Let's see if we can talk to them," said Tanwen. "Maybe they can tell us about the mage."

They crept around the side of the shed. Tanwen peeked around the edge. Aithne sat in the opposite corner, arms wrapped around her drawn-up knees. Muirne and Lassair flanked her, huddled close for warmth.

Tanwen stepped into their line of vision. Aithne's face lit up and she rolled to her feet. Two long steps brought her as close as she could get. The other two girls followed, passing Aithne to where their mother, Greer, stood.

"Mama, I knew you'd come." Her voice was muffled, and she started to cry.

Briant took a step back. It was hard to see Aithne cry when he couldn't do anything to help. Instead, he scanned the crowd for Liam and the others he knew. He saw Aithne and Lassair point in the same direction, and a moment later, Aithne pulled her training beacon out of her tunic.

Tanwen nodded and turned away. She motioned to the others and they all gathered nearby. She swallowed hard and said, "Aithne says the shields were made by an earth mage who stays in the woods to the northeast."

"That's what Lassair said, too," said Greer. "Looks like we

CHAPTER 24

have to find the mage before we can dispel the shield."

"That's what Torquil said," added Moira. "The men all banded together to overpower it, and they couldn't. There's no dropping the shield without dropping the mage."

"Should we pair up and search?" asked Skye.

"I think so," said Tanwen, "But I think a couple of us should stay to protect the captives when the shield falls. The trolls might know it's down and come out to contain them. They don't have weapons that I can see. No doubt the girls are a long-term food source for them."

"I'll stay," said Briant. "I'll see when the shield falls, and I can lead them to the dragons."

"Good thinking," said Tanwen. "Moira, you're the best hand-to-hand fighter we've got."

Moira grinned. "Nice of you to say so. I'll stay if you want me to, or I'll go and you can stay. We all know how much you love the woods."

Tanwen shuddered. "I have to go. I can't stay rational here with Aithne inside the shield. Can you two handle it, or should we leave a couple more?"

"We can handle it, can't we, Briant?"

"Yes, and you'll need people in the woods. It's pretty big."

"It is." Tanwen shuddered. "When the shield drops, tell the men we have warriors heading for the hunting site with horses. Everyone who doesn't want to ride a dragon needs to rendezvous there."

"Some of them are injured," said Briant. "Should I go with them? Maybe Vask could circle and keep an eye out for danger? If nothing else I have weapons to share."

"If Vask is agreeable, I am, too. Good thinking. All right, girls, let's go."

Briant watched them go until Moira nudged his shoulder. "Let's guard the cave entrance, kid. They'll be easier to kill if they don't know we're hiding by the door, and their bodies will create a barrier."

Briant nodded, and they took positions, one on each side of the entrance.

She looked at him across the opening. "Good strategy. I'm pretty sure none of us would have thought to accompany the men. Maybe having one on the council will be helpful after all."

Briant snorted. "I didn't come to be a hindrance."

"I know you didn't. When the shield falls, you handle the men. I'll get the girls to the dragons. Speaking of which, you'd better coordinate with Vask."

He stopped himself from smacking his forehead. He'd almost left a team member out of the loop. *Vask, we have a change of plans. When the shield falls, Moira is going to herd the girls your direction. I'm going to gather the men and head back to the hunting site to rendezvous with the warriors who hopefully will be there to meet them, and we need you to fly reconnaissance if you don't mind.*

I do not. It is a sound strategy. Nicely done.

Thank you, but how do you know it was my idea?

The women would not think of such a thing. They would assume the men are strong and able to escape on their own, even if they are injured, malnourished, and weaponless.

I wonder why? It's clear to anyone who looks.

When people do things the same way for several generations, they can become blind to reality. I will await instruction.

"Vask is on board. Does Tanwen not like the woods?" he whispered.

CHAPTER 24

Moira shook her head. "She avoids them whenever possible. I don't know why. I don't think she knows why. All I know is she must be about to come apart if she voluntarily went into the woods rather than stay here with Aithne."

Briant glanced at the shield. "I think my mother would have done the same thing."

"I think you're right."

He looked at Moira. "You knew my mother?"

"We trained together. It broke my heart when she left. We all knew she wouldn't be able to partner with another dragon, but we would have taken care of her."

"She misses Aegon a lot. She won't talk about him. She'll talk about Da and other people she's lost, but not Aegon."

"The bond is strong. That's why it's common for the rider to die if the dragon does. I don't know how she's made it this long. Cover the entrance. I'm going to tell the captives the plan so when the shield drops, maybe we'll be able to get everyone to safety."

She walked away and talked to the nearest group, and then came back. The captives dispersed among the others, spreading the word.

Briant and Moira stood by the cave entrance for what seemed like an hour. Inside the shield, the captives stood facing different directions, looking for dragons.

Movement caught his attention. One of the warrior trainees stood near the shield, waving his arms. Briant pointed him out to Moira, who nodded, and Briant walked over.

"Briant, is there a good point where we should meet?"

"Yes, there's a path down there, and it passes by an eroded place in the rock. It's like a porch with a roof. It's not too far."

"Is it far enough?"

"Let's hope so."

"Any chance you could leave your bow and arrows next to the shield? You won't need them at close range with stone trolls."

"No, I won't." He laid them on the ground. "I'm leaving it to you to see that someone takes them when we go."

"I'll grab them myself."

Briant nodded and turned back to the cave.

* * *

Greer matched Tanwen's pace, their footfalls muffled in the powdery snow, weapons at the ready, as the woods got denser and darker. Tanwen expected the mage would be in the densest part, probably in a shelter of fir trees and well hidden. She pushed back against the knot in her stomach that grew larger the further they ventured. She breathed deeply, focusing her will, ignoring the oppression of the woods.

Greer picked up his trail and pointed it out to her. Sure enough, it led to a grove of fir trees, and smoke rose from the center.

"Got him," Greer mouthed to her, and Tanwen nodded.

Greer whistled the alarm call of a redwing blackbird to signal the others. A second later, she fell backwards, blood gushing from her shoulder.

"Greer!"

Greer slapped her hand against the wound. "It was a magic bolt! Go get him! I'll be fine."

Running toward the fir grove, she bellowed, "Wybrens!"

She heard a faint whistle and dove to the ground. Tree bark exploded behind her. She rolled to her feet and kept running.

CHAPTER 24

When she reached the grove, she took cover behind a large tree trunk and looked around it.

She saw a large fire in the middle, but no people. She knew he had to be there. Magic didn't shoot itself. She pulled her sword from the scabbard and moved around the tree. There were footprints in the snow, too many to indicate which direction he would come from. There was a dark object near the fire. She took a long look around the grove before creeping toward the flames. When she got close, she saw Liam's leather fighting vest. He'd been wearing it when he left, and she knew it was his because she'd done the decorative tooling. It had been her gift to him when they paired.

She started to reach for it when something flashed through her vision and wrapped around her neck. It tightened, pulling her off balance against a man's chest. She dropped her sword and reached for the ligature, trying to get her fingers under it. It tightened more and she gasped for breath. Her lungs started to burn and she flailed against him, trying to get her feet under herself for leverage.

The ligature loosened for a heartbeat and she gasped, greedy for air. She stepped on his foot accidentally and had an idea. Shifting her weight, she picked up her foot and stomped hard on his. He didn't make a sound, but the ligature loosened a little and she tried to breathe as deeply as she could before it tightened again.

She reached behind, groping for some part of him to grab for leverage, preferably someplace very sensitive. Her arm brushed the hilt of her dagger, and she grabbed it, pulling it free with her right hand, reversing the blade, and plunging it into his side. She expected blood to gush into her hand, but it didn't. She tried to pull the dagger out to strike again, but she couldn't get it out all the way. His answer was to tighten the ligature more.

The edges of her vision began to go black, and she thought of Aithne, hoping she wouldn't be there when they found her body.

Somewhere nearby, someone screamed, "Wybrens!"

She heard a thud and the ligature loosened and dropped to the ground. Her attacker ran past her, the dagger in his side and a crossbow bolt in his back. She fell to her knees and wrapped her hands around her throat, gasping and coughing. At the edge of the woods, he stopped in a shadow and pulled out the dagger. He turned and threw it in the snow. In the dim light, she saw his face and her mouth went dry.

"Tanwen!" Skye ran to her and knelt in front of her. "Are you all right?"

She nodded and closed her eyes, trying to take a deep breath. When she opened them, he was gone.

Skye took her arm. "Come on, we have to get to cover. He could come back."

"What did you do to him?"

"I shot him in the back, and he ran away."

She looked at Skye. "What do you mean?"

"I mean I put a crossbow bolt in the middle of his back, and he ran away. Whatever that thing was, it wasn't human."

They made their way to the boughs of the nearest fir tree, and Tanwen sank to the ground.

"I'll be right back. I'm going to get your weapons." She ducked out and came back with Tanwen's sword and dagger. Tanwen nodded her thanks and sheathed them. "I thought I stabbed him but I must have gotten his armor. There's no blood."

CHAPTER 24

"He pulled it out and dropped it right before he ran away. It looked like it was really stuck in there. I think you got him, but it was one of those things we've been finding. It didn't bleed when I shot it."

"Did you get a look at his face?"

"No, but he had dark hair."

"He had Liam's fighting vest, too."

"Did he? How could you tell?"

"It was in the snow by the fire."

"Stay here." She ducked out of the tree and came back with the vest. "This one? Are you sure it's his?"

"Of course I'm sure. I made it."

"Can you walk? We should find the others."

She wanted to say no. She wanted to lie down in the snow and stay there, but she struggled to her feet and shrugged her arms into Liam's vest. "I won't guarantee any kind of speed."

* * *

Briant glanced at the shield in time to see it fall, starting at the top and melting away like snow. "Moira! The shield!"

She squinted at it and ran a few steps toward it. "Dragons are to the west! If you're not riding, go south to Briant's rendezvous point!"

Three warriors ran to Moira. "They have people in the cave."

Moira nodded. "We know. Go with the others. Briant and I will look for them." They hesitated, and she added, "Do you have any useful weapons?"

"They probably took them in there with them," said Fergus. Briant stepped forward to join them. "They left them at the hunting site. This doesn't make sense to you, leaving the riders to clear the cave, but we want to save as many of you as possible. It's been more than a week since you've had a proper meal or sleep, right?"

"He's right," said Ruy. "Good luck. We'll meet you at the rendezvous point."

They stepped into the cave and peered into the inky darkness. "How about a light wisp?"

He was glad she couldn't see his reddening face. "It's not much. My magic is weak."

"Any light is better than what we have."

He swallowed hard and conjured a light wisp. It barely glowed, and he sent it a few steps ahead.

Moira sighed. "So the rumors are true. Come on, then."

They advanced slowly. Their eyes adjusted to the deep twilight of Briant's light wisp.

Moira paused when she saw a jumble of rocks and nudged Briant. They crept closer and he saw the rocks were three sleeping stone trolls. He wanted to back away, but Moira edged past them. He swallowed hard and followed.

They passed three more piles of sleeping stone trolls before reaching the back of the cave. He looked closely for tunnels or exits and found nothing. When Moira signaled, he followed her out.

The daylight was blinding and he shaded his eyes with his hand. "Did that seem odd to you?"

"Not finding any humans or an exit? I'll say it was odd. Remember everything you saw. You'll have to report to the councils when you get back. The closer your report matches mine, the quicker you'll be taken seriously. How many stone trolls did you see?"

"A dozen."

CHAPTER 24

"Good. Go rendezvous with the men. Get back safe."

"You, too. See you in a couple days."

She laughed. "If you're not back in a couple days, I'll personally be riding recon." She grasped his wrist. "See you soon."

He grasped hers back, and then she let go and spun off to run west.

Vask, we cleared the cave and I'm heading to the rendezvous point.

Did you find anyone?

No, and we didn't find any exits, either.

How odd.

Briant snorted and scrambled down the path. *That's one word for it. I wonder if I should get the wounded to the rendezvous point and then come back up with a couple other guys to check it more thoroughly? My light might have been too dim. We might have missed something.*

Allow me to relay your idea to the council. They will have an answer for you later today.

Briant sighed. *That's not exactly what I meant, but if that's the way we do things, I'll wait for their decision.*

Would it make a difference if I told you Lucas is in the group meeting you at the hunting site?

That depends on what the council says. What's the penalty if they say no, and I go anyway?

I would advise you not to disobey orders at this point. You must be trusted first. I will advocate for you.

Thanks. I'm almost to the rendezvous point.

* * *

Aithne ran, heart pounding. She didn't know how far she had to go, and her mother was nowhere in sight.

She stopped, trying to think of the best place to find her. Her training beacon vibrated and she looked around. Muirne stood a few feet from her, beacon in her palm.

"Muirne, what are you doing? The dragons can't land here!" She ran over and slapped the beacon out of Muirne's hand.

"Hey!"

"Think!" She waved her arms at the trees. They weren't dense but there wasn't enough open space. "How are they going to get to you? Drop a rope for you to climb? Come on." She grabbed Muirne's arm and headed the direction her mother told her to go.

Muirne jerked her arm away and bent to pick up the beacon, but put it in her belt pouch and followed Aithne. They moved as quickly as they could over the rocky terrain, looking for a clearing big enough for the dragons.

Moira came up from behind them. "Come on, girls, there's an easier trail this way." She shook her head as a couple of trainee dragons flew by looking for a place to land. "Whoever summoned the dragons made life a lot harder for the rest of us. I hope we can gather everyone before dark."

Muirne looked at Aithne, her eyes wide, and shook her head. Aithne rolled her eyes and followed Moira uphill.

A quarter of an hour later, the trail led to a clearing. Three people came from the other side and looked around. One stepped into a shaft of sunlight and her red hair glowed.

"Mother!" Aithne sprinted as Tanwen turned. She paused when she saw angry red marks around Tanwen's neck. "Mother, what happened to you? Why are you wearing Papa's vest?"

CHAPTER 24

Tanwen's arms clasped Aithne tightly. "Just a fight. I'll be fine."

Skye grabbed Tanwen's arm. "There's Quillon. Get Aithne home and gather the Keep Council. I'll stay with Moira and make sure everyone gets back."

Tanwen nodded and they ran to meet Quillon as he landed. Tanwen pushed Aithne into her saddle, shoved Liam's tunic in the saddle bag, and climbed onto Quillon's back behind her. Quickly fastening the straps around them both, she shouted at Quillon to go.

Aithne held on as Quillon launched. Razo flew past with Peio as they circled to land.

Tanwen held on to the front of the saddle until Quillon leveled, and then pressed herself against Aithne's back.

25

Briant heard wings flapping and looked up. Several dragons flew toward the Keep with riders. Quillon had two. Good. They got Aithne. He rounded the ledge and found the men waiting. "Is everyone here?"

They turned and looked at him, and Fergus said, "Where are the others?"

"We didn't find anyone. Just sleeping stone trolls."

"But they had to be there somewhere," said Fergus. "People don't just disappear. I knew we shouldn't have left it to riders to clear the cave."

"Fergus, that's enough," said Ruy. "The mage probably has secret passages and such. Briant, did you see any indication?"

"I didn't, sir. I saw a dozen sleeping stone trolls and no signs of any people."

"But they were there!" said Fergus.

Ruy swung to face him. "If you don't shut your hot-headed mouth, I'm going to shut it for you. Keep whatever issues you have with Briant to yourself because now is not the time!" He turned back to Briant. "We saw them taken into the cave. If they aren't there, how might they have gotten out?"

"I don't know, but clearing the cave was too easy. We went around the trolls, and they didn't wake up. We walked to the back of the cave and out again unmolested. I hope the Dragon Council allows me to go back once we've rendezvoused with the warriors meeting us at the hunting site. They should be there later today."

Ruy patted his shoulder. "Well done, lad. We'd better go if we're to beat them to the hunting site." Fergus started to object, and Ruy glanced sideways at him. "We need supplies if we are to conduct a full investigation. I will consult with whoever is meeting us and we will decide what course of action to take. Staying here would be foolish, considering none of us have had adequate food, water, or shelter for a week. Now let's go." He strode down the mountain, and the others followed. Briant let them go and took rear guard. He hoped Fergus would be allowed to go back with the search team, since he likely wouldn't be allowed. Two days traveling with him would be unpleasant.

They reached the hunting site near dark and found half a dozen men, two dozen horses, and a hot meal. He followed the captive men into camp and breathed a sigh of relief.

Lucas walked toward him. "There's the glory hound!"

Briant snorted. "This is glory? It feels like tired and thirsty."

Lucas laughed. "Come on, we have dinner ready. I want to hear what happened. Is this everyone?"

He followed Lucas toward the fire. "Except the girls, of course. They're probably all in the bathhouse by now."

"What about the rest of the men?"

"We couldn't find them. They said the stone trolls took them, and Moira and I cleared the cave, but we didn't find them. I'm baffled. It's like they disappeared or something."

"There weren't any tunnels they could have gone down?"

Briant took a water skin from a pile. "Don't you think we'd have checked out any tunnels we found?"

"Yes, I guess you would have. Go sit by that tree. I'll get you some food."

"You don't have to."

"If I don't, you're going to fall over. Go."

Briant stumbled to the tree and sank down beside it, leaning against the trunk. He closed his eyes, weariness a boulder on his chest.

"Briant." Lucas kicked his foot, and Briant opened his eyes. Lucas handed him a bowl before dropping to the ground across from him. "Eat first, then sleep."

Briant dug into the stew. On the other side of the fire, Ruy and two other men stood in a tight circle. "What's going on there?"

Lucas twisted to look. "Oh. They're deciding whether to send a few men back to try to find where the missing men were taken, or if it's better to go back and return with a larger group."

Vask? Any word from the Dragon Council?

They request you return to report to them.

I figured as much.

He sighed. "Whatever they decide, I won't be with them. It's probably for the best. I won't be much help."

"Why?"

"My magic is too weak. It would just be embarrassing anyway."

"Don't say that, Briant. Come on, eat and get some rest. You'll feel better in the morning."

26

Two days later, Aithne walked through the Keep. People passed her, talking loudly, but she didn't listen.

The whole Keep buzzed with news and activity as the captives returned and reported to the council. Rumors flew aimlessly, like butterflies.

Aithne ignored it all. She waited for one specific piece of news, and it hadn't come. Wouldn't come.

She walked into the courtyard and out the gate without pausing. It was quieter outside the wall, and she headed for Brigid's pool.

When she got close, she paused to take off her boots. The grass was cool and she felt a tiny trickle of peace.

At the pool, she dropped her boots and sank to the ground. She started to dip her fingers in the water and ask Brigid to bring Liam home safely, but it didn't seem like enough. Asking the goddess of hearth and home for a rescue? Wouldn't that be Laoch's job? Or Maccha's? She sat back for a moment, unsure of what to do.

The sun was warm on her head, and a butterfly landed on

one of the stones surrounding the pool. She watched it settle as the breeze rippled the water. She closed her eyes and thought of Arwyne telling her class the story of Balphrahn when she was a child, about how Cruthadair, Mother Creator, saw the world and formed it into a life-giving planet, filled with food and comfort and love.

She dipped her fingers into the water. "Cruthadair, if you still care about us at all, if there is anything good in me that makes you happy, please bring Papa home. Please don't let him be dead, too. I can't bear to lose another father."

Even as she said it, she didn't dare to hope. Two groups had searched the cave he'd been taken into. No one found any trace of the missing men.

She heard a shuffling sound and glanced over her shoulder. Briant walked toward her carrying his boots. Lovely. Company was exactly what she wanted.

He chose a spot several feet from her and didn't talk for a few minutes. Finally, he asked, "Does it help? Coming here?"

"Not really. Maybe a little."

"Has your mother told you anything?"

"Only that no one knows anything." He fidgeted.

She looked up. "No one knows anything, right? Haven't you been sitting in on the Dragon Council?"

"I have, on the condition that I observe and don't speak."

"Have you observed something?"

"I don't know. No one else seems to have made the connections I'm seeing, so maybe I'm wrong."

"What connections?"

"When the warriors went back to check the cave again, my friend was with them. They saw what I saw - sleeping stone trolls and the back of the cave. But Lucas described every

CHAPTER 26

detail as I saw it. I asked him about it outside the council chamber, and it sounds like the stone trolls were in exactly the same places as where I saw them."

Aithne shrugged. "I always sleep in the same place. Why shouldn't they?"

"I guess, but something about it is bugging me. What if their positions aren't because that's where they sleep, but because they're hiding something?"

"Hiding what? An opening big enough for at least one man to go through?"

"I don't know. Something about the magic in that place felt different." He shook his head. "This must be why they didn't want me to talk. I'll just muddy the water and make the interviews take longer."

"Have you told Mama this?"

"Why would I waste her time?"

"You might have the missing link."

"I might also have a half-cooked theory that she doesn't need to deal with right now."

Aithne sighed and rolled to her feet. "Protocol states that when you have information, you should tell the pertinent person. Come on."

"Where?"

"To find my mother." She picked up her boots and strode barefoot toward the Keep.

Briant scrambled after her. "I don't want to bother her, Aithne. I shouldn't have bothered you. None of the news we've gotten is good for your family."

"And that's supposed to stop you from sharing it? Mama and I both chose this life. Being a Wybren doesn't mean you get to withhold possibly important information to spare someone's feelings. Besides, maybe that's one reason Vask chose you."

"I think he chose me because I'm not afraid of him."

"None of the women are afraid of him. He could have Chosen any of us, but he hasn't taken a new rider in years. I think it's because women have been running the show for so long we don't know how to think like a man. Maybe that's what we need now."

* * *

Tanwen pinched the bridge of her nose. "Is that everything?"

Briant tried not to fidget. "Yes, Wybren Tanwen."

She sighed and opened her eyes. She looked like she hadn't slept in a week. "All right. I guess we should go find Cadell and Siril. They'd know better than I would if any of this means something."

"I can go find them myself," said Briant. "I'm just going to end up telling them all of it again anyway."

"No, I'm the liaison. I need to hear their thoughts from them, not second-hand from you. Not that I think you wouldn't do a good job. It will save time. Trust me. Aithne, you can come along, too, if you'd like."

"Mama, let us go find them and bring them to you. You're the liaison. Rank has its privileges."

Tanwen chuckled. "You're too smart by half. Fine. Go find them and bring them to my study. Hurry up."

Aithne leaned to kiss her cheek. "We'll be as fast as we can."

* * *

Aithne strode down the hall toward the courtyard with Briant

CHAPTER 26

trailing behind her. "I think we should start with the pells."

"Why? Practice ended an hour ago."

"I know, but sometimes they stay and practice."

"Are you sure they wouldn't be at the armory?"

She clenched her jaw and spun to face him, taking perverse pleasure when he stepped back, eyes wide. "Do you have to challenge every little thing? Can't you just play nice once in a while?" She held up her hand when he tried to speak. "Fine. You go to the armory, I'll go to the pells. We'll probably find them faster if we split up anyway."

She turned on her heel without waiting for an answer and jogged to the pells. As she expected, Cadell and Siril shot arrows into the line of targets, moving from one to the next from opposite ends.

Aithne waited until they met in the middle. Despite her hurry, she knew better than to interrupt them. As they shot their last arrows, she strode over.

Cadell laughed at something Siril said and glanced toward her. "Yes, Aithne?"

"I'm sorry to interrupt, but my mother sent me to fetch you both."

"Is something amiss?" asked Cadell.

"Briant has a theory and she thinks you two might be the best authority."

Siril looked around. "Where is Briant? With your mother?"

"No, he's looking for you in the armory. I can fetch him and meet you in Mama's study."

"If you're going to the armory," said Siril, handing her his bow.

Cadell laughed. "Go on then, Siril. The girl can't carry all the quivers herself. Aithne, take what you can. I'll fetch the

181

arrows and the rest of the quivers and be along in a trice."

Siril walked away with a grin. "Don't be too long."

Cadell snorted. "I've a mind to leave everything here and come back for it later so I can beat him there."

Aithne laughed. "If you do, I'll come back and help you."

Cadell grinned. "I'll hold you to that, and young Briant, too."

She took off at a dead run, taking the alternate route into the Keep.

Aithne picked up her bow and all the quivers nearby and headed for the armory.

She shouldered the door open and headed for the third door on the right. As she passed the second doors she heard laughter and stopped.

Briant and Muirne stood in the sword room. He had evidently just hung a practice sword. His arms were up, and Muirne had stepped closer to him.

She reached toward him, and he skipped back. She laughed again.

Aithne tasted bitterness and bit back her irritation. "Briant, I found them. They'll be waiting for us."

His face went red, and Muirne turned and sneered. "You're such a killjoy." She turned on her heel and brushed past Aithne to leave the armory.

Aithne continued to the archery room and hung the bows. She heard Briant follow but didn't acknowledge it.

"So I guess you were right after all. You found Siril and Cadell, and I found Muirne."

She didn't answer as she hung the quivers.

He shuffled his feet. "Funny, I didn't think she liked me before. In fact, I thought she'd be the last girl to like me. Do you need any help?"

CHAPTER 26

Aithne clenched her jaw and hung the last quiver. "I'm done. We shouldn't keep them waiting. Let's get back to the Keep."

She jogged back. He kept pace with her and ran ahead a few paces every time they came to do a door to open them for her.

When they reached the corridor to Tanwen's study they slowed to a walk.

He knocked on the door and opened it for her. Siril and Cadell lounged in Tanwen's sitting area, having apparently enjoyed a joke. Tanwen sat with them, smiling, but Aithne could see how the weeks since they'd left for the hunt, since the start of their ordeal, had worn on her. She knew her mother wasn't sleeping much. She heard her pacing at night.

Cadell turned to Briant. "So, there is a facet to your adventure we've yet to hear about?"

"I'm not sure. My friend, Lucas, went back to the stone troll cave. What he described was exactly what I saw. I questioned him about it later. As near as we could both remember, it's like the sleeping stone trolls hadn't moved, like maybe they were dead. Also, that magic felt wrong."

"Wrong how?" asked Siril.

He searched for the right word. "Malevolent, maybe. I've never felt anything like it."

"Are ye sure, lad? None of the warriors mentioned it in their reports, did they?"

"No, sir, but Lucas felt it, too."

"That's odd," said Tanwen. "Could the warriors not have noticed it because they'd sensed it before? Everyone on the team except Lucas has seen real battle."

Siril frowned. "Maybe. Briant, you can get back to the cave, can't you?"

"Yes."

"Might we borrow him for a few days, Tanwen? We should take Lucas, too."

"That sounds like a good idea." She glanced out the window. "You have half the day left. Can you assemble your team and be ready to go in the morning?"

Cadell nodded. "It sounds as if we need to be."

* * *

"Briant!"

He stopped on the last flight of stairs and turned. Aithne trotted down to meet him.

His heart skipped a beat, and then he remembered Muirne's attention, how he'd been attracted and repulsed at the same time, and shame pinged. "You're up early." *That's the best you can do, Briant? Smooth. Real smooth.*

She nodded. "I knew you'd be leaving early. Do you know who else is going?"

"Siril and Lucas. I'm not sure about anyone else."

"You'll be careful, right?"

He felt his face heating. "Sure, but is that what you want? It seems like I've been a thorn in everyone's side since Vask found me."

Her face turned pink, too, but he was pretty sure he won the brightness prize. "No, you haven't."

He snorted. "Come on, Aithne, the other riders tolerate me at best, and we've had our differences."

"It's just taken a little time to get over the shock. None of us ever thought there would be a boy in our ranks."

Boy? "Sorry to break up the all-girls club. I'll see you next week. We need to get back to our training."

CHAPTER 26

"We do. Briant, thanks for stepping up. You've given me hope of getting Papa back."

He swallowed hard. "You're welcome. I have to go."

"See you soon."

He started down the stairs again. His heart pounded and his chest felt tight. When he got to the landing, he jogged into the courtyard. He didn't want to get left behind.

27

Briant slid off his horse and looked up. Vask rode the thermals high above. The other men were intentionally ignoring Vask. Briant kept his amusement carefully hidden. He admired their courage, of course, but watching dragons fly was one of Briant's favorite things. Briant had considered asking if he could ride Vask and meet the others there, but had decided it would be better to travel with the others. He'd learned you could get to know people better when you traveled together, and he was desperately short of friends.

They reached the hunting site in one day. The plan was to get up at dawn and start up the mountain on foot, leaving the horses in the care of a pair of grooms who traveled with them. They allowed three days to get to the cave, explore it, and get back.

He pulled the tack off his horse and carried it to the pile of saddles and bridles while one of the grooms slipped a lead rope over the horse's head and led him and two others to the stream.

CHAPTER 27

Briant and Lucas followed to collect firewood while others organized the camp.

"The trip isn't very much faster on horseback, but my feet sure don't hurt like they did when we hiked here," said Lucas.

"While carrying all our supplies on our backs," added Briant.

Lucas laughed. "Exactly."

"Is it normal to travel with grooms? They really look like they know what they're doing."

"They do, and yes, the warriors usually take a groom for every five horses. They're responsible for making sure they're fed and protected from predators while the warriors are away fighting."

"So they routinely keep the horses away from the fighting?"

"Usually, unless the ground is favorable and the enemy outnumbers us. Our stable has grown in the last couple of decades, but we only have so many horses, so we have to protect them."

"Makes sense. Anyway, we both know the horses wouldn't make it to the cave."

Lucas hoisted his bundle higher in his arms. "We know better than anyone. I hope they listen to us when we get there."

* * *

"There's the cave," said Lucas when they topped the last ridge.

The climb to the cave was still long, but it was easier with food and water.

"Right," said Siril. "We'll let Briant and Lucas take point. I want to know if anything has changed from what you remember. Dermod and Murchad, we need to pay special attention to magic traces. Any questions?" Everyone shook their heads.

"Let's go, then." He unsheathed his sword and everyone else followed suit.

Briant glanced at Lucas and turned for the cave. Lucas followed a step behind. "We're going to need your light wisp," muttered Briant.

"I know."

They entered the cave, and Lucas' light wisp brightened. They stood for a moment, getting their bearings.

It smelled musty and Briant rubbed his nose to keep from sneezing. Lucas sent his light higher and ahead. They stepped in further, and the others filed in behind them.

The first group of stone trolls sprawled to Briant's left. The musty smell got stronger. Something skittered across his path, too fast for him to make out what it was.

Behind him, someone muttered, "Evil magic."

"Briant," whispered Lucas and lowered his light wisp. It illuminated what looked like a pile of rocks. "Lucas, turn it up."

The light got brighter and Briant stepped closer. "What happens to stone trolls when they die?"

Siril stepped closer. "They decompose in much the same manner we do." He poked at the pile. The stone troll corpse tipped over, disturbing a pair of rats that ran off with what looked like fingers, and the air filled with a musty stench.

Siril's eyes went wide and his light wisp flared. He looked over his shoulder. "Murchad, do you sense what I do?"

Murchad nodded. "Necromancy."

Briant's legs went weak. Lucas' face was white. No one wanted to speculate about what it meant for the missing men. Siril turned to them. "Let's move the rocks, but be careful.

"We don't know what the mage left behind. Briant, you work with me. Lucas, I want you paired with Murchad."

CHAPTER 27

"Yes, sir," they said together.

Siril turned to the pile in front of them while the others moved further back. He and Briant pulled on leather gloves. They moved the rocks aside and found two more troll fingers but nothing else.

Siril straightened and placed his hands on his back, stretching, when someone in the back of the cave yelled.

Briant leaped over the rocks in front of him, Siril hot on his heels. Murchad and Dermod stood amid a large pile of rocks in front of a cleft in the stone.

Murchad turned. "Siril, the magic trail leads this way. It's strong, and it's not just necromancy. I think the men were spelled, but might have been lucid enough to leave a magic trail to follow."

Siril walked over and peered at the cleft. "That's awfully narrow."

"It was probably magically widened to allow them to pass through."

"That can be done?" asked Briant.

Lucas pushed his shoulder. "Probably not by you."

Siril reached for the edge of the cleft. His hand passed through it. Eyes wide, he looked at Dermod, who reached for the other side. They moved their hands in opposite directions while Lucas and Murchad moved their light wisps.

When their hands stopping moving, they were far enough apart to get a stone troll through.

Siril grunted. "Let's go back outside for a minute." He started toward the mouth of the cave before anyone could object, and they followed him.

They stood in a circle beside the cave, out of the wind. It had started to snow lightly, and Briant shivered.

"Lucas, Briant, did you sense the different magics?"

"I did," said Lucas.

"It all felt like a big mess to me," said Briant.

Siril nodded and turned to the veterans. "Thoughts?"

"We should follow it, see where it leads. Let me and Murchad scout it out. We'll either come to a wall and stop, or it will lead out of the cave. Briant, can Vask see us?"

Vask, can you see us?

Somewhat, but I am higher than I need to be for reconnaissance.

"He can see us, but he needs to come lower for recon."

"Ask him to," said Siril. "You two go and see what you can find. We'll wait for word until three hours before dark."

"That should give us enough time," said Dermod. He clapped Murchad on his shoulder.

"Let's go."

Briant watched them disappear into the cave. *Vask, two of us have gone back in. We found a cleft at the back of the cave, and it might lead to an opening somewhere nearby. Will you keep an eye out and tell me if and where they come out?*

Certainly. You have advised them I will need to decrease altitude?

I have.

"Vask is going to watch for them."

"Let's find some shelter nearby, then. Not that cursed cave."

"We know a place," said Lucas. "It's this way."

They settled into the outcropping, cloaks pulled tight, and watched the snow.

"Briant," said Siril, "I noticed you didn't use a light wisp in the cave."

Briant's face grew hot, and Lucas looked away. "No, sir, I didn't. The truth is, I didn't want anyone to see it." Siril's eyebrows raised. "Might I ask why?"

CHAPTER 27

"It's not bright at all. My magical ability is pretty limited and I've never been able to figure out why."

Siril turned toward him. "Really. Interesting. Let's see it."

Briant frowned, and Lucas laughed. "Congratulations, Briant, you've just become a puzzle. Siril loves puzzles."

Siril glanced over his shoulder. "Hush, boy." He turned back to Briant. "The light wisp, if you please?"

Briant gritted his teeth and produced a lit wisp. He turned it up to maximum brightness, and it glowed like a cheap wax candle.

"That's as bright as it goes?" asked Siril.

"Yes, sir."

"That's odd. You do fine with the accuracy spell."

"That's the only one I do fine with."

Siril frowned. "I'm sure it must have something to do with your dragon riding capabilities, but I've seen naught like it." He swiveled around and leaned on the wall. "I'll have to think about it."

Briant nodded and banished his light wisp. *Vask, does it sound right to you that my magic is weak because I'm not afraid of you?*

It is logical, although not the only reason. Before the curse, some people had weak magic. Some of those people had it grow stronger after a traumatic event, and others never came into their magic at all.

So the curse changed that?

So it would seem. This would account for your lack of ability. I wonder if there's anything we can do about it, short of trauma. Allow me to consult Raine.

Briant pulled his cloak closer and leaned his head against the rock. "Vask says it might have something to do with the

191

dragon thing. He's going to ask Raine if she knows of any way to fix it."

Siril closed his eyes. "If anyone would know, it's Vask and Raine."

* * *

Briant.

He jolted awake, staring wide-eyed at the snow. Siril chuckled. "Must have been some dream."

"I don't remember falling asleep. I heard my name."

I did not mean to startle you.

Briant snorted. "Vask." He leaned against the rock again, his heart pounding.

You asked me to tell you when I saw the others. They have emerged from a cave two leagues from you, on the west side of the mountain. It appears they are studying the area to get their bearings in order to return to you.

Thanks.

"Siril, have you ever thought about having dragon riders travel with the warriors, like we're doing now? Vask sighted the others, but of course there's no way to communicate with them. If we had another rider, we could communicate through the dragons."

"It's a good thought. We've used that tactic from time to time, but only when the Aramachs become particularly aggressive. We've been trying not to overwork the dragons and riders, so we don't send them on skirmishes like this."

"Maybe, if they're going to look for the captives, or what's left of them, we should coordinate with them about the route? Maybe have riders rendezvous with them from time to time?

CHAPTER 27

Or maybe I should go with them since I'm already here."

"Perhaps. Any idea how far away they are?"

"About two leagues."

Siril rolled to his feet. "Come on, then. We have daylight left. Maybe we can meet them halfway. Vask can guide us to them. Beats sitting here on the cold stone getting snowed on."

28

Guided by Vask, they rendezvoused with the others in a surprisingly short amount of time. Murchad and Dermod didn't seem surprised to see them. They made camp and settled around the fire for a dinner of travel rations and water.

Siril looked at Dermod. "What's next, do you think?"

Dermod took his time chewing. "The trail seems to head due west. It might turn once we get off the mountain. Murchad and I were talking, and we think the best strategy would be for us to split up. We need a couple people to go back to the hunting site and bring a groom and some horses as close as they can west of here. If Vask is agreeable, he could circle a rendezvous location. We will follow the trail while the rest of you report back to Wybren Tanwen."

"I can go fetch horses," said Briant. "Why not take me west with you? I can communicate with Vask, and he can report back to the Dragon Council and have reinforcements sent if we need them."

Murchad leaned back on his elbows and crossed his ankles.

CHAPTER 28

"Makes sense. Who knows what we'll find? It might be good to have fresh troops coming."

Lucas leaned forward. "The mage did brag about how the captives should be honored because they'd be joining a great army."

Murchad and Dermod looked at each other. "That can't be good. Briant, can you have Vask request reinforcements leave as soon as possible?"

"Of course." *Vask?*

I have been listening.

What? You can do that?

Vask chuckled in his head. *I will explain later. I will contact Raine. It might take a little time to get the message to the appropriate people.*

Briant shook his head. "He's contacting Raine."

"That was fast," said Lucas.

"Apparently he was listening to our conversation. I didn't know he could."

Lucas laughed. "You're going to have to watch what you say every moment for the rest of your life!"

29

Aithne balanced the tray of arda and pastries as she walked down the hall to her mother's study. When she was three doors away she heard shouting and stopped.

"That's preposterous! You know me! How could you think I would recommend this only because Liam is involved? I'd go myself if I thought it would make a difference."

There was a lower murmur.

Tanwen's voice was lower when she answered, but Aithne recognized the tone and gripped the tray as her heart rate ratcheted up.

The door opened, and Sir Donovan strode out, his face red. He nodded to Aithne as he strode off in the opposite direction. Aithne swallowed hard and walked to the door. Her mother sat in the window seat looking out.

"Mama?"

Tanwen jumped, one hand reaching for her sword, the other fluttering to settle on her chest like a bird. "Aithne. You startled me."

CHAPTER 29

"I'm sorry. I thought you might need a break. You haven't left your study since early this morning."

Tanwen nodded, walking around the desk. "And how would you know?"

"No one has seen you all day, and people have started asking me how you're doing. Why was Sir Donovan here?"

Tanwen closed the door and motioned to the sitting area. Aithne put the tray on the low table in the middle of the circle of upholstered chairs.

"We had a message from Vask. The warriors have picked up the trail of the missing men and are going to follow it. They want warriors for back up to leave immediately, along with dragon reconnaissance between their location and the border to carry messages and provide support if needed. Some members of the royal council question whether extra support is worth the cost."

"What border are they talking about?"

"Western."

Aithne sank into the nearest chair. "Where the Shunned went?"

"Yes. Did you hear the mage bragging about how you were going to be part of a great army?"

Aithne nodded. "Yes, it was sinister."

"Briant and Lucas heard it, too, and the trail so far is leading west." Tanwen poured a cup of arda and wrapped her hands around it. She sank into the chair beside Aithne's. "I probably don't need to be drinking this, but I'm so tired."

"I know you haven't been sleeping well."

"Neither have you."

Aithne swallowed hard. It was true. "I was trying not to be noisy."

"You weren't."

"Every time I go to sleep I dream about him telling me he'd protect me and then disappearing."

"Is that what happened?"

"More or less. I was afraid after they took Ruan, and he said he wouldn't let them take me. They took him two days later, just before dawn. If I'd been awake I might have stopped them, or gotten someone else to help me."

"I doubt it," said Tanwen. "I've talked to the others who were with you, and everyone said the mage spelled you with immobility every time the shield dropped. If you'd been awake, you wouldn't have been able to move."

Aithne sniffled and leaned back. "I could have tried."

Tanwen brushed her hand over Aithne's hair. "You are right. You should talk to Sine about a sleep aid tonight."

"So should you."

Tanwen shook her head. "I can't, not with the situation as fluid as it is right now. I have to be able to respond at a moment's notice."

"Are you going to be able to if you're exhausted?"

"I have before."

"But for this long? Mama, if you said you'd had a full night's sleep in the last three weeks, I wouldn't believe you. Surely there must be something you can do to get some sleep that will allow you to wake up quickly."

"If there is, I don't know what it is, but Sine might. Help me eat these pastries, and when you take the tray back, see what she says, eh?"

"Is that a direct order?"

Tanwen laughed. "Yes."

30

"There they are," said Lucas, pointing.

"Good catch," muttered Siril. "I hope they've set up camp."

Briant, there is a large clearing one half league north. Please meet me there at your convenience.

"Let's go find out so I can help if needed. Vask has requested an audience half a league north of here."

Siril waved a hand at him. "Go meet him. We've enough hands to set up camp from scratch, and you don't want to keep a dragon waiting."

"He didn't sound like he was in a hurry."

Lucas narrowed his eyes. "There's a dragon on the ground half a league away. You might be comfortable with that, but none of the rest of us are."

Briant's face warmed. "I'll go see what he wants." He reined his horse around Siril and Lucas, heading north.

Half an hour later, his horse started to balk. "I guess we're close, eh?" He patted the horse's neck and took him back several yards before dismounting and tying the reins to a tree.

"You graze, and I'll be back soon."

He broke through the tree line and grinned at how short the distance had been. Vask crouched at the far end of the clearing, but it was far closer than any other horse he'd ridden would get to a dragon. He made a mental note to feed him an apple and tell the grooms as he jogged across the clearing.

That was fast, said Vask in his head.

"The guys want me to take care of it so you can get back in the air."

Vask chuckled. "I am too close for their comfort. Your horse is braver than your companions."

Briant laughed. "So why do you need to see me in person?"

"This requires physical contact."

"Oh. All right." He walked over and sat on Vask's paw.

Do you hear how loud my voice is in your head?

Yes.

It's louder than it was when you were in the air. I am whispering to you. In the air, I was shouting.

Briant frowned. "So proximity affects our communication."

Indeed. What I am about to suggest is unorthodox at best. At worst, it could get us both in trouble. However, I believe it may expedite the process of recovering our captives.

What is it?

Tell the others I've spoken to the Dragon Council, and you have been ordered to accompany the men heading west in order to have dragon reconnaissance.

I guess I haven't actually been ordered?

I have not consulted the council. The younger dragons do not agree it is needed. They do not have the years or experience I do. While you travel, I want you to look for a stone you like particularly. It should be larger than your thumb but smaller than your hand, and you should find it aesthetically pleasing. When you find it, tell me so we can meet.

CHAPTER 30

Why would it be a problem for me to look at stones?

You're looking for your beacon stone.

Now? But I haven't finished training yet. Vask, if I jump the line I'll never hear the end of it. Aithne will never speak to me again, and it's not going to help me fit in with the other women, either.

Those rules are new. They've only been in place a hundred or so years.

That's new?

For me, yes. Briant, this is important. If you have your beacon we will be able to communicate over greater distance. It could be the difference between bringing them home safely or bringing home corpses. We don't have time for formalities.

Briant swallowed hard. *This is going to be bad when we get home, isn't it?*

I will bear the responsibility.

I have a feeling I will, too.

31

"They've what?"

Tanwen stood in the middle of the dining room. Quillon's timing was usually better.

"Mama?"

She noted the concern in Aithne's eyes, and then noticed the people around her staring. "I'm sure it's nothing, but I need to go see what Quillon is yammering about. Finish up here, sweetie. I'll be up soon."

Without waiting for an answer, she pushed in her chair and strode from the room.

Tanwen, please, I never yammer.

She started down the stairs. *Maybe not, but your timing is terrible. What do you mean, Vask and Briant have gone rogue?*

Siril and his group are on their way back. Razo noted them. Briant and Vask are not with them, but Lucas is.

I thought Lucas was going with them. Has anyone contacted Vask?

All he will say is this is for the best.

Tanwen groaned. *Who else knows?*

CHAPTER 31

Razo and Raine. They only told me because you need to be privy, also.

She stopped and leaned against the wall. Closing her eyes, she rubbed her face with both hands. She didn't need this. What she needed was a week of sleep, which wouldn't happen anytime soon.

Tanwen, we must assume Siril has no idea Briant was supposed to return.

Siril won't be the one in trouble.

"Wybren, are you all right?"

She startled and dropped her hands. A warrior trainee stood in front of her, concern etched on his face. She inhaled and forced a smile. "Yes, thank you. Aiden, isn't it?"

"Yes, Wybren."

"Are you busy?"

"No, not at the moment."

"Excellent. How would you like a bit of adventure?"

Aiden grinned. "How can I help?"

"Siril and his party should be returning soon. I'd like you to wait for them outside the gate, maybe in the trees around the first bend in the road. When they arrive, I want you to send them directly to my study. It's imperative they not stop anywhere, not even the stable, first. Tell them I'll have food and drink waiting for them."

Aiden nodded. "I'll go wait for them now."

"That's perfect, thank you."

Her smile was more genuine as the boy sketched a salute, turned on his heel, and ran down the hall to the courtyard. She heard a shout as he cleared the gates and chuckled. Time enough to finish dinner with Aithne, and she needed to have Sine make a large tray to send to her study. *Quillon, is anyone*

flying around the area?
No, but I would like to stretch my wings. How much notice would you like of their arrival?
A quarter hour should suffice.
I will see to it if you go finish eating dinner with Aithne.
My thoughts exactly.

* * *

Siril trudged into her study behind Lucas. "I hope you don't mind, but I sent Aherin to the stable to see to the horses. He wasn't privy to any of our conversations with Briant."

Tanwen motioned them to the comfortable seats and pushed the tray of food and arda across the low table toward them.

"That's fine. What's going on?" She picked up Arwyne's beacon and settled across from them, rubbing her thumb over the beacon's smooth surface.

Siril poured two cups of arda and passed one to Lucas. He took a moment to breathe in the steam and smiled beatifically. "This is what I miss most when I'm away."

Tanwen chuckled. "Arda is what you miss most?"

"No one makes it like Sine. Sorry. That's not why you asked us up. The men are heading west, following the trail we found in the cave. Think of it as a scent trail, except it's magic. Briant is riding with the men, and Vask is flying reconnaissance. Their rationale, or at least the one they're going with, is it will speed communication between them and the Keep."

"Seems reasonable. Why do you think they're really doing it?"

"I got no idea. It all seemed logical to me, so much so I was a little mad I didn't think of it myself. But I did get the

CHAPTER 31

feeling there was something Briant wasn't saying, which is odd, because he's been forthright with me, even when it doesn't cast him in a good light."

Lucas, who had been stuffing meat into a roll, met her eyes. "Briant gave me a message, but he said I should tell you and Aithne."

"At the same time?"

Lucas frowned. "He didn't specify."

Siril rolled his eyes. "Tell Wybren Tanwen, then. You can find Aithne later."

"Or have her brought here," said Tanwen. "First I need to know what it is in case I need to act on it."

"He said to tell you this is what Vask told him to do. He is concerned this will affect his status with the Wybrens, although Vask says it won't. I think he wants to believe Vask, but he talks about how Aithne has been so strict about following the rules, and he doesn't want to disappoint anyone. I think he also feels guilty about Liam's capture, though there's no way he could have stopped it. It seems important to him to be on the team trying to get him back."

"I see. Maybe That's what you thought he was hiding, Siril."

Siril sat back. "Might be. Makes sense he wouldn't want to disappoint Aithne."

Tanwen cocked her head. "Does it?"

"It does," breathed Lucas. "I didn't put it together until just now."

"Put what together? They never seemed anything but uncomfortable together."

"That's how it starts at that age, doesn't it?" asked Siril. "You're afraid of looking stupid, and it makes you look more stupid. I remember being awkward with girls, especially pretty ones, when I was a lad."

Tanwen sat back and looked at the ceiling. "You're right. That's how I remember it, too. I was glad I was in Wybren training because it meant I was too busy for boys and didn't have to deal with them in classes much." She sighed. "Time enough to worry about it later. What else can you tell me? I guess Briant's hunch about the stone trolls was right."

Lucas nodded. "It was spot on. They were all dead, and their bodies were piled up to hide escape routes."

"Were you able to tell from the magic who was taken?"

Siril shook his head. "It was too mixed up, and it wasn't just our men who were in the magic trail."

"I figured as much. I'll pass the information to the councils, but you should both be prepared to be summoned tomorrow, just in case. Lucas, do you need to deliver your message personally? Or do you trust me to do it?"

Lucas stared into his cup for a few seconds. "I trust you to do it, but tell her to find me if she has any questions."

Tanwen bit back a smile. "I'll make sure she knows." She sat back. "I sure wish there was a way to analyze the trail. Separate one magic from another so we could identify people."

Siril leaned toward her. "I know you're worried, but he's a fighter."

She looked away. "I'm not sure he was in the group that was taken."

"Why?"

She glanced at Lucas and away again. "Call it a hunch."

Lucas looked from Tanwen to Siril and back. "Umm, why don't I go find Aithne? It might be better if I tell her after all."

Tanwen forced a smile. "You might be right. Thank you. Try the dining hall or our quarters."

CHAPTER 31

Lucas nodded, picked up his cup, and left the study.

Siril leaned back and squinted at her. "When did you last get a full night of sleep?"

She rubbed her face with both hands. "I don't know. A couple weeks, I guess."

"About the time we got word they were missing?"

"Yes."

He leaned forward again. "You can't lose hope. You know he's strong."

"I'm not convinced he's alive. Did you sense necromancy in the cave?"

Siril's eyes widened. "How did you know? How did you even know to ask?"

Tanwen closed her eyes and swallowed hard. "I saw him. He tried to kill me."

"I'm sorry, I can't have heard right."

She wanted to slide out of her chair onto the floor and sleep for a week. Instead, she stood up and walked to the window to perch in the window seat where the cool air might wake her up. "When we went to rescue the captives, the mage wasn't around. We knew we had to take him out to drop the shield, so some of us went looking for him. Greer and I thought we found him. It turned out to be Liam, but not Liam. Skye said he was a *tanad.* He didn't speak, and he almost killed me before Skye shot him. He didn't bleed."

"That's where you got the bruises."

"Yes. Aithne doesn't know. Nobody does, except Quillon, and he only knows because he lives in my head. I couldn't bring myself to tell the councils. Part of me wants to believe the mage is so skilled he can make a *tanad* to look like someone without hurting them. Part of me is terrified of facing an opponent so powerful."

"You haven't lost hope. You don't know what to hope for."

"Yes."

He walked over and leaned against her desk, arms crossed over his chest. "You have to get some sleep."

"I can't. I've tried."

"Have you talked to Sine?"

"Not you, too! Siril, you know I can't walk away from this for a minute, and you know why!"

He nodded. "I totally understand. I ever tell you about my granther? My father's father?"

"No."

"He was a Wreiddon, too. Good one. Runs in the family. He was an advisor to the king. During the Aramach Conflict, Granther thought he had to be on alert all the time in case dispatches came in from the field. He didn't trust anyone else to do it right, to know which ones he could deal with and which ones needed to go to the king. Ran himself right ragged, from what I was told."

"What happened?"

"It killed him."

Tanwen's jaw sagged.

"You heard me right. In the middle of a council meeting, he dropped dead of exhaustion. So tell me, Tanwen, are you ready to leave Aithne? She's all but grown now, practically a Wybren in her own right. She's all done but the Choosing and getting her beacon stone."

Tanwen pinched the bridge of her nose. "No. I'm not ready to leave her."

Siril leaned forward and took her free hand. "I know the situation is fluid, but there has to be someone who can stand

CHAPTER 31

in your stead for a day or two at a time. You can't go on like this."

She nodded, swallowing hard against the emotion roiling in her gut. "Can you do me a favor?"

"Anything in my power."

"Can you have Cadell sent to me?"

"Excellent choice. I'll get Sine, too."

* * *

Aithne looked up at the knock on the door. "Come in." The door opened, and Lucas peeked around it. She grinned and put her book aside. "When did you get back?"

He entered and shut the door. "Just now."

"I thought you were going with the search party. Where's Briant?"

"Briant went with the search party."

Aithne blinked, vaguely surprised by the stab to the gut. "Why?"

"Vask is flying recon so he can communicate with the council here."

"Oh. I heard the warriors had requested it, but I didn't know they'd assigned Briant. I guess it makes sense. I mean, he was already there, and it's not like I can teach him much more anyway. He practically didn't need training at all."

He sat in the chair across from her. "He asked me to give you a message."

"A message?"

"He said to tell you Vask said this was all right, but he doesn't want to disappoint you by breaking the rules. He knows it's against protocol for him to do this when he hasn't finished training, but Vask assures him there will be no repercussions."

She shrugged. "I don't know why he'd be worried about disappointing me. I think he likes Muirne."

"Muirne?"

"I saw them in the armory the other night."

Lucas frowned. "I don't know, but he didn't give me a message for her. He only said I should tell you and your mother. Besides, why would he be attracted to Muirne? She's not his type at all. Maybe he's her type, but trust me, he never talks about her."

Aithne snorted. "Like he goes on and on about me?"

"Maybe not on and on, but he does talk about you. He dreams about you, too."

A flash of heat crossed her face. "He told you?"

"He didn't have to. He talks in his sleep."

32

Briant slid out of the saddle and handed the reins off to Owen. They walked together to the nearby stream, and Briant went upstream a little to refill his water skins. There were pebbles on the shore and some in the water, but they were too small.

When the skins were full, he stoppered and slung them over his shoulder, walking a little further upstream. He'd done this for three days, and the others were starting to look at him like they wanted to ask what he was doing, but didn't know how. He'd been trying to cover it by skipping stones in the water to cover his real purpose. If he was traveling on foot, he might have found his stone by now. Of course, he wouldn't be nearly so far along, but distance wouldn't matter if he was only looking for a stupid rock.

He picked up a small flat stone to skip, and something underneath glinted. Frowning, he sank to his haunches and moved other stones out of the way to dig it out. It was almost rectangular and about the size of a bay laurel leaf. Different shades of brown striped the surface, and gold flecks sparkled in the sun. He turned it over and saw a circle of lighter brown in the top left corner. The edges were worn and craggy.

"Find something good, Briant?" called Owen.

"I think so," he answered, turning to walk toward him.

Owen looked at it. "I've never seen anything like it, but it's not a good skipper."

Briant grinned. "This one isn't going to skip. It's coming with me."

"Why?"

"It's special." He grinned and tucked it into his belt pouch.

"Let me help you walk the horses."

Vask, I found the stone.

Excellent! I will find a place for us to meet.

Are you sure we should do this? I can just hold on to it.

Are you unsure because you are having second thoughts about our partnership?

No, I'm having second thoughts about having to work with a bunch of women who are going to give me grief about not doing it the right way.

Women? Or woman?

Briant sighed. *I would be lying if I said Aithne wasn't a consideration. She's the one who would give me the most grief. You know how she is about rules.*

I do, but I also know she wants Liam back, as does Tanwen. Ruan and Colum also have families who want them back. The ends will justify the means.

If we have a positive outcome.

It will be enough that we did all we could even if there is not a positive outcome.

You're really calling this due diligence?

That is a human term with which I am unfamiliar.

CHAPTER 32

You're saying we're doing all we can?
I am.
Briant swallowed hard. His heart hammered. *All right. Find a place.*

* * *

Two days later, Vask told Briant how to get to the rendezvous point. Briant road up beside Dermod. "I might have to take a little side trip tonight."

"What are you talking about?"

"Vask needs to meet."

"In person? Why?"

"He has an idea that will increase our communication range. It will allow him to scout further and fly higher."

"Where are you supposed to meet?"

"There's a clearing with a stream running through it about a league from here."

Dermod squinted at the sky. "If you deviate, and we ride on, can Vask guide you to us when you're done?"

"Of course."

"Carry on, then. If there's a stream, you can refill water skins while you're there."

* * *

Vask was in the clearing when Briant arrived, having tied his horse a quarter league back.

"All right, let's get this done. The others are riding on and I'll have to catch up."

I will see to it you are reunited with them safely. Place the stone on the flat rock beside the stream.

Briant took the stone out of his belt pouch and laid it on the rock.

Vask tilted his head to look at it. *Very nice. Please take several steps back.* When Briant was far enough back, Vask blew fire on the stone.

When he was done, Briant stepped forward to look at it. It was more or less the same shape, but charred black.

Do not touch it yet.

As they watched, the black began to flake off in the breeze until the stone glittered gold in the setting sun.

You chose well.

"Thank you. Is it safe to touch now?"

I believe it is.

Briant reached down and tapped it gingerly a couple of times. It was warm, but not too hot to pick up. He turned it over a couple times, looking at it from different angles. "This is it? The famous beacon I'm going to catch so much grief over?"

It is. All that remains is to test it.

"How do we do that?"

I will fly further afield than usual, gradually, of course, and when you can barely hear me, you will tell me.

"All right. Is it safe for me to go back to the others? Or do I need to stay here in case it didn't work?"

It worked. You may return.

"Vask, do you think there even a chance we can bring them home alive?"

We have to hope there is.

Briant scoffed. "That's not an answer. You have to know something I don't, or why are we going to all this trouble?"

CHAPTER 32

What I know is too many good men have been left in precarious situations to get out on their own. Or not. When they do manage to survive, they are often damaged in the process. Is that what you want for Aithne?

"Of course not."

"Then we must try. You have a trail to follow, and the advantage of a dragon keeping watch from the air. It is more than some men have gotten."

"All right. Good night, Vask."

"Travel safely, Briant."

He tucked the beacon in his belt pouch and hiked back to his horse. He was nearly to the road when a rush of wind came from behind him. He patted his horse's neck, soothing him as Vask took to the air. Pointing his horse west, he nudged to a canter to catch up with the others.

* * *

When he caught up, they were outside a farmstead. Dermod was talking to the farmer, while the others stood nearby.

Briant rode to Owen. "I didn't expect to find this here."

"Nor did we," said Owen.

"Dermod is negotiating some fresh provisions and a place in his barn overnight."

"You don't seem happy with the prospect of having a roof over our heads."

"There's something that feels amiss - and have you ever seen anything like that before?" He nodded toward the barn.

Following the direction of his gaze, Briant saw a large tree branded on the side of the house. He frowned. "No, I haven't. Maybe it's the family sigil?"

"It looks fresh."

Vask, I don't suppose you can see through my eyes, can you?

I cannot. What do you see?

There's a fir tree branded on the side of the barn. It's big; it almost covers the whole side.

That is curious, and it seems familiar. I will relay it to Raine but there is probably nothing to fear.

Briant nodded. "Vask will tell Raine. You're right, though, something feels off."

Dermod rode back. "He's agreed to sell us some food, but he won't let us stay overnight. Apparently, he doesn't like strangers."

Owen's shoulders dropped a little. "Maybe Briant and I should scout ahead a little and find a campsite."

"Good idea. Stay on the path. We'll be along shortly." Briant nodded and followed Owen away from the others. "Did the thing with Vask work?"

"He says it did. I hope it helps."

"I wish I knew why that place felt so strange."

"It felt like the stone troll cave."

Owen looked back at him. "Did it? You should tell the others when they catch up."

"I'm pretty sure they'll have figured it out. They were in the cave, too."

"Tell them about it anyway. Did you hear them talking? They had an odd accent. It was almost like they were speaking an old version of our language. I've never heard it, but my brother is a scribe, and he sometimes makes fun of the wording in old documents he reads. I'd say it's because they live so far away from everyone, but so did you, and you don't talk funny."

Briant laughed. "Thank you, I think."

33

Briant added wood to the fire to cook breakfast. They'd ridden almost to the mountains. So far there was no sign of them, and he hoped they didn't have to go through the pass. Something about going through the same pass as the Shunned made his skin crawl. The Shunned had never tried to return. What if it wasn't because they all died, but because the pass somehow prevented them from returning? Were there such things as one-way portals?

They had been traveling for a week. The border loomed closer, and Vask ventured a little further each day. Briant rubbed his cold hands together and reached for the sheet metal frying pan to start the bacon.

I might see something.

Briant paused, holding the pan over the fire. *What?*

A curious blur in the woods over the border.

A blur? Are you sure it's not just a trick of your old eyes?

Vask chuckled in his head. *It might be, youngling. Let us wait a bit and see if this mysterious blur makes footprints in the snow.* Briant jiggled the pan into a stable spot in the fire and reached in the nearest provision bag. The others were up and breaking camp. Owen led the horses, two at a time to the creek. Dermod and Murchad folded the tarps and blankets they'd slept on and stuffed them in packs while Briant cooked. He was the best cook of all of them, but that wasn't saying much.

They finished their chores and gathered around the fire. They were all tired and cold, and no one said anything as they ate.

I see them.

Briant stopped chewing. ***Where?***

You will need to turn south. There is a pass in the mountains at the border. It appears they will be through it today, but you should be able to intercept them tomorrow.

"What's Vask saying?" asked Owen. Briant looked at him, startled. "How—"

"You get a look on your face when he talks to you."

Briant shook his head to clear the cobwebs and relayed Vask's message.

Dermod grinned. "Maybe we can all be home by the end of the week."

"Let's hope it goes that well," said Murchad.

They finished breakfast, and Briant rinsed the dishes off over the fire to put it out.

Near lunch, Dermod turned to Murchad. "Do you smell smoke?"

Murchad took a deep breath and nodded. "I can't tell where it's coming from."

Vask?

There is another homestead less than a league ahead of you. It doesn't have that tree on the side, does it?

CHAPTER 33

I cannot see the sides of the buildings unless I fly low enough to alarm the residents and their livestock.

Never mind. Briant chuckled. "There's another homestead a league ahead of us. Vask says he can fly lower to see if the barn is branded with that tree, but he'll alarm the residents and livestock."

Murchad's eyebrows flew up. "He's not going to, is he?"

"No."

"Good. We might need information from them."

They rode on and soon came into a clearing with a small house and barn and a large yard surrounded by a split rail fence. In the yard, a little girl was feeding chickens. When she saw them, she dropped the bucket of feed and ran between the buildings. A moment later, a man and a woman came from around the far side.

Murchad nodded to Briant. "Come with me. If Vask can hear what's said, he might be helpful."

"He can."

"Good. Dermod, Owen, I don't see a tree, but maybe you could look around a little."

Dermod nodded. "Just what I was thinking."

They dismounted, and Briant handed his reins to Owen. The man met them at the fence, and Briant and Murchad raised their hands.

"Good day," said Murchad. "Might you have any food we could buy?"

"No," said the man, "I am storing the food against the winter. Why are you so far from home?"

Briant glanced at Murchad, paying close attention to the man's accent.

Murchad smiled. "We are looking for some lost friends. You

haven't seen anyone come by here recently have you? In the last few weeks, maybe?"

"I have seen no people in many months. I lose count of how many."

Murchad nodded. "I wish you a bountiful harvest and a warm hearth this winter."

"May Maccha bless your search."

Murchad stiffened and his eyebrows raised. He inclined his head. "Thank you." As they turned away and started back to the horses, he touched his left shoulder with his left hand and brushed it diagonally across his torso to ward off evil.

Briant made the same gesture and whispered, "Do you think he really meant that as a blessing, or was it a backhanded curse?"

"No idea."

Did he wish Maccha's blessing on our search? asked Vask.
He did. Does that mean something to you?
People used to say that long ago, before the curse.
That's odd.
Indeed. When you are well away from that farm, you should tell the others.
I don't plan to do it now.

When they were well out of earshot, Murchad said, "He had the same strange accent as the last people we talked to."

Briant nodded. "The mage who kidnapped the others had the same one. Also, Vask said no one has wished Maccha's blessing on anything since before the curse as far as he knows."

Dermod shuddered. "Maccha's blessing? Does she actually bless anything?" He and Owen brushed their left hands across their torsos at the same time.

Murchad nodded. "That's what we wondered. Has Vask relayed that to the Keep?"

CHAPTER 33

Briant got instant affirmation from Vask. "He has."

"Good," said Murchad. "Now we're all on the same page. You're pretty handy to have around, kid."

34

While Briant and the others made camp, Vask flew back to the pass. As he'd suspected, the footprints were closer to Slan. He didn't see the men, but he guessed they were magically shielded. Their progress was slowing but steady. He circled them before landing on a rocky ledge.

Since they were shielded, he could not be sure they were the men they sought. There was every chance that they were, but they could also be descendants of the Shunned, if any had survived.

Crossing his paws, he said, "I am Vask. Please lower your shields."

The footprints stopped, and one by one, the men he sought came into view.

"Please remain where you are and allow me to assist you. There is a cave on the other side of the pass you may rest in if it is unoccupied. I will alert you if danger approaches."

He took a deep breath and torched the pass, melting the snow to ease their journey. They hurried toward the spot.

CHAPTER 34

When they reached the cave, Colum sent a light wisp in and pronounced it empty and dry. They went inside and slumped to the ground.

Vask reached out to Briant, who also seemed to be settling in for the night. *They are through the pass and resting in a cave. I will keep watch tonight.*

They're alive? That's great! Do they look all right? Is anyone wounded?

It does not appear so. Very thin and dirty, but not wounded in any way I can tell without getting closer, which they will not appreciate. I will lead them east tomorrow. When they are under way I will circle and try to lead both groups together.

Sounds good. Thanks for the news!

"Guys, Vask found them! They're through the pass, resting in a cave. Vask will lead them east tomorrow so we can rendezvous."

Murchad grinned. "That calls for a drink! Who brought the spirits?"

Dermod snorted. "You know we don't have spirits. It would have cursed the outcome, and it still might if you don't stop talking about it."

Owen shrugged. "I don't mind not talking about it, but it won't stop me from being excited about finally being able to go home and get warm again!"

Briant nodded. "I'm so glad they're alive."

* * *

The moon was high when Vask saw Colum wake Liam and Ruan. A moment later, Liam stepped into the pass. His body was tense and his eyes were closed as he said. "Vask, do you hear dogs barking?"

Vask lifted his head and listened. All he heard were the wind and the rustling of small animals. "I do not."

"We all hear it, and it's not the first time. Those dogs chased us all the way here. None of us are going to sleep anymore, so we're going to move on. Which way should we go?"

"East. I will find you some food and keep watch."

Liam nodded, and Ruan and Colum came out of the cave. Vask watched them until they disappeared into the trees. Ruan was limping a bit, but he was the oldest of the three and might be stiff from sleep. Otherwise they appeared to be in relatively good condition. When they were well away, he launched and flew west, listening for dogs. He heard a wolf howl, but nothing that would have alarmed the men. As he turned east, he saw some deer heading for the pass, attracted by the smell of scorched earth. He swooped noiselessly and grabbed a young buck before it knew he was there.

He continued east and passed the men. They were following the edge of the mountains, going more south than east. Clearly he needed to keep an eye on them to keep them from going too far out of the way. If they kept to their course, they would reach Annwn in a few days.

He dropped the carcass in their path before landing on an outcropping to blow flame on it, then launched and started circling east. He watched as they put out the flames and cut into the charred flesh. They must have found at least part of it edible.

He felt Briant stirring at the edge of his mind. He waited to see if he was truly awake, or simply in temporary wakefulness. When he was sure, he touched Briant's mind, feather light.

The touch back was meant to be light, but still groggy and

CHAPTER 34

clumsy. Amusement rumbled through him. Humans were so entertaining.

Did something happen? asked Briant.

They chose to travel instead of sleep.

Maybe they want to get home.

Perhaps. I dropped a deer for them. They are eating.

You dropped a deer? What do you mean? You killed it and gave it to them?

Vask scoffed in Briant's head. *I would never do half the job, Briant. Humans like their meat charred, so I killed it, dropped it, and set it on fire.*

Briant shuddered. *You do know you skipped a couple steps, right? Like gutting and skinning?*

I lack the fine dexterity for such things. I did the best I could. Besides, dragon fire would take care of the skin.

I'm sure they appreciate it. Should I wake everyone up?

Not yet. I will monitor the situation.

Give me a little notice, would you? We need a little time to pack up and move.

Certainly.

* * *

Liam poked at the deer haunch and belched. "It's not the worst meal I've ever had."

Colum nodded. "My mother always said you have to cook venison fast and hot so it's not gamey, but she always cooked it with onions. Vask won't win any cooking contests, but I do feel more ready to press on."

Ruan nodded. "Should we try to take some of this with us? We might get some properly cooked off the shoulder."

Liam looked at the carcass. The top shoulder was charred. He grabbed a leg and rolled it onto the back. "Bottom is raw. Let's see what we can get from the top, then roll it over and let the scavengers have it."

They used the dagger to cut off what meat they thought they could use. While Ruan stowed it in his pack, Colum and Liam turned the carcass over.

"Maybe this will slow those dogs down," said Colum.

"That would be ideal. Let's go."

They turned toward the rising sun and set off at a brisk walk. The terrain angled down gently, and by mid-day they'd crossed out of the snow line and the woods got denser. They paused in a clearing to eat the rest of the venison, and Liam saw Vask riding the thermals.

"Do either of you have anything reflective?"

Ruan pulled his sword and rubbed the flat of the blade with his sleeve. "Will this do?"

"I don't know." Liam took the sword and angled it toward the sun, trying to get the light to reflect off it to signal their location. After a few minutes of trying, he nearly blinded himself and the others. Vask circled the clearing once and turned north.

"I wonder if we're supposed to follow him?" said Ruan.

Liam shook his head. "If we turn, he might lose us in the trees. It's more likely he's headed back to where the searchers are so he can lead them to us."

"If there are searchers," said Colum.

"Briant is nearby. Vask wouldn't come without him," said Liam.

"Makes sense. You'd know better than I would, since you're joined with a Wybren."

CHAPTER 34

They were getting ready to move on when Vask returned and started to circle the clearing. He blew a short burst of flame east.

Colum chuckled. "Looks like you're right, Liam. He's herding us."

"I've never felt so much like a sheep in my life," said Ruan.

* * *

Briant guessed they had about two hours of day light left when they reached a small clearing.

Dermod pulled his horse to a stop. "Looks like as good a place as any to set up camp. I wonder if there is water nearby?"

"Let me check," said Briant. *Vask, is there water near this clearing?*

There is a stream, but it is half a league east. However, our friends are set to intercept this spot shortly.

Briant nodded. "Vask says the water is half a league east but we should make camp here. It's our rendezvous point."

Owen grinned. "Let's unload. I'll take the horses and skins to the water while you guys get ready for our guests."

They all dismounted and set to work. Briant found a small bare spot in the earth and dug away the surrounding vegetation before going to gather wood. *Vask, any idea how long it will take them to get here?*

Perhaps an hour. It is difficult to determine due to the density of the woods, but I know where they are, which makes them easier to follow.

You'll let us know if they deviate? I shall.

Half an hour later, he had the fire going. Murchad and Dermod had tents set up, and Owen returned with the horses.

"Briant, can Vask tell how far out they are?" asked Dermod.

"I asked him a while ago and he said about an hour."
"They're traveling east?"
"Yes."
"Are you up for a ride?"
Briant shrugged. "Sure."
They saddled two pack horses and headed west into the woods.
Vask, we're going to try to intercept them.
I see.
Briant rolled his eyes and refrained from comment. They rode in silence for a while, stopping occasionally to listen. Dermod's horse was the first to notice sounds coming from the opposite direction. Dermond waved at Briant and pointed to his horse's ears.

Briant nodded. *Vask, can you see them, or is it too dense?*
It is too dense, but you should intercept them momentarily.
"Vask says it's probably them," Briant whispered.

Dermod nodded, cupped his hands around his mouth, and hooted like an owl. They heard two answering hoots.

Briant grinned and followed Dermod at the fastest trot they could manage in the woods. A few minutes later, he saw them and called, "Liam!"

Liam's head jerked up and he waved.

They rode a little closer before sliding out of their saddles and leading the horses to them. Liam grabbed Briant around the shoulders and pulled him into a bear hug.

"Am I ever glad to see you! Is Aithne all right?" Briant nodded against his shoulder. "She's fine."

Liam let go and his shoulders sagged. "Thank Brigid. I've been worried about her."

"She and Tanwen have been worried about you. They'll be glad to know you're safe. What happened to your hand?"

Liam shrugged. "I don't know. I woke up in a cell somewhere

CHAPTER 34

in Dorchada with a finger missing."

Briant's eyebrows flew up. "Dorchada? There's a place with a name beyond the mountains?"

"There are a lot of things we didn't know about, and we need to get back so we can tell the council."

Briant nodded. "Of course. Come on, we have camp set up. You can ride my horse."

Liam shook his head. "Let Ruan or Colum ride. I'll walk with you. I need you to relay some information for Vask to pass along to the other dragons. There's a chance Slan could come under attack."

35

Three days later they crested a hill and saw the Western Keep. Owen let out a whoop and said, "We should be able to sleep in our beds tonight!"

Liam turned to Briant. "You should ride Vask in. There's a clearing on the way where you can meet him."

"I don't mind riding a horse the rest of the way."

"No, you should have your moment of glory."

Briant's gut tensed. How could they know he dreaded returning? He hadn't told them he and Vask had flaunted tradition again when they made the beacon, and he dreaded having to face the consequences.

The others agreed, though, and he couldn't think of a reason to delay. *Vask, they're telling me we should meet in the clearing halfway between here and the Keep so I can fly in with you.*

Is that what you wish?

I wish I knew what was waiting for us with the Dragon Council, and I can't think of a reason not to go back.

I shall meet you in the clearing. Have you forgotten the head of the Dragon Council is my sister? I shall take the responsibility. Let

CHAPTER 35

us fly back together.
All right.

* * *

He met Vask in the meadow, and the others went on without him. They waited a while to let the others get ahead before Briant mounted and Vask lumbered out of the clearing into the sky.

Briant's stomach flipped, but it had nothing to do with the cumbersome launch or the lack of a saddle. He'd tried not to miss Aithne while he was away. During the day he steadfastly avoided thinking about her, but at night she flitted around the edges of his dreams, elusive but ever present. He couldn't bear to think about how upset she'd be when she learned he'd skipped tradition. Again.

Vask circled the returning warriors, breathing flame to announce their arrival. There were already crowds on the battlement, courtyard, and in front of the gates. Wonderful.

At last, they reached the Keep. Briant could hear the cheering a hundred feet in the air. ***Vask, any chance we could land soon? I'm dying for a bath, and it's getting chilly up here without my leathers.***

Certainly.

Vask circled around to the landing pad as people screamed and scattered. He ignored them and dropped delicately onto the platform. *Get some rest, beloved.*

I will. You, too. Briant dismounted and scrambled down the steps, standing beside the base of the platform as Vask launched again, even though there was no one coming in behind him. Briant shook his head as Vask circled the Keep again, breathing fire in celebration.

The crowd surrounded him, cheering and touching his

231

back and shoulders, congratulating his good work. It was good work, but he didn't know if it would be enough.

He waded through the crowd to the stairs, smiling at well-wishers as anxiety curled like a snake in his gut.

At the bottom of the second flight, he turned toward the dining hall in search of arda and caught a flash of red hair.

"Briant!"

He turned and faked a smile. "Hi, Aithne."

She rushed toward him and pulled up short, as if she'd wanted to hug him but decided not to at the last second. "Is it true? They're all home safe? Mama said Vask told Quillon, but is it really true?"

"It's true. They should be close to the gate by now."

"Are you coming down?"

Briant grinned. "I'm going down to the bathhouse. I have weeks of dirt to scrub off."

"But you'll come after, right, so we can celebrate your victory with you? I need to thank you properly."

"No need. I'm glad I could be a part of it."

"But – "

"You should be at the gate when they get here. Liam was worried about you."

"He was?"

"Of course he was. He didn't know you were safe. I thought he might weep when I told him we'd found you. Go on so he can see for himself."

"You've put my family back together. I don't know how I can thank you."

He swallowed hard. "Don't. Not yet. Not until you know everything. If you want to thank me when you know all the facts, then you can figure something out."

CHAPTER 35

"What do you mean?"

"It's really better if you get all the facts first, and I can't talk about it now. Liam will be here any minute. Go be with your family." He turned on his heel and strode the other direction toward his quarters, arda forgotten. Gathering up his clothes, he took the back stairs to the bathhouse, avoiding as many people as possible.

* * *

Liam's heart pounded as they rode up to the gate. He scanned the crowd, looking for red hair. He didn't see them. Surely they'd gotten the news. Tanwen would have gotten it from Quillon if nothing else. For a brief second he was grateful for her connection to the dragons. At least they'd been able to stop worrying about if he was alive.

There.

A woman with red hair pushed through the crowd, paused, and broke into a run, her hair flying like a banner.

He pushed his horse to a canter and drew ahead of the others.

"Papa!"

His heart broke. He reined in the horse and slid out of the saddle. He ran the remaining yards and caught her.

Tears slid down his cheeks as Aithne sobbed against his chest.

"I was so afraid you were dead!"

He laughed and held her tighter. "I was afraid you were dead. Oh, baby girl, I don't think I could live through losing you."

She sniffled and pulled back, wiping her face with both hands. "Yes you could. You just wouldn't like it."

He laughed and drew her back against him. "Let's not find out who's right." He heard footsteps and looked up. More people were coming, and he saw Tanwen. "There's your mom."

"Don't tell her she looks tired. She's barely slept since you went missing."

He stepped forward to meet her, not caring that he was still crying.

She melted into his arms and he was struck, again, with amazement at how their bodies fit together like puzzle pieces.

"I'm sorry," he murmured into her hair.

"Me, too."

"You have no reason to be sorry."

She pulled back and looked at him with tears in her eyes. "Yes I do. I'm the new liaison."

He nodded slowly. "I expected as much. Right now, I don't care. It will keep you off the circuit, and I'll come to your study to ravish you if I have to."

She laughed. "Oh, Liam, I do love you."

"You think I won't do it, but just wait. You'll see."

"I can't wait."

36

*B**riant.*
He startled awake and sat up. Sunlight spilled across his floor and he rubbed his eyes, wondering how late it was.

It is late, nearly mid-day. I cannot avoid Raine any longer.
Do I need to come down?
No, but I will tell you if it changes.

Briant sighed and rolled out of bed. Putting on clean clothes felt luxurious, and he headed for the dining hall in search of food.

Sine was in the middle of preparing the mid-day meal, but she gave him cold meat, cheese, and melon, and a cup of arda before kicking him out of the kitchen. He took his food to the battlement, hoping to avoid people for as long as he could.

Despite his anxiety, he finished eating in record time and settled into a niche out of the way of the patrolling guards. The sunlight relaxed him, and he felt drowsy despite having just gotten out of bed.

Briant? You should come down. Raine would like a word.

His contentment evaporated like a puddle blasted with dragon fire. He swallowed hard. *I'm on my way.*

He trotted down the stairs. Everyone he passed welcomed him home, and he smiled despite himself. He hoped he wouldn't be sent away because it was starting to feel like home. Raine and Vask waited for him in the Dragon Council room. As usual, he was awestruck by the size of the cavern and wished he had a light wisp strong enough to illuminate the ceiling.

He walked over to the dragons, and Raine lowered her head. "There is our rogue now."

He felt his face blaze. "Please don't send me away."

She cocked her head. "Why? If we send you away, we must also send Vask away. Besides, there is a reason you are here. I thought it best to try to figure it out before the council convenes this afternoon."

"This afternoon?" His heart pounded. "At least I won't have to worry about the results for too long."

"I will not deceive you. The other riders will not be happy. You have not done anything in the traditional manner, and some will want you to leave. If we can extrapolate your purpose, we will have logical reasons for you to stay."

"The riders have no power to expel us," said Vask. "Especially when I am taking the responsibility."

"You will take all you can," said Raine. "Briant also bears some responsibility, although I will be the first to agree the ends justified the means. What we have are traditions, not laws. The traditions are old by human standards, but Vask and I remember when they did not exist. What you have done falls far below the threshold for exile, although I will admit some of the women

CHAPTER 36

will want to do so and may even personally shun you. It will not be easy for you in the coming weeks, I suspect, but things will settle down eventually."

Briant sank to the floor, sitting cross-legged in front of the dragons. "It hasn't really been easy since I got here, so I might not even notice the difference. How do we figure out my purpose before the council meets?"

"I am not sure if time will allow us to find the whole purpose, but let us start with some questions."

"All right."

"We can assume you have a purpose because you do not fear us. Even the bravest warriors, those who can communicate with us, are afraid. We can feel it. We get no such sense from you. That is fact number one. The second is, because you were not raised here, you do not think as our people do. They dislike it, but it can be an asset."

Vask growled in assent. "Was it not you who suggested that you travel with the warriors so I could fly reconnaissance? None of them would have considered that."

"True," said Raine. "Did you observe anything on your journey indicating trouble from the west, or a reason they abducted our warriors?"

Briant shook his head. "I didn't see anything, but they might be able to tell you more."

"They will tell their tale to the Keep Council soon. However, we will not get their answers before our council meeting."

"It is safe to assume there might be trouble from the west," said Vask. "Surely Briant's ability to think differently will be an asset if and when it happens. Is it not enough for that to be his purpose?"

"I think not, brother," said Raine. "Some of them are offended that he is becoming part of what women have done well for some time. I think you forget how short-sighted humans are sometimes, and some of the riders assume they are of superior intelligence because they were Chosen."

Briant stood and took a few steps. "How do you Choose? I mean, is there a standard set of criteria you follow?"

"No," said Raine. "First, you must stop assuming all dragons are of equal intellect. Like humans, we gain experience as we age. Therefore, a young dragon may not choose particularly wisely. We advise young dragons before they Choose for the first time, but they do not always heed our advice. We make the best choices we can before allowing a dragon to join the council, but we all change as we age, and some not for the better."

"Wait," said Briant, "You make it sound like not all dragons get to Choose."

"They do not. They must pass their training standards just as the riders do. There are no limits on how long it takes to pass the training, but not all of them do."

"What happens to the ones who don't pass?"

"They are allowed to stay and work or contribute to the breeding program. Obviously, we cannot allow those who cannot pass the training to teach others, and there are not a lot of ways a dragon can be productive here aside from helping shepherds to keep predators from the flocks and suchlike. Most decide to leave. None of this is helping us discern your purpose."

"Sorry. You're right."

Vask and Raine looked at each other at the same time, and Briant heard the now-familiar buzz of telepathy between them. When it ended, Vask looked back at Briant. "It seems you

CHAPTER 36

will have a short reprieve. Your presence is required in the council chamber in one hour. The Keep Council would like the Dragon Council to sit in on the captives' report."

"So I'll be in there so you can listen in?"

"And in case they have questions for you, since you were on the rescue team. Go and prepare yourself. Joint sessions last several hours, and you have meals to catch up on."

37

"I'm really sorry to do this to you." Tanwen brushed the hair off Liam's forehead.

He tried to smile. His maimed left hand throbbed, and he cradled it in his right arm, worrying a fray in the bandage. "It will be more efficient this way."

"Just a few more hours and you can sleep all you want."

He snorted. "I don't know if it will happen anytime soon." He got up and walked to the window. "I really didn't think I was going to make it home again."

"I'm so glad you did. Are you ready?"

He nodded. "Let's get started so we can get it over with."

She held his hand and walked into the Great Hall. "If you get tense or anything, just look at me. Tell me the story."

He nodded and walked toward the side of the dais toward Ruan. Tanwen took her place with the Keep Council.

The reeve and his advisors walked in from the other side of the dais. Dinsmore's chair had been removed and replaced with three cushioned chairs. He walked to the center of the dais and turned to those in attendance.

CHAPTER 37

"Thank you for coming. Gentlemen, if you will come up, we will begin our interview."

Liam, Colum, and Ruan stepped onto the dais and took their seats.

The three of them looked at each other, and they nodded at him. Liam turned to the council. "None of us remembers being taken away from the group. The first thing I remember is waking up in a cell feeling like the fifth day of a four-day drunk."

Ruan and Colum nodded, but no one laughed like they would have under other circumstances.

"We didn't know where we were. At some point, a maid came and gave us food and water. Apparently, she wasn't supposed to. She never said why, only that she couldn't abide starving us to death, but now that we've had a chance to talk among ourselves, it doesn't make sense that they intended to let us die, at least not right away."

Ruan nodded. "That might have been the goal initially, but maybe they changed their minds at some point. Nothing about it really makes sense to me."

"Or me," said Colum.

"Whatever their motives, we went on like that for a few days. I don't know how many. Maybe four or five?" He looked at the others, and they nodded. "One day I woke up tied to a chair, and the light was unnaturally bright, like someone figured out how to make the daylight brighter. I thought it would burn my eyes. Someone, a man, I think, was in there, and he asked me about the king."

"The king?" gasped Councilor Briaca. "Why would they ask about the king?"

"I do not know, Councilor. He said something about his

master being heavily invested in seeing justice served. They knew about our families, even though none of us talked about them at all after the stone trolls took us. He offered to let me stay and join the cause for justice for the Shunned."

He heard several gasps, and Tanwen's face paled. He swallowed hard, wishing he didn't have to deliver bad news, but grateful that they had warning and could plan.

"At that point, my head was throbbing from the light, and it didn't seem surprising that they were the ones holding us, even though we didn't know they even existed. I asked what their ancestors being shunned had to do with us, since we weren't the ones who did it. He asked if I would welcome them back. I said I would, personally, if they came in peace, but if they came armed and demanding retribution, I wouldn't be the only one taking up arms against them. At that point, the pain became agonizing. Someone untied me, and I fell out of the chair and covered my head with my arms. Someone outside the door asked if it was done, and the man said, 'Yes, Raca.' When I opened my eyes, everything was gone and the light was back to normal."

"Colum, Ruan, was your experience similar?" asked Dinsmore.

They both nodded, and Colum said, "They knew the names of our wives and children, but they didn't seem to know anything about the king or any councilors."

"That's something positive, I suppose," said Dinsmore. "You mentioned someone named 'Raca.' Do you know who that is?"

"We aren't sure," said Liam. "A couple days after they interrogated us, they moved us to another room and brought us food and clothing. They told us to clean up for our audience with the Raca. The person they took us to was a man—big,

CHAPTER 37

burly, looked like an old fighter, the kind no one wants to challenge. He asked us if we were from the Western Keep. We didn't answer, and he assumed it meant yes. They said if we resisted, they would come for our families and add them to the pool of material for the necromancers."

Dinsmore nodded. "Vask reported that much when you were found. We have already increased security and started other preparations, so don't let that concern you."

"It does concern me," said Ruan. "We've seen what those people can do, and bumping up security isn't enough."

"I'd like to hear your thoughts, but let's do that after you've had a chance to rest," said Dinsmore.

Liam nodded. "He said our magical ability had been assessed, and he had big plans for us, but if we gave him trouble, he'd give us to the necromancers. That was it. They took us back to the room and locked us in."

"They didn't want to know anything about the Keep itself, or how many fighters we had, or anything," said Colum.

"That's when we knew we had to escape or die trying," said Ruan. "We had to try to find a way to get word back here."

"We decided the best way to start was to eat and rest for a few hours since we didn't have much information. The place they held us in was a maze of hallways, and we didn't have a clear indication of where the exits were or how they were guarded. That night, the maid who'd been sneaking us food came to our room and offered to help us escape if we took her with us. She said they'd figured out what she was doing, and they would punish her for it. It seemed like our best chance, so we took it. She got us out of the castle. We passed through a city to a tavern in the trade district, and we got out of the city through a smuggling tunnel. We traveled through woods all night and most of the next day. It was snowing, and we needed to get as far away as possible before we left a trail. Turns out they trailed us with dogs, so we couldn't rest as long as we wanted. We headed east. Maccha—that was the maid's name—told us about the pass the Shunned had taken. So we headed that way. I think it was the third day, or maybe the fourth, when they caught up with us. We'd just come to the edge of the woods, and we could see the space in the mountains a couple leagues ahead. We were following the tree line to avoid leaving footprints in the open, and they came out of the trees ahead of us. We ran for the woods. I climbed as high in a tree as I could and shielded. I tried to get Maccha to follow me, but they caught her. The dogs killed her. I heard one of the men say he'd get her back to see if the necromancers could get any information from her before it was too late.

"When they were gone, we headed east as fast as we could, which wasn't that fast with the snow. We're lucky Vask was looking for us, and I never thought I would say I was happy to see a dragon. We were almost to the pass at that point, and he melted the snow so we could move faster. He found us a cave to rest in, and when the dogs woke us up that night, he kept track of where we were and killed a deer for us the next morning. That night we rendezvoused with the team looking for us."

"Thank you," said Dinsmore. "It was quite an ordeal for you, and a lot of information for us to process. Does anyone have questions now?"

"What about the men who went to bring them back? Did they see anything? We haven't heard anything from them. Are any of them here?" asked Councilor Briaca.

Briant stood slowly and looked around. No one else was

there.

"What is your name, son?" asked the reeve.

"Briant, sir. I'm the Wybren. Or, I will be, I guess. I'm not sure what my status is right now, but I ride Vask."

"Of course, I should have known. Please come up here and answer the councilor's questions."

His face flamed as he walked to the dais and stepped up. "I did not personally see anything having to do with magic or those who abducted our men. I rode with the rescue team and Vask provided aerial reconnaissance, which enabled us to locate the men more easily." He paused, then added, "Vask tells me he didn't hear the dogs the men heard after they crossed through the pass. Liam asked if Vask heard them, and he didn't, but the men did."

"That is odd," said the reeve. "Does Vask have a plausible reason?"

"No, sir. He would expect the opposite to happen—that he would hear them before the men did."

"Any other questions for Briant?"

Skye stood up. "How were you able to communicate with Vask while he was flying? The two of you haven't been together long."

Briant hesitated. "With this." He pulled the beacon out of his belt pouch.

Tanwen's stomach clenched as others among the Wybren ranks gasped. Not good.

"Vask said if we made my beacon, it would increase the range for our communication, and we might find them faster. It seems to have worked."

The reeve stepped onto the dais and clenched Briant's shoulder. "Seems like everything you do ruffles feathers, young man. This is a matter for the Dragon Council to deal with privately. Are there any other pertinent questions for Briant?"

The room fell silent.

"We've been at this long enough, I think. Gentlemen, the councils will need some time to talk through your account, but I can tell you most assuredly we will have more questions for you later. In the meantime, I recommend we send a summary of these proceedings to the king as soon as possible."

The other councilors agreed, and the reeve adjourned the meeting. Briant bolted off the dais and out the door.

Tanwen rushed to the dais as Liam stood and took his arm as he stepped down.

"Are you hungry?"

"Famished."

Aithne appeared on his other side. "I asked Sine for dinner in our quarters. She said she'd have a page bring it."

Liam managed a brief smile. "That's my girl."

They walked in a tight unit back to their quarters, and Liam sagged as soon as the door shut. "I'm going to lie down until dinner."

* * *

Tanwen watched him limp into the bedroom and shut the door.

"Mama, is he going to be all right?"

She draped an arm around Aithne's shoulder. "Sure he will. He's been through a lot, and it's going to take a little time, That's all."

"I hope so. It just seems like they're all more beaten down than I thought they'd be from the stories they told. Maybe it's

CHAPTER 37

because I've never been through something so physically and mentally taxing."

"It takes a toll. He just needs some time and rest, and we need to be gentle with him for a while."

"So no picking fights?"

"No picking fights."

"What about with Briant?"

Tanwen sighed and drew Aithne onto the couch beside her. "There is a lot we don't know. Until we do, here's what we need to remember. First, Briant is young and knows only what he's learned here about being a Wybren. Second, Vask is old. It's entirely possible Vask told him to do it without him knowing there should be a ceremony. Vask was around before there was a ceremony, and the older dragons are quicker to dispense with formalities. Third, it's a tradition. It's not a law. It's going to tick some of the girls off, but there isn't really a reason to punish him. Fourth, and most importantly, what if they were right? What if the increased communication really did get them home faster? If Briant and Vask hadn't been there, if they hadn't broken a tradition, maybe Liam would be out there instead of napping before supper."

Aithne sighed and leaned against Tanwen's shoulder. "I guess you're right. I mean, I like him. He's a good person, but he has no regard whatsoever for the rules, and I don't like that."

"I know. But you grew up with the rules. He's still learning them. You can't blame him for breaking rules he doesn't know about."

"I guess I'll just have to give him the benefit of the doubt until we know more. That explains what he said to me yesterday, though."

"What did he say?"

"I wanted to thank him for bringing Papa home, and he told me not to until I knew all the facts. It must be what he was talking about."

"It must be."

"I wonder if I should go find him?"

"He could probably use a friend right now. If you can be a friend, I'd say yes. If you find him in time, you could bring him back for dinner."

"All right."

38

Aithne knocked on Briant's door. There was no answer, but the door across the hall opened and a warrior trainee poked his head out. "Looking for Briant?"

"Yes."

"I saw him head for the battlements."

"Thanks." The door shut and she headed down the hall to the stairs.

She found him sitting in a niche looking east. "Thinking about going home?"

He startled. "Just wondering what they're doing right now."

She leaned against the battlement across from him. "I understand now why you said what you did yesterday."

"I'm surprised you're not yelling at me."

She blushed. "I talked to Mama first. She told me to invite you to have dinner with us if you want."

"I don't know if I can face the people in the dining hall."

"Why not? Mama says you didn't do anything wrong. It's a tradition, not a law."

"Do you agree?"

"I'll admit, the rule follower in me is a bit put out, but you can't be blamed for breaking a rule you didn't know about."

"I knew about the beacon ceremony, or at least I knew there was one. But Vask made a good argument, and I believe we found them faster because he could fly further."

"The ends justified the means."

"I think so."

"I might be biased, or maybe grateful, but I agree. And sometimes we have to change to make things better. Maybe we need to look how we do things. As for dinner, we're eating in our quarters tonight, and you do need to eat. Will you come join us?"

He nodded. "I'd like that."

"Come on, then." She turned toward the stairs and heard his footsteps behind her.

"Just to clarify, you don't hate me because I cheated on the beacon?"

"It wasn't a cheat, exactly. You are supposed to be alone, but under the circumstances it was probably close enough. Did the others know what you were doing?"

He followed her down the stairs. "No, I didn't tell them anything, not even when I had the beacon finished."

"At the end of the day, you got the job done."

"Wow."

She looked at him. "What?"

"I thought you would hate me forever."

"I guess you'll have to try harder next time." She grinned and flipped her hair.

"I'm not sure I could handle it."

She laughed and turned down the corridor toward her family's quarters.

"How's Liam?"

CHAPTER 38

"He's tired. Hopefully he'll wake up for dinner."

"Are you sure this is a good night for me to join you?"

"Sure, he'll be glad to see you. And it's not like we're having a full-scale party."

"As long as I'm not in the way."

She pushed open the door and peeked inside. "Mama?"

She heard a gasp, and Tanwen sat up on the couch, rubbing her face. "Is dinner here?"

She walked in and held the door for Briant. "The page is just coming down the hall, and I have Briant."

"Oh, you found him. That's good." She turned and put her feet on the floor. "I guess I'm more tired than I gave myself credit for. Hi, Briant."

"Thanks for inviting me, Wybren Tanwen."

She flapped her hand at him. "It's just Tanwen tonight. All the Wybren business is going to get cumbersome, as you'll soon find out for yourself."

"I will?"

"You have a dragon and a beacon. We just need to figure out how to make it all official since you refuse to follow protocol." She grinned and winked.

Aithne took the tray from the page and brought it to the table.

Tanwen stood. "I'll get Liam." She disappeared into the bedroom.

Briant walked to the table and helped Aithne lay out dishes. A few minutes later Tanwen and Liam came out.

"Briant!" Liam walked over and squeezed his shoulder. "It's good to see you."

"I hope I'm not intruding."

"Not at all. You probably need a safe place to hide from all the women."

Briant laughed. "I admit I was trying to decide if it was worth eating when Aithne found me."

"Aithne found you? Huh."

"Papa, he didn't just turn up on his own."

"I saw your face when he pulled out the beacon."

Aithne looked across the table at him. "If I want to be a Wybren, I have to learn to put my feelings aside and look at facts, right? Feelings aren't always right."

Tanwen sat at the table. "So true. The trick is learning to distinguish between feelings and instinct. You have to know when to trust your gut."

Liam sat across from her. "Right now, my gut is telling me this food won't stay hot all night. Come on, younglings, let's eat."

* * *

The next morning, Briant walked into the Dragon Council chamber better rested and fed than he thought he'd be. He'd woken up to someone tapping on his door, and opened it to find a page with a tray Tanwen had ordered for him.

Vask and Raine were alone in the chamber. "Good day, Briant," said Raine. "Are you ready to face the meeting?"

"More ready than I was yesterday. I had a strange dream about that necromancer. You don't think he's coming here, do you, Vask?"

"I would not rule out the possibility, but there are extra guards on duty, and the trainees have begun flying reconnaissance patrols."

"That's a relief. I think the interruption yesterday may have

CHAPTER 38

been good."

"Agreed. The worst of the news is out, and the Wybrens have had the night to consider the ramifications."

"I hope that's a good thing."

Vask lowered his head. "I will address the council first, if it is agreeable."

"I don't mind. Tell me where to stand and what I need to do."

"Stand with me," said Vask, "As the other Wybrens will do. I will address the council first, after which Raine will invite you to tell your version of events. You may choose ahead of time whether to take questions as they come up, or to answer them all at the end."

"Seems reasonable."

"I would advise full disclosure."

Briant frowned. "Why wouldn't I tell them everything?"

"Tell them about your magic."

His stomach clenched. "Vask, I don't know if that's a good idea."

"I know them better than you do. It will put you on more of an even playing field with them if they know you do not have a strong advantage. It is possible your weak magic is a result of the Curse's lack of effect on you."

"All right, I'll tell them."

The other dragons began to file in, and a moment later the other Wybrens started arriving. Everyone except Tanwen looked stoic and ready for a fight, and Briant's heart rate ratcheted up.

When everyone was assembled, Raine called them to order and turned the floor over to Vask.

"Thank you, Raine. I would like to begin by acknowledging that some, perhaps most, of you are angry with Briant for not following the procedures you did to become a Wybren. The fault is mine. He was unaware of the path taken to become a Wybren and so should not bear the blame for not taking it. He was unable to, in any case, since his family lived in isolation. Rest assured, he did all of the necessary training anyway as a matter of survival. I chose him because I believe there may come a time when our current ways of thinking will hinder us. You dislike that Briant does not think as you do, but I say it is his biggest advantage.

"As to the beacon issue, it was entirely my idea. Briant was hesitant to acquiesce to my suggestion, but ultimately agreed it would aid in the search and recovery of those we sought. I stand by my decision and firmly believe it was instrumental in the success of our mission, but I do apologize to those of you who love the tradition. I shall now turn the floor over to Briant."

He wiped his palms on his thighs and stepped forward. "Thank you, Vask. I'm not really sure where to start."

"How did you come to be on the mission?" asked Raine.

"I was present. Siril was going to send me back here and allow the warriors to conduct the search since they found the magic trail. I suggested it might be helpful to have aerial reconnaissance and offered to ride with the warriors to relay information to them."

"Why?" asked Raine.

"It made sense to me at the time. Vask and I are able to communicate telepathically, and he would be more likely to see what was ahead, especially since a lot of our journey was through woods. Except for making the beacon, most of the trip was uneventful. We followed the warriors, who followed the trail."

CHAPTER 38

"You could not sense the trail?" asked Raine.

He shook his head. "I couldn't. My magic is weak. It always has been."

"What?" gasped Skye.

Moira caught his eye and winked at him.

Briant nodded and made a light wisp. It glowed dull blue and did nothing to illuminate the room. "It's true. This is the best I can do."

"How is that even possible?" asked Greer.

Vask answered. "We suspect it is related to his lack of fear of dragons. Before the Curse, magical ability was not limited by gender. There were men and women who exhibited little ability. It is rare in this age to see limited ability in men, but it does happen."

"Briant, can you jump ahead to the beacon," asked Tanwen, "Or did something important happen before that?"

"We discovered pretty quickly that Vask couldn't fly very far without losing contact with me. We didn't know if the men were in immediate danger, so he suggested the beacon to increase his range. He's right. I didn't want to do it at first. I wanted to do it right, but I agreed to it because it allowed Vask to scout further. Our communication ability more than doubled after we made the beacon."

"It nearly tripled," said Vask, and some of the women gasped. "It is the only way I was able to arrive at the pass half a day ahead of Briant's party and melt a path in the snow to aid the warriors' escape."

"Forgive me, Vask," said Gautier, "But is that assessment truly accurate? The range seems overlong."

"It is true."

"I am also skeptical," said Razo.

"Perhaps we can test it," said Raine. "The last step to becoming a Wybren is the beacon test. The response of the dragon is when we acknowledge the passage of trainee to Wybren. Briant's beacon test was not witnessed. I would therefore suggest we send Briant and a group of Wybrens a day's ride away. The escorts should activate their beacons one by one to test the range before Briant activates his. It might be we all have that range and have never realized it."

"I agree," said Quillon. "It is time to begin questioning what we know and testing its validity."

Tanwen stepped forward. "I also agree and would like to be in the escort."

"So would I," said Skye.

"Me, too," said Moira.

Raine looked around the circle. "It is decided, then. We will commence the experiment tomorrow morning. If there are no further questions, or if Briant has nothing more to add, I hereby adjourn this meeting."

Tanwen grinned and walked over to Briant. "What a handy solution to our dilemma. You get to do it the normal way this time."

"What a relief!"

* * *

They rode out the next morning at dawn with two grooms to bring back the horses.

"Which way, Briant," called Tanwen.

He looked around. "Let's go south. I've never been that way before."

They turned south along the road toward Mevan.

"Colum wanted to come with us this morning to ride escort

CHAPTER 38

for the escort," said Moira.

"So did Liam," said Tanwen. "The three of them are convinced there's going to be an attack. I finally told him the dragons would know before another happened. They've started using trainees to fly circuits around the Keep, looking for trouble. He doesn't seem to understand he needs to rest."

Skye chuckled. "Men."

"We should make it interesting," said Moira. "The dragons will be able to sense our direction for a while. Let's ride for an hour or so and turn east. We need to be away from populated areas when we summon them. I know a big meadow we can use."

Briant shrugged. "Sounds good to me."

"I've been thinking about your magic issue," Moira said. "Have you talked about it with Siril?"

"I have. He said he's going to think about a solution."

"Have you tried to do any magic since you made your beacon?"

He frowned. "No, I've gotten so used to living without it I never thought to try it."

"Maybe you should."

He shrugged and made a light wisp. It seemed a little brighter, but not much.

Moira shrugged. "It was worth a shot. Try it when you're flying sometime. Maybe contact with Vask will help. You should talk to Siril about getting Cadell and Vask involved, too. Between them they might figure out if there is a workaround. Being able to use magic from the air would be really useful, even if it makes the rest of us jealous."

"Magic weapons don't work for you?"

"Only warriors get magic weapons."

Briant frowned. "Why? Is it because of the Curse?"

Moira's brow furrowed. "I don't know. It can't be, though, because I know women in the warrior ranks who can use them. Hey, Tanwen, why don't we get magic weapons?"

Tanwen laughed. "Because no one besides Briant thought to ask."

Moira rolled her eyes. "Good job, kid. I bet you can guess what I'll be doing when we get back."

* * *

Just past noon, they found the clearing. They waited until the grooms left to water the horse sat a nearby spring before going to the middle of the field.

Tanwen took out her beacon and held it, palm up for a few minutes. "I sure hope this works."

Moira and Skye joined her.

"Camp will be cozy if it doesn't," said Briant, waiting until the others put their beacons away before activating his own. "More importantly, Vask and I will look silly if it doesn't."

* * *

Briant?

Startled, Briant rolled to his feet.

"Is it Vask?" asked Tanwen.

"Yes!" *Vask! Where are you?*

Flying south. Activate your beacon again. I couldn't pinpoint your location from that distance.

"He needs the beacon again. Apparently he heard it, but it was too far to pinpoint the location."

"That's incredible," said Skye. She jumped up and followed

CHAPTER 38

him. "What about our dragons?"

Is anyone with you?

Everyone is coming, but we agreed I would get a head start. Tell the girls to activate their beacons, too. It appears we are about an hour out. The others will communicate with their riders when they hear the beacons.

"Hold up your beacon, Skye!" He waved to the others. "Hold up your beacons!"

Tanwen and Moira jogged into the field and held up the beacons.

'Vask said your dragons will tell you when they hear them."

Tanwen grinned. "I heard from Quillon! It's faint, but he heard me. How far out are they?"

'Vask is about an hour, and the others gave him a head start before following."

They sat down, watching the sky with their beacons in the air.

"There's Raine!" said Moira.

"And Oriel!" said Skye. "This is amazing!"

Almost an hour later, they heard dragon wings. The grooms gathered the horses and led them deeper into the woods so they wouldn't be spooked. Vask landed in the field, and Briant ran to him.

He collapsed against Vask's neck. "Am I ever glad to see you. I was afraid I'd look like an idiot again."

The women jogged over and Tanwen threw her arms around Briant. "Welcome to the ranks, Wybren Briant!"

"If I'm dreaming, don't wake me up!"

Vask raised his head. "I do not wish to bring the celebration to an end, but Quillon reports a group of people coming this way from the south in a wagon. One is riding a horse. He says they resemble your family, Briant."

Briant's heart ran cold. "Why would my family be here? Did he say it's them, or it looks like them?"

"He said it looks like them. Would you like me to fly over myself?"

"Would you?"

"Certainly."

They backed away, and Vask launched.

"I'm sure it's not actually them, Briant."

"I hope not. If it is, it can't mean anything good."

A few minutes later, Vask brushed his mind. *Briant, I'm afraid it's two of your brothers and their families. They will intercept you in approximately half an hour.*

Are they coming from due south of here?

Yes.

"I need a horse. It's my brothers."

Tanwen turned to the grooms. "Saddle our horses, please, gents. We need to ride to intercept Briant's family."

* * *

They rode as quickly as they dared through the woods. Briant's heart pounded and he focused on his breathing to try to calm the panic. When they saw the group approaching, Briant waved his arm. Brice was driving the farm wagon with one plow horse, while Aengus rode the other.

"Aengus? What is it? What's wrong?"

"Briant, what are you doing out here?"

"I'm working. Why are you here?"

"The homestead was attacked."

Briant's legs went watery. "What?"

CHAPTER 38

Aengus scrubbed his free hand over his face. "There was an attack. By people, or something like them. I think they used to be people, but they didn't bleed when we wounded them."

Tanwen's face went white. "You'd better come with us." She turned to the other women. "I'll have Quillon notify Raine. Can you tell your dragons to circle?"

They nodded.

Briant turned back to Aengus. "Where is everyone else?"

Aengus' face crumpled. "Dead. They're all dead, Briant."

His pulse roared in his ears. "Mam?"

"She went down fighting. I saw it. Come on, we'd better do as your friend said."

Briant nodded, but sat still in the saddle, not comprehending.

Tanwen rode to them. "I'm sorry to have to do this now, but I need to ask some questions about the attack."

"Should we do that here, though," asked Brice. "They could be following us."

"Our dragons are watching for anyone coming this way." Brice and Aengus looked at each other and nodded. "Good. My name is Tanwen, and – "

Aengus' eyes went wide. "You're Tanwen? *The* Tanwen?"

The corner of her mouth quirked up. "I'm the only one I know of, although I'm sure there must be others. I knew your mother."

Aengus stared at her. "I remember you. You were with child, and you let me feel the baby kick."

"That was a long time ago. Can you tell me what happened? I know it's very soon, and it's hard to talk about, but the more details we can get while they're fresh, the more we'll know what we're up against."

Aengus nodded. "I was in the barn when it started. I heard a scream and was heading out to see what was amiss when Fiona ran in with Lilea and Malcolm." Fiona, sitting beside him, took his hand. "She told me some men attacked Morag and Sorcha at the river. They'd been gathering herbs against the winter. I'm not sure how it all happened. All I know is I hid Fiona and the children in the hayloft and ran out with a scythe. There were six of them, I think, all warriors from the look of them, but Brice shot one of them with his crossbow." He swallowed hard. "He didn't bleed. Just slumped to the ground. Same thing with the one I decapitated. No blood. They fought like demons. We're all that's left." He shook his head and turned to Briant. "You should have seen Mam. I've never seen her so fierce—came barreling out of the house screaming 'Wybrens' with a cleaver in her good hand. She took two down before they got her." His voice thickened and tears streamed down his face. "I'm sure if she hadn't been crippled from the fall, she would have taken them all single-handedly and cooked dinner afterward."

"Had you seen them before? Did you kill them all?"

"No. Some got away. I can't say how many, but it seemed like a lot."

"One of them branded the house," said Lilea.

"He did what, sweetling?" asked Tanwen.

"I saw him. I was looking out the window in the hayloft. Fire shot out of his hand, and it burned a tree in the side of the house, but it didn't burn the house down."

Briant shuddered. "I need to go out there. We need to bury them."

Tanwen nodded. "I think we should have the grooms take your family to the Keep while we fly to the homestead. After

CHAPTER 38

we've seen what happened, I can fly back to report, and someone can fly reconnaissance to get everyone there safely."

Briant nodded. "Is there anything you need me to bring back?"

His sister-in-law, Karleen, nodded. "Malcolm left Bunny behind."

His two-year-old nephew's eyes welled with tears. "I didn't mean to!"

Briant reached over and squeezed his shoulder gently.

"Don't worry, I'll find him and bring him back."

39

They landed in the clearing, and Briant slid off Vask's back as Tanwen came to his side. "Briant, are you sure you need to be here? You're likely to see things you won't be able to forget."

He nodded. "I need to be here. Mam would want me to bear witness, to let it fuel me for what needs to be done."

"All right, but if you need to leave, come back here and wait for us." She nodded to Skye and Moira. They unsheathed their swords and left the clearing on silent feet.

He could smell the carnage long before they saw it. Blood and smoke filled the air, but when they broke the tree line he was unprepared for the sight. A dozen bodies lay scattered between the house, garden, and barn.

Bracing himself, he turned over the nearest body. He didn't know the person. His throat had been cut, but there was no blood. "Uffern!"

Tanwen looked over his shoulder and nodded. "It's what we were afraid of, girls. *Tanad.* Briant, I need you to check them all to see if any are your family. I'm sorry, but it has to be you."

CHAPTER 39

He nodded and checked them all, finding only his sister-in-law, niece and infant nephew. "Where's Hamish? And Dougal? They're not here, and neither is Mam."

The women looked at each other, and Skye said, "Where might your nephew's bunny be?"

Briant blinked. "Umm, in their cottage, probably. The first one beyond the barn. Why would their bodies not be here?"

Skye and Moira headed toward the other cottage, and Tanwen said, "It's best not to speculate right now. Come on. They left in a hurry. Let's gather the things they left behind so we can get back."

"Tanwen!"

Moira's voice came from Ian's cottage, and Tanwen sprinted toward it. Briant followed close on her heels.

Moira was standing near the woods. "They left a trail!"

Briant ran over to look. "Maybe we can catch them! Let's go! It's only been a few hours, they can't have gotten far."

"Moira, you and Skye follow the trail. We'll gather what needs to go back and follow."

"I should go," said Briant. "I'm a good tracker."

"So are Skye and Moira. We need to gather the things your family will want. It's likely they won't want to come back here."

"But where will they go?"

"There's no need to worry about it now. Come on, we need to find Bunny."

He sighed. Moira and Skye were already gone. There was no use arguing. He walked into Ian's cabin.

"Let's gather what we're taking with us on the table."

He nodded and picked up Fiona's favorite shawl, Ian's pipe, and the Lilea's favorite book, and took them to the table. "I can't find Bunny." He climbed the ladder to the loft. Everything was neat and orderly with no sign of the toy. "Maybe he was at someone else's cottage when the attack started?"

"Maybe." He went to Aengus' next, gathered a few sentimental trinkets, and added them to the small pile before moving on to Dougal's, and then Mam's. He took a few things from the loft he'd shared with Hamish before going to Mam's room. "I don't see anything in here she would have wanted to keep, but I'll bet Fiona would like the rolling pin Da made. She borrowed it all the time." He went to the kitchen to get it and stopped. Bunny sat in the middle of the hearth in a wine goblet, one ear flopped over and one straight.

"Tanwen!"

She came in, and he pointed.

"He was here. He came here, and he hurt my family because of me."

"Briant, you can't be sure."

He whirled to face her. "It's my nephew's rabbit—not his horse or my niece's doll. It's deliberately placed. That goblet was the only thing she took from the Eastern Keep, and none of us were allowed to touch it. Malcolm would never leave his bunny in it, and she would never leave it on the hearth. No, this is a message to me. He knows about me, and he has my family. He must have seen me in the mountains and knew I wanted to stop his plan, so he took them to get back at me." He snatched up the rabbit and stuffed it in his pocket. "We have to go find them before he hurts them."

She nodded, placing everything in Fiona's shawl and tying the corners. "Let's see if we can find Skye and Moira."

They have returned, said Vask.

He scooped up the bundle of his family's belongings and

CHAPTER 39

Tanwen closed the door as they left. A few minutes later, they entered the clearing, and Skye jogged toward them.

"We think we know where they are, but it's too far on foot. We were getting ready to do some aerial reconnaissance, but our dragons said you were on your way here."

Briant started toward Vask. "Where do you think they are?"

Skye strode after him. "It's not good. The trail leads toward the ruins at Nokton."

Briant swallowed hard. "Nokton? Are you sure?"

"As sure as we can be at this point."

Tanwen squeezed his shoulder. "If that's the case, we're going to need back-up. A lot of it. Even in its ruined state, Nokton won't be an easy target. Stow the bundle and let's see if it's even a possibility. Maybe he took them toward Nokton, but not to it."

He stuffed the bundle in the nearest saddlebag as the others mounted and launched. Vask was last, and he gripped the front of the saddle with both hands and leaned forward against the sharp upward trajectory. His stomach lurched as Vask climbed and tears burned his eyes.

The others had been circling, waiting for Vask, and as he leveled out, they turned west toward Nokton. The ruins had once been a formidable citadel and was said to be haunted by the ghosts of those who perished in its defense. Rumors of those who went said they never returned. It seemed like the perfect place for a mage to hole up.

Even from the air, the place was terrifying. The forest, once kept back from the citadel, had reclaimed it. Trees and brush clung to the walls, and ivy climbed all the way up and over the ramparts. In some places, it was the only thing holding the wall up. Parts of the roof had fallen in, and the open bailey was littered with stone and bones.

After circling the citadel a few times, the dragons broke off and flew east.

Wait, Vask, why are we leaving? Isn't my mother there?

We don't know, but the magic inside the citadel is powerful and dark. I'm sorry, but we have to assume he's taken them there, and you won't like what he does to his captured.

Briant swallowed hard. *Then shouldn't we be trying to get them out?*

It will take more of us. We will have to hurry.

40

"Briant!" He turned to see Aithne running down the hall. "I'm glad I caught you in time. Here." She handed him a leather thong with a pendant dangling from it. "It's my good luck charm."

He tried to hand it back. "I don't want to take this. What if something happens and I lose it?"

She took it and looped it over his head. "Don't let that happen. Come back safe." She stepped back as her cheeks flushed pink. "Please come back safe."

He swallowed hard and nodded. "I will." He tucked the pendant into his tunic. It was warm against his chest. He nodded, turned and jogged down the hall.

Ten minutes later he strapped into his saddle and Vask launched off the tower. His stomach lurched, and he wondered if he'd ever get used to it.

It had been a day and a half since their reconnaissance. He had chafed at every passing second. His family had tried to comfort him, but he knew what they didn't: Their mother might not be dead, and it might not be good. They'd all prefer she have a clean death rather than torture. He couldn't bring himself to burden them, but the truth festered inside him.

As they neared the citadel, he could see the path cleared by the Wreiddons. They'd left the morning before to prepare for the ground assault. He didn't know their plan. All he knew was he and Vask were to join the aerial assault. He was armed with arrows spelled to return to his quiver, as well as small bags of caltrops and small jars of oil, and Siril had taught him a shorter accuracy spell.

They flew over a clearing in time to see grooms leading horses into the woods so they wouldn't be spooked by the dragons. Past the clearing, the path seemed narrower. He saw bodies scattered along it, some in pools of blood and some with no blood at all. He shivered, glad to be passing quickly from above.

The citadel came into view, shrouded in smoke. A few of the Wreiddons were burning away the brush and ivy. Even from fifty feet up, Briant could smell the blood in the smoke. He looked down to see some warriors dragging bodies away from the citadel, and healers bent over wounded fighters. He couldn't tell which ones, if any, were *tanad*, but he hoped a lot of them were.

Vask started to circle with the others while Quillon veered off toward the citadel.

Why aren't we going with her?

Because, beloved, our orders are to circle. Tanwen knows your mother, and your brothers should be easy enough to recognize since they were the only ones taken.

But we don't know. What if they've hit other homesteads?

Then we will soon know.

He clenched the front of the saddle in frustration.

CHAPTER 40

They were half-way through the second circle, near the portcullis, when someone threw a flask into the brush. Fire erupted in a wide column that shot straight up, passing the battlement by twenty feet and barely missing Quillon. Some of the Wreiddons were far enough away to leap back, shouting, their magic shields rippling. Several fell back burning.

Vask chuckled in his mind. *I wish you could hear Quillon. It is not every day a dragon curses so prolifically.*

Briant wanted to smile at the amusement in Vask's voice, but his stomach roiled with the smell of burning flesh.

They circled around again, and Briant saw a swarm of what appeared to be people enter the bailey. Their movements were all exactly the same—every step, the swing of every arm was perfectly in tandem. ***Tanad.*** Their clothes were ragged, and they all looked ill, but their movements were purposeful and strong. Something else about them spooked Briant, but he couldn't say what it was.

Some climbed the steps to the battlement. The rest headed toward the gate in a single wave and pulled it open. The hinges shrieked, and more ***tanad*** joined them to force them open.

Briant's heart hammered. *What are they doing?*

It appears they plan to attack. I cannot see where they are coming from. There must be tunnels underground. The citadel is too small for that number of bodies.

The ***tanad*** poured through the gate and slammed into the remaining warriors. Briant looked around, trying to see where they were coming from, but he couldn't tell. He swallowed hard, trying not to listen to the screams of wounded Wreiddons.

Someone shouted, and those still on their feet backed away, swinging swords. Quillon swooped low to blow dragon fire on the far side of the citadel, incinerating a portion of the enemy army. His efforts barely made a dent. As the warriors backed toward the clearing, the *tanad* continued to pour out, moving to flank the still retreating Wreiddons.

Something flashed at the edge of his vision and he turned. The roof of the citadel glowed blue.

Vask! He pointed.

Yes?

Briant realized Vask couldn't see him pointing and clenched his jaw. *Look at the roof of the citadel!*

The light burst brightly for two or three seconds and went out. The other riders saw it, too, and were shouting and pointing. Greer waved her hands, and the others circled in closer. Quillon blew dragon fire on the roof, and the dry beams erupted in flame. The other riders threw small pouches of caltrops or flasks of oil through the fire.

Vask, are they sure he's in there?

Where else would he be? Get your oil ready.

Vask swooped low over some trees so Briant could toss oil bottles into the hole in the roof to incinerate the mage. Briant got three in on the first pass, and the flames grew, but the blue light started again.

Gautier and Oriel flew close to the flames. Skye and Finley were ready with oil, but before they could drop them, flames shot up from the center of the citadel. For a moment, the fire was so bright Briant couldn't see anything, but the sounds of women and dragons screaming together turned his blood cold.

The dragons veered away. Skye fell from the saddle, burning, as Oriel shrieked. He caught her with his claws and she made no sound as he dove unsteadily on charred wings.

CHAPTER 40

Briant watched in horror as Gautier followed him. Finley was still in the saddle and appeared to be burned. *Holy Laoch! Vask, are they all right?*

I cannot say yet. Do you have any oil left?

Briant reached into the saddle bag. *Yes, three flasks.*

I am going to swoop low. I need you to throw them in and strengthen their power with magic.

Vask! He's shooting fire out of the roof! Did you not just see what happened?

I did. That is why we need your magic. We need to kill the mage. Briant, you must trust me.

Vask circled around, coming in lower. His tail clipped the top off a pair of fir trees near the citadel wall. Briant heard a shout but didn't take time to look around to find its source. When they were almost over the hole, he dropped the bottles of oil together, shouting a strengthening spell as they fell.

Go, Vask!

Vask flapped his wings hard and thrust his tail down, lifting away from the hole as the oil exploded. The blue light wavered and dimmed, and the other riders cheered.

An arrow bounced off Vask's scales and Briant lobbed an arrow in the attacker's direction, shouting the accuracy spell. The spelled arrow hit his target in the eye and as she fell, he realized he shot his mother.

No! Vask, go back!

Vask turned and flew over. His mother's body lay on the battlement, riddled with arrow holes, limbs splayed, with no blood. The arrow vibrated and freed itself to return to Briant's quiver.

She is not bleeding, Briant. She was already dead. You did her a kindness.

He laid his bow across the front of his saddle and dashed away tears with the back of his hand. *No. I killed her when I went to the Keep. I killed her when I refused to come home. The mage found me, and he went after my family. I led them there. It's all my fault. All of it.*

No, it is the mage's fault.

The other riders were bombarding the citadel, and the blue light faded.

Despair settled on him like a sodden cloak, so he didn't pay attention when a loud rumble started.

Vask turned and flew away from the citadel. *Good. Thanks, Vask. I don't want to be here anymore.*

We are not leaving. Look left.

Another *tanad* army was coming through the trees from the west. They swarmed in, surrounding the Wreiddons. They trampled the wounded and the Wreiddons scrambled back, forming a circle around the healers with their backs to the inside, pikes and swords ready.

The *tanad* pressed in, oblivious to the weapons. The nearest ones were impaled and fell, only to be replaced by others. The bodies stacked up around the Wreiddons circle.

Raine and Quillon banked toward the horde, breathing fire at the back ranks and moving forward. They decimated the rear two-thirds of the army, but could not get all of them without killing the Wreiddons. The *tanad* pressed the warriors hard, breaking through the ranks. They scrambled to protect the healers. Magic shields rippled and more Wreiddons fell.

Vask banked toward them over the fir trees. As they passed, Briant caught a glimpse of something he couldn't identify.

Vask, circle around and take me back to the fir trees! I think I saw something.

CHAPTER 40

We must help the Wreiddons!
I think I saw a shield in a tree! Why would there be one in a tree?
Vask circled around, slowing as he approached.

Briant leaned over to look, and a bright beam of light flew toward his face. He jerked back, almost falling out of the saddle on the other side. He righted himself, but the bow slipped out of this grasp and plunged to the earth. "Burn the trees, Vask!"

They erupted like a torch, and Briant saw someone drop out and start running.

He shouted a fireball spell, pointing at the fleeing figure. It shot out of his hand, small and compact, more precise than an arrow, and struck the person in the back. He flew forward several feet and landed with a thump, as limp as a rag doll.

All the *tanad* fell. The blue light went out. Everyone looked around, trying to figure out what happened.

Vask, can you land?
Certainly.

Vask dropped to the ground, and Briant slid out of the saddle. He ran to the body, face down on the grass, with singe marks on his clothes. The soles of his feet smoldered as if he'd been struck by lightning.

Briant hunched over the body as Quillon landed nearby, stirring up a sudden gale force wind. Briant rolled the body over. The man's eyes were glassy, and blood ran out of his mouth and nose.

Briant's stomach clenched hard. The man had been alive moments ago, before Briant had killed him with magic he didn't know he had. His hands trembled, and for a horrible moment, he thought he might vomit. Taking a deep breath, he closed his eyes and stood.

Tanwen ran over. "Are you all right?"

He nodded and took another step away from the body. Tanwen knelt and opened the leather pouch the man wore.

She pulled out several small vials and a book with magic symbols on the cover. She held them up toward Briant. "Magic components?"

He nodded.

The commander of the Wreiddons ran up. "What happened?"

"It's him," said Tanwen. "He has a spell book and components on him, and he was shielded in a fir tree. Could there be more mages? What about the light from the citadel?"

The Wreiddon looked around. "Everything stopped when he went down. Must have been a spell."

Tanwen grinned and shouted, "Briant killed the mage!" She hugged Briant hard. "You saved us!"

* * *

The dragons blew fire in the air as they flew back to the Keep. As they approached, Briant saw several people on the parapet. He picked Aithne out immediately. Part of him wanted to wave to her, but mostly he wanted to hide. When she found out he'd killed his own mother, she'd never speak to him again. Quillon landed first. Vask followed him, and Briant scrambled for the stairs.

"Tanwen?" He ran down the first flight as she paused on the landing. "Have you heard anything about Skye and Finley?"

She blinked hard. "Finley is badly burned. Skye didn't make it."

"What? No, she can't be dead."

CHAPTER 40

"She is, and so is Oriel. They were together a long time, longer than Quillon and me. The thing we need to focus on is that it could have been worse. We lost a lot of people, but there could have been more."

"It is worse." He swallowed hard, and his face heated as his voice grew hoarse. "I saw my mother. I put an arrow in her head."

Tanwen hugged him. "Briant, honey, that wasn't your mother. The part that made her your mother was long gone." She stepped back and held his shoulders. "I want you to come to my study tomorrow, after you've had some rest. I'll tell you how I know that. Come on, your family is waiting for the news."

He nodded and they walked down the stairs. His family waited for him outside the dining room, looking at him expectantly.

He tried to smile. "We got him. The mage who killed Mam and the others is dead."

They broke into a cheer as Aithne skidded around the corner.

"What happened?"

Tanwen stepped up beside him. "He killed the mage, that's what happened!"

Moira came down the steps. "Oh, Aithne, I wish you could have seen it! Mister I-Don't-Have-Magic tossed a lightning bolt off Vask's back and nailed him. It was great!"

Brice and Aengus stared at him for a few seconds, jaws slacked, before rushing forward and lifting Briant off his feet, dancing him around.

"Hey! Put me down! It's not as good as you think. I tried to throw a fireball!"

They put him back on his feet, laughing, and turned to pick up the children.

Aithne took his hands. Her face lit up with joy as she gazed at him with sincerity and respect. "The mage is dead, no matter what spell you used. I knew you could do it. Never doubted for a second. Nicely done, Wybren Briant."

THE END

Epilogue

Briant stood outside Tanwen's study door with butterflies in his stomach. He didn't want to talk about this, but he knew he had to. Before he could change his mind, he knocked. When she answered, he pushed the door open. It felt like it weighed twice as much as the last time he'd been there.

"Hello, Briant." She stood and gestured to the sitting area. "Did you get some rest?"

He forced himself to choose a chair and sit up straight.

"Some. I guess nightmares are to be expected?"

"Yes. Talk to Sine if you need help sleeping."

"I will."

"I can tell you're not as well as you'd like me to believe."

"I shot my mother. How well do you think I'd be?"

She leaned toward him, perched on the edge of her seat with her forearms on her knees. "Briant, do you remember how I came back from the rescue mission with bruises on my neck?"

"Yes, but you never said how you got them."

"I didn't, because the person who tried to kill me looked like Liam."

Briant scoffed. "Liam would never hurt you."

"No, he wouldn't. Skye shot my attacker with a crossbow bolt after I put my dagger in his side. He ran away, and he didn't bleed."

"But how could a *tanad* look like Liam?"

She looked at the floor for a few seconds before looking back at him. "Did you notice during the battle that some of the *tanad* looked like each other?"

Briant frowned. "Now that you mention it, I think I did. There was something about them that seemed creepy. But I couldn't put my finger on it."

"I'm afraid the mage may have figured out how to make multiple *tanad* from one body. I think he did it with Liam."

"But how? Liam is alive."

"And missing a finger."

Briant's stomach clenched. "You think the mage was powerful enough to make a whole man out of one finger?"

"I don't know, but it's the only thing I can think of. I just started researching it, but it's going to take me some time."

"But the mage is dead. Does it even matter now?"

"We don't know where he was from, or what he wanted. We don't know if he made more of them, or if he's the only one who knew how to do it. I hope I'm wrong, but I have a bad feeling we might not have seen the end of this yet."

Briant swallowed hard. "That's why you think my mother wasn't really my mother."

"That's how I know it wasn't, just like I know it wasn't my husband who tried to kill me."

"Is there anything we can do?"

"I don't know for sure yet. Quillon told the other dragons. I hope they'll have some ideas. In the meantime, you should talk to Sine about something to help you sleep. If I'm right about this, if it's not over after all, we could have a lot of work ahead of us."

* * *

The crystal ball in the center of the table went black. One moment, Bron could see the whole of the small room bathed in its light as the battle played out. Then fire erupted around Balgram and the fool fell from the tree. Another flash of light, a large winged shadow, and the whole thing went dark.

She reached toward the ball and stroked it with one finger. "Balgram, Balgram, did I not warn you about hubris? You always did overestimate yourself. Fool!" She picked it up and threw it against the far wall.

With a flick of her hand, the candelabras lit. The shelf on the wall lined with crystal balls nestled in black velvet sparkled to life. Bron strode across the room, boots crunching on broken glass, and jerked the door open. A scrawny girl cowered outside.

"Clean up that mess, and do not touch anything else!"

"Yes, Raca," the girl whispered.

"Apprentices! Report!"

Bron stomped into the throne room and poured a mug of ale from the table near the cold fireplace, taking it to the window to watch a corpse on a rope swing lazily in the breeze on the other side of the glass. The shuffling of feet announced the apprentices' arrival.

"Balgram failed. What is the status of our army?"

"Our current numbers are small, but the necromancers can produce soldiers quickly. Their training progresses and they are developing spells to raise more undead with each casting."

"Ensure they do not become complacent." Bron studied them in the reflection of the window. "I dislike complacency."

They all shuddered. Good.

<<<>>>

About the Author

Wendy Blanton has been writing since she learned to string words into sentences. She is a U. S. Air Force veteran with a long and eclectic resume. In addition to writing, she tells Celtic folk tales at Scottish festivals and other venues. When she's not mired in stories of one form or another, she enjoys reading, camping, gardening, and drinking coffee. She lives in Chicago with her husband and three geriatric cats.

About the Publisher

Bear Publications seeks unique story concepts in science fiction, fantasy, and horror anthologies and novels. Find out more at: www.bearpublicatiions.com